Shadows of BRIERLEY

A Distant Shore

VOLUME THREE

Shadows *of* BRIERLEY

A Distant Shore

VOLUME THREE

a novel

ANITA STANSFIELD

Covenant Communications, Inc.

Cover: To Wander at *Twilight* © Daniel F. Gerhartz. For more information go to www.danielgerhartz.com.

Cover design copyright © 2011 by Covenant Communications, Inc.

Published by Covenant Communications, Inc.
American Fork, Utah

Printed in the United States of America
First Printing: August 2011

17 16 15 14 13 12 11   10 9 8 7 6 5 4 3 2 1

ISBN: 978-1-60861-450-9

For my eternal companion

Chapter One
The Call

Nauvoo, Illinois—1842

Ian walked briskly up the street, his thoughts distracted by the happenings at home and his desire to return there quickly and see that all was well, especially with his sweet wife. Wren was ready to have a baby any day now, or as the doctor had said just yesterday, "Any minute." In time with Ian's steps he repeated a familiar inner dialogue, where a part of himself worked very hard to convince another part of himself that he needed to trust in God and believe that everything would be fine.

He knew well enough that childbirth in and of itself was a distinct medical risk. Women came through it just fine all the time. But some women died; women who were otherwise strong and healthy could be snatched away in a heartbeat. Ian had experienced many losses in his life, but the very idea of losing his precious Wren was too unbearable for him to even consider. And yet he found himself considering it all the time, then scolding himself for even allowing such a thought to enter his head.

Close on the heels of his fear of losing Wren was his fear that the child might not be healthy, that it might not live longer than a handful of heartbeats. It had been just a few years since he and Wren had lost their first baby, their dear little Joy, who had lived only minutes after her birth. He'd had mixed feelings ever since about Wren's desire to have many children. She'd given birth to a healthy boy since they'd lost their little girl. Everything had gone well, and it had all turned out just the way it should. They'd named the boy Donnan, after Ian's brother who lived in Scotland, and little Donnan had brought a great deal of happiness into their home—as had Gillian, the daughter of Wren's deceased sister, who they were raising as their own. Ian couldn't disagree with Wren's desire to have many children. They both loved being parents, and he'd been blessed with an abundant inheritance that made it possible for him to provide amply for his family. His only issue with this plan was the very fact that Wren had to descend into the valley of the shadow of death in order to bring each child into the world, and this deep concern was accompanied by his fear that the life of the child was equally as vulnerable as the life of the mother. For all that he'd prayed very hard to come to terms with the death of little Joy, having to once again face the reality of bringing a child into the world brought back painful recollections of losing her.

As lost as Ian was in his thoughts, he still remained mindful of the faces of the passersby he encountered as he walked past the lovely, thriving businesses of Nauvoo. He recognized some faces, and even knew some by name. Others he didn't recognize at all, but he greeted each person with a smile and a warm "hello" or a kind "good day." He nodded and smiled at a man he didn't recognize until after the man had passed by, and then a more distant memory stopped Ian abruptly. He turned back before the memory had fully taken hold. He didn't know *where* he had seen that man, but he knew it hadn't been here in Nauvoo.

"Excuse me," Ian said and ran back a few steps to put his hand on the man's arm to stop him. "Forgive me." He chuckled tensely. "You just . . . seem so familiar, and . . . I wonder where . . ."

"Willis Tyler," the man said, smiling and holding out his hand with the offer of a friendly handshake. But then, most people in this town greeted others that way. Friends and strangers alike lived in this place for a common reason, and most people were eager to share in that brotherhood.

"Ian Brierley," he said in response, and they exchanged a firm handshake. Holding the man's hand in his seemed to strengthen the memory, but he still couldn't place it. Reluctant to let go, he said, "I could swear I've met you before, but . . ."

"You look familiar to me too," Brother Tyler said, "but I can't put a finger on it."

Still holding to Willis Tyler's hand, the memory rushed into Ian's mind and took his breath away. "Good heavens!" Ian said. "Did you serve a mission . . . in England . . . some years ago?"

"I did!" Brother Tyler said with enthusiasm, and the sting of tears briefly blurred Ian's vision.

"London!" Ian said. "I met you in London! Only briefly." He was so breathless he could hardly spit his words out. That moment had changed his life. He couldn't believe *this* moment was happening now. "I heard you preaching. What you said had . . . such an impact on me. I bought a Book of Mormon from you, and . . ." Ian laughed, still holding Brother Tyler's hand, shaking it again. "That book changed my life; it brought me here. And now . . ." He laughed again. "Here you are!"

"And here *you* are!" Brother Tyler said, laughing as well. "I remember you, Brother Brierley. I do. I remember wishing we could have talked. I remember thinking you looked . . . so . . . lost."

"Indeed I was!" Ian said, finally letting go of Willis's hand.

"You look much better now," Brother Tyler said.

"I'm sure I do." Ian chuckled, self-consciously putting a hand through his dark, curly hair, recalling how unruly it had been while in London; how he'd been unshaven and dirty. At least now he didn't feel like a heathen. Realizing that Brother Tyler's implication was likely more in reference to his spiritual or emotional state, Ian added quickly, "Oh, I am much better!"

He wanted to stand there on the street and talk indefinitely, then he remembered Wren at home with the children and said, "Could I tell you where I live so that we can meet again? I must get home to my wife, but . . . we must talk!"

"We certainly must!" Brother Tyler was equally eager to do so. He fortunately had a little notepad and pencil in the pocket of his jacket, and the two wrote down their names and the locations of their homes.

"Is your wife not well?" Brother Tyler asked while he was writing.

Ian felt momentarily disoriented while he too was writing. "Oh, my wife. She's ready to have a baby any time now, and I don't want to leave her alone."

"Congratulations are in order, then," Brother Tyler said.

"Indeed," Ian said, refraining from saying that congratulations should wait until the birth was over and all was well.

The two men parted ways with another firm handshake and a brotherly embrace, then Ian hurried on toward home, smiling to think of encountering the man who had changed his life. After all these years! It was a miracle! He hoped that he would see Brother Tyler again soon, then his thoughts returned to Wren, and he quickened his pace.

Upon arriving at home, Ian entered through the back door of the lovely two-story, red brick home and found his very pregnant wife sitting at the large table in the kitchen, shelling peas that he'd picked from the garden earlier that morning. Her rich, dark hair was gathered, as usual, in a bun at the back of her head. The size of the bun indicated the thickness and length of her hair that always looked so beautiful at night when she brushed it out. She looked up at him with her green eyes that were so dark they were almost black. Her eyes still had the ability to take him aback at certain moments. She smiled at him, and he couldn't deny this was one of those moments. She was alone, which happened rarely in such a busy household, and he took advantage of the opportunity to bend over and give her an especially warm and lengthy kiss in greeting.

"Oh, hello, Mr. Brierley," she said with a smile of pleasant surprise and a sparkle in her eyes.

"Hello, Mrs. Brierley," he said and kissed her again. The delightful sounds of children playing in the next room reminded him that they were *not* alone, and he had to settle for just one more kiss before he asked, "How are you feeling?"

"Beyond the usual aches and pains of being *great with child,* I'm as fine as I was before ye left. Ye mustn't worry so much, dear husband."

"Perhaps not," he said, "but it's difficult not to when . . ." He let the sentence fade and was glad she ignored it when he was regretting that he'd even started such a sentiment.

"Ward and Patricia are doing well at keeping the little ones occupied," she said to divert attention from the topic. "What we would ever do without them, I can't imagine!"

"Nor can I!" Ian said. "Perhaps I should see if they need rescuing."

"Perhaps ye should," she said and laughed softly. He kissed her once more quickly and went up the hall to the main parlor of the house. It was spacious and more than adequate for a variety of gatherings, the greatest being the way his own family gathered here with that of their dear friends, Ward and Patricia, who actually lived under the same roof in their own private portion of the house; they all spent a great deal of time interacting despite separate living areas. Ian and Wren had met Ward Mickel in Liverpool just before embarking on their journey to America. He had been traveling with his mother, Millie, who was now deceased, and he had been very taken with Wren's sister, Bethia, who was also now deceased. Ian and Ward had very quickly become close friends, and they had all just as quickly become as good as family. Ward made up for the brother that Ian had left behind in Scotland, and Ian made up for the brother that Ward had never had. After enduring many hardships together, they had finally arrived in Nauvoo a couple of years ago, and they had quickly made plans to build a home. The decision to build a dwelling where they could all live together had mostly been based on the fact that Ward was blind and could not live without some kind of assistance. Following Millie's death in a carriage accident, Ian had quickly taken over her role of doing many little things for Ward that he could not do for himself. Both men had ample financial resources, and so together they had planned a home that would suit their unique needs, and they had hired the proper builders to accomplish the task. When Ward had met Patricia and quickly fallen in love with her, they had all unanimously decided to proceed with the house plans. While Patricia had taken over the majority of duties in caring for Ward, they all felt better about having others nearby in the same house so that someone would always be around to help watch out for him.

It wasn't that Ward was, by any means, completely debilitated by his limitations. Quite the opposite, in fact. As long as the furnishings and contents of the house were mostly kept in order and where they belonged, Ward could move around on his own and find much of what he needed. He did well at caring for himself as much as it was possible. He could also be very helpful in the kitchen and even in caring for the children, as long as certain things were put within his reach and someone was nearby in case any difficulties arose. Ward was a positive and cheerful man, with hair as dark as Ian's, but it was as straight as Ian's was curly. He was not as tall as Ian, but he was still taller than average. He was nice looking, and his eyes didn't appear at all abnormal.

Patricia was a lovely woman who had endured many hardships. She had lost every member of her family in one way or another as a result of the persecution the Saints had endured in the years prior to their coming to live in Nauvoo. She was slight of build with brown hair, and the majority of one side of her face bore a dark red splotch—a birthmark. Between her wounded spirit and her self-consciousness over the mark on her face, she had been a timid and troubled young woman when she had first met Ward. But his ability to see her in ways others did not had a swift and sure healing effect. They had soon married, and now they were the parents of a beautiful daughter, Millicent June—Millicent after Ward's mother, who had shortened it to Millie for her own use, and June for the month in which she was born. Little June had just barely passed her first birthday. She was a cheerful baby who brought a great deal of happiness to their home. Ward and Patricia were very good parents, and between the two of them they were also very adept at helping with Ian and Wren's two children, especially since Wren had reached the stage in her pregnancy when it was difficult for her to move around or lift the children.

Gillian would be three before the end of the summer, and Little Donnan was barely eighteen months. The two of them were continually finding ways to make a mess or destroy something if they weren't watched constantly. Parts of the house had been secured with nothing breakable or valuable within their reach, but neither of them could be left alone for more than a minute unless they were asleep. For this and many other reasons, Ian was grateful to have Patricia and Ward living under the same roof. Patricia loved the children and was gifted at helping care for them. And Ward, despite his limitations, was very good at entertaining children with a variety of silly antics. While Ward and Patricia had their own little parlor and a small cooking area, along with a few bedrooms at the other end of the house, they were most often here in the living areas of the main part of the house during waking hours, and they all agreed that they preferred it that way.

"Papa!" Gillian squealed with exuberance and jumped up from her scattered toys to run and leap into Ian's arms when he entered the room.

"How's my little angel?" he asked and twirled her around, making her giggle.

She embarked on a lengthy oratory telling him what she'd been doing, with words that were surprisingly clear for a child her age. Ian engaged in a fairly mature conversation with Gillian before she finally got down and returned to her playing. Ward then asked Ian, "Did you accomplish your errands, then?"

"I did," Ian said, sitting across the room from Ward. "And I had a surprise encounter in town as well that . . ." He was interrupted by Gillian and little Donnan fighting over a toy, both their voices rising in volume by the second as the battle heightened. Ian got up to settle the dispute and said loudly enough to be heard over the din, "I think I'll save that story for supper when we can all sit down together."

"Very wise," Patricia said, jumping to her feet from where she'd been sitting on the carpet with little June on her lap. June loved to watch the other children play, and she was best entertained when they were nearby. "And now that you're back, Ward and I will go and see to our own errands. We should be back before lunch."

"And hopefully before it gets too hot out there," Ward said, standing up. Patricia immediately took his outstretched hand and put it on her shoulder so she could hold the baby and at the same time guide him while he walked.

"You'd better hurry," Ian said facetiously. "It's already warming up considerably."

After Ward and Patricia left the house, taking June with them, Ian checked on Wren and found her lying down in their upstairs bedroom with all the windows open to let in the summer breezes. Unfortunately there wasn't much of a breeze, and the white curtains barely showed any sign of a flutter. Fortunately, the house had been built conveniently close to an already existing cluster of large trees, and this part of the house was nicely shaded most of the day. Once he was sure that Wren was fine, Ian took Gillian and little Donnan outside to play in the shade of those trees, amazed at what a few simple toys, a pleasant stretch of grass, and a lot of silliness could do to entertain children. Little Donnan was an adorable boy with a chubby face and dark, curly hair—much like his father's. Gillian was blonde, which made her stand out differently in her coloring, but her mother had been as blonde as Wren was dark—in spite of their being full-blooded sisters. Gillian bore a strong resemblance to both of her blood parents. It was impossible to look at her and not recall Greer, her father, who had also been Ian's closest friend through most of his life—except that little Gillian's eyes were very much like her mother's.

Bethia's eyes had been beautiful, but in an unusual kind of way, and Gillian definitely had that look. Occasionally Ian would look at Gillian and be reminded of her parents and the tragedy and drama that had surrounded each of their deaths, but more and more he could look at her and be reminded only of the pleasant memories and the good times. Or perhaps he was finally coming to see her as her individual self without thinking of her blood parents at all. Gillian was their daughter to raise and care for in this world, and she was every bit as loved and adored as the other children in the house.

That evening at supper, Ian told the others about his encounter in town with Willis Tyler. They all knew very well the story of how Ian had encountered Mormon missionaries in London at a time in his life when he'd been as low as a man could get. Ian knew beyond any doubt that God had led his feet to cross paths with these men who had been preaching in the streets. He knew it as surely as he knew the Book of Mormon had been guided into his hands, and that the book was absolutely true. And his sharing that knowledge with Wren, and later with Ward, had led them to each discover their own personal witness to these truths. This knowledge had brought them to the city of Nauvoo. Here in Nauvoo, Ward had found Patricia, who had long before come to know of such truths for herself. They were all here now because they shared a common bond in the power and glory of gospel truths. The others were thrilled to hear of Ian's encounter earlier in the day, and given the growing population of Nauvoo, they all felt certain that it hadn't been a coincidence.

"Ye must go and see him," Wren said to her husband. "Ye must learn more about him, especially when he's the man who took such a long journey to find ye there in England when ye needed him."

"I'm not leaving you alone long enough to go visiting *anyone*," Ian said, "until after this baby is born, and that's that."

"I'm fine," Wren insisted. "I've got Patricia and Ward here t' help when—"

"I'm *not*!" Ian declared, and Wren acquiesced with a quiet smile.

"Then why not have Brother Tyler and his family over here for dinner?" Patricia said with enthusiasm. "I'd be happy to do the cooking if you men will watch out for the children. Then we can all have a chance to visit with them. Oh, it would be delightful!"

"And what if Wren goes into labor just before they're meant to arrive?" Ian asked. "Or what if—"

"We can certainly send word to them if there's a change," Ward said, "and I'm certain they would understand. But it could still be many days before the baby comes. I'm afraid I must cast my vote with my lovely wife."

"It's a grand idea!" Wren said. "I'm not completely disabled. I can certainly help with the meal." She turned directly to Ian who knew that he'd been undone *and* outvoted. "So, why don't ye pay a quick visit in the morning t' the Tyler home and invite them t' dinner. It will be lovely! Ye'll see."

"Provided you don't go into labor in the middle of dessert," Ian said drolly.

The next morning Wren still had no signs of labor beginning, so Ian rode his horse to the location that Willis Tyler had written down for him. Brother Tyler wasn't at home, but Ian met his wife, Arla, and offered the invitation to dinner the following evening. She was thrilled and felt confident her husband would be too, and she also made it clear that they would entirely understand if Sister Brierley went into labor in the meantime, making it necessary to postpone the dinner. When Ian asked how many they could expect for dinner, she told him that their children were all grown and it would just be the two of them.

Ian almost hoped through the remainder of the day that Wren would go into labor and prevent the dinner party from happening. It wasn't that he didn't want to visit with Brother Tyler and his wife; in fact, he wanted very much to do that. It was more a desire to get this baby here and have it over with. When Wren was still going along normally the following morning, Ian shifted his thoughts—and even his prayers—toward having a pleasant evening with their intended company, including his hope that the baby's coming would be delayed. And of course, as always, he prayed fervently that all would be well with Wren and the baby that was about to join their family.

Early in the afternoon, Ian went to answer a knock at the door, since the women were busy in the kitchen.

"Brother Joseph!" Ian said, wishing he'd managed to suppress his surprise and enthusiasm just a little. It wasn't the first time he'd opened the door to see the Prophet standing there, but it had been a very *long* time since he'd encountered him personally. Joseph Smith was likely the busiest man on the planet; therefore, Ian knew this was not likely a social call.

"Brother Ian!" Joseph said with equal enthusiasm, and as always he was genuinely sincere. "I wonder if we might sit down and have a word."

"Of course," Ian said, wondering what the Prophet might ask him to do, what project he might be called on to participate in. The last time Joseph had personally asked for assistance, it had involved a clever matchmaking scheme that had brought Ward and Patricia together. Ian knew this man was a prophet, and he knew from witnessing and hearing of many miracles that he was truly inspired in the work he did. He felt a thrill of anticipation in wondering what this visit could be about.

"Come in," Ian said, motioning with his arm. "Did you wish to speak alone, or—"

"I was actually hoping that we might speak with Brother Ward as well, and your lovely wives if they are available." He put a hand on Ian's shoulder as Ian closed the door. "Last I heard the baby hadn't come yet. Is that still—"

"Not yet," Ian said, "but it will likely be soon."

"I'm certain everything will go well," Joseph said, and Ian wondered if that was simply a kind wish, or if it held some tiny degree of prophecy in it. He hoped it was the latter.

"Thank you," Ian said. Then, trying to add some of his own faith to the matter, he added, "I'm certain it will too."

Ian invited Joseph into the parlor where Ward was sitting with little June in his arms. She was relaxed and appearing tempted toward sleep. Gillian and Little Donnan were both napping, which made the house unusually quiet. Joseph greeted Ward warmly, in a quiet voice that didn't distract June away from her calm state. Ian went to get Wren and Patricia, who quickly rinsed their hands and removed their aprons. Patricia went ahead, and Ian helped Wren move more slowly up the hall.

After kind greetings were exchanged and they were all seated, Ian said, "What is it we can do for you, Brother Joseph?"

"First of all," Joseph said, "I want to express my appreciation to your household for the support you give in the building of the Lord's house."

Ian's heart was warmed by Joseph's reference to the temple presently being erected in Nauvoo. Ian personally was blessed with the privilege of not having to work for a living; therefore, he'd been able to put in many hours at the temple site. Sometimes Ward went with him and was given odd jobs that he was capable of doing with minimal guidance, jobs that offered support to the many workers who were putting in long hours of manual labor. The women too had made generous contributions. They had helped prepare meals for the workers and had also sewn clothes for them. Wren was especially good at the latter with her expertise in being raised as a tailor's daughter. They had all agreed many times that they were glad for the opportunity to be a part of such a great endeavor, but Ian was glad to be able to officially assure the Prophet, "We consider it a privilege to contribute to the building of the temple in any way."

"And you will surely be blessed for your efforts," Joseph said. Then his expression changed abruptly. Something subtle in the Prophet's expression warned that what he was about to say might not be easy to hear, but Ian didn't have time to think about the possibilities before Joseph said straightly and without apology, "The Lord has made known to me that he has a special call for you, Brother Ian—and you, Brother Ward—for the two of you to go together and share the gospel of Jesus Christ with the people of your homeland."

The silence became so thick that no one even seemed to be breathing—except for little June, whose eyes were getting heavy with sleep. Ian wanted to ask if he'd heard correctly. But Joseph had no trouble articulating his words, and Ian did not have a hearing problem. He knew well enough how this worked. He'd witnessed other men being called away from their families and asked to serve in faraway places. He'd simply hoped and prayed it wouldn't happen to him, and he'd pushed it thoroughly away from his thoughts, not wanting to acknowledge that it could even be a possibility. Putting in many hours of his best work on the temple had strengthened his hope that he could remain here at home and still serve the Lord.

Ian wanted to yell at this man and tell him that Wren needed him; she needed his help with the children—especially the new baby. He wanted to tell him that he didn't want to miss a day seeing his children grow and change. But how could he even consider putting a voice to those kinds of thoughts? Not to such a man as this! He couldn't even imagine the sacrifices this man had made on behalf of the gospel cause. He had likely been separated from his sweet Emma and their children more than they had been together, sometimes for reasons that were horribly unspeakable. How could Ian express the utter faithlessness of his thoughts?

Ian saw movement and turned slightly to see Patricia reach for Ward's hand; her own was trembling. At the very same moment, he felt Wren's trembling hand slip into his own. Ward broke the silence with a courage and conviction that was not surprising. "Of course I will do whatever you ask of me, Brother Joseph."

"Your willingness is appreciated, Brother Ward, but it is not me asking this of you. The call comes from the Lord. But you all know well enough that you do not need to rely on my word alone. You are each entitled to your own witness that this is right. By the power of the Holy Ghost you may know the truth of all things." Joseph turned to look directly at Ian with eyes that bore the power of a prophet and the empathy of a man who knew *exactly* how Ian was feeling, without a word being said. "Of course you should be here to make certain the baby comes safely and that your household is in order. But you should leave as soon as possible after that."

Again Ian wanted to scream. Images of his journey to America rushed through his mind like a stormy sea threatening to capsize his reason and sanity. How could he do it all in reverse? Memories of the traumas that had occurred during the journey didn't help him at all in trying to find any sensibility to the situation.

Ward spoke again, and Ian was grateful, given his own inability to find his voice. "How long should we anticipate being gone, Brother Joseph?"

"You will both know when your mission is complete and it's time to return to your families," Joseph said.

He then looked at Patricia as if to ask a question, but before he could do so she said, "I will support my husband in whatever is necessary."

"Thank you, Sister," Joseph said. "Your faith has always been inspiring to me."

Patricia forced a smile, but tears overtook it and she looked down. "And the same for me," Wren said. "I will do whatever is necessary."

Ian looked at his wife, admiring her faith and courage as much as he wanted to scream at her, as well. This was madness! How could he leave her? How could he do it? Especially when there was so much uncertainty in such a journey—both here and abroad!

"Brother Ian?" Joseph asked in a gentle voice, and Ian snapped his gaze toward the Prophet. He was the only one who hadn't spoken. He knew that in comparison to the others in the room, his faith was lacking, but he still regretted how his silence had seemed to accentuate that fact.

Ian cleared his throat and fought for a steady voice without succeeding. "I will do whatever the Lord asks of me." He thought he might feel better having said it, but he didn't. He felt like he was lying, promising something he couldn't give. But what could he say? How could he dispute it? And yet, how could he possibly do it? How? Why? He didn't understand!

"You have great faith, Brother Ian," Joseph said, and Ian wanted to accuse *him* of lying. He reminded himself that this man was a prophet, and he just listened. "You *all* have great faith." He talked for several minutes about the glory of taking the gospel to the world, the blessings that had come to many for the sacrifices they had made, and he told them more specifically what would be expected of them. He welcomed any questions, but no one had anything to say. For minutes after Joseph left, they all sat together in the parlor, not one of them uttering a single syllable.

Ian finally rose to leave, fearing the silence would suffocate him to the point that he truly would scream. He'd wake the baby. He'd cause a scene. And he would convince his loved ones all the more that he simply didn't have nearly as much faith as they did. He hurried upstairs to the bedroom, closed the door—quietly so as not to wake his own children—and dropped to his knees beside the bed. He clasped his hands and started to shake. The only words he could get out of his mouth were, "I can't do it, Father. I just can't do it!" In his mind he imagined the journey that he and Ward would have to take, without the comfort and company of their sweet wives, and the delight and laughter of their children. He imagined their wives and children here on their own, with no man in the house to do the things that men do. Who would chop the wood and build the fires and clean out the ashes? Who would care for the horses and keep the yard in order? The list of his usual chores and duties filed through his mind. And then, for no apparent rhyme or reason, Ian's thoughts drifted to a cold alley in London, and a version of himself wandering and alone, lost and confused, rescued and saved by men who had left their families and traveled thousands of miles to give *him* the Book of Mormon. How could he *not* do it? But how *could* he?

Ian didn't hear Wren come into the room, and he had no awareness of her kneeling beside him. Only when she pressed her hand over his face to push his hair back from his eyes did he become aware of her presence. He urged her into his arms, then held to her desperately, already anticipating an inevitable separation that tore his heart to pieces.

"How can we do this, Wren?" he whispered.

"God has blessed us so very much, Ian."

Ian couldn't dispute that, but he didn't particularly like the answer, because it only enhanced his guilt in not wanting to do this.

At Wren's suggestion they prayed together, but Ian still didn't feel any better. They sat together for a long while, but neither of them had much to say. The children woke up and demanded that their parents proceed with the normalcy of life, while Ian watched them as if he might never see them again. He kept glancing at the clock, wondering how many hours until he would have to leave them for some hideously long, indeterminate length of time. Then it dawned on both Ian and Wren at almost exactly the same moment that they had invited company over for dinner. They found Patricia already busy in the kitchen, looking somber and saying little. Ward was sitting at the table, carefully cutting some potatoes that had been put within his reach. His expression was similar to Patricia's and perfectly mirrored what Ian was feeling, but no one had anything to say. June was awake and sitting on the floor, playing with some toys. Gillian and little Donnan quickly joined her, and the typical noises of the children helped buffer the strained silence as the Prophet's words kept echoing around the room in a soundless tornado of sacrifice and potential blessings all whirling painfully around each other in a tormented dance.

Patricia finally rallied the troops by declaring, "We all have a great deal to think about, but I think it's best we put all of that away for now. We have company coming and would do well to receive them properly."

"Ye're right, of course," Wren said.

"Of course," Ward said. Ian didn't comment.

Patricia enthusiastically kept her promise and put on a lovely meal with a little help from Wren, while Ian and Ward took care of the children. Brother and Sister Tyler arrived at five minutes past the appointed time. Introductions were quickly made, and they were all comfortably on a first-name basis within minutes. As they chatted in the parlor and then moved to the dining room for their meal, Ian was amazed at what great actors they could all be when necessary. There was no hint of the dark cloud hovering in the house or with any of its occupants. It was about halfway through dinner when Ian looked across the table at Willis Tyler and fully began to accept what this man had done for him. Surely this gathering was not coincidental in its timing or its main topic of conversation in light of the Prophet's visit earlier today. Ian listened, as the others did, as Willis told them how he had been called to share the gospel in England and of his personal sacrifices, as well as those of his wife and his children at the time.

A question occurred to Ian that he felt compelled to ask, but it mulled around in his head for many minutes before it found the courage to come to his lips, as if he already knew he didn't want to know the answer. But apparently he *needed* to know.

"What of the other man who was in England with you?" Ian asked Willis. "I didn't speak to him, but I heard him preaching. The two of you traveled far together; you must have become very good friends."

"We did indeed become *very* good friends," Willis said, but a shadow passed through his eyes when he said it. Ian didn't have to wonder over the reason very long when Willis quickly added, "Brother Givan passed away not long after our return." Willis looked down and fidgeted with his napkin. "He became ill on the passage back, you see, and . . . he never recovered. He did make it back to his dear wife and son before he passed, and she's married again and doing well last I heard, but . . ." His words faded into the difficulty of his memories while Ian felt sobered and perhaps mildly nauseous at the thought of what this man had sacrificed to share the gospel with others. He wanted to know more about the widow and child, but didn't know how to ask. Given his own experience in encountering Brothers Tyler and Givan in England, he almost felt personally responsible, as if Brother Givan's life had been given in a literal sacrifice so that Ian could have the gospel in his life.

"Would ye excuse me a moment," Wren said as if she'd just remembered that she had left a kettle boiling on the stove. She gracefully stood from the table and left the room, but Ian heard her going upstairs and wondered if she was all right.

"Forgive me," he said, rising himself. "With the baby and all, I should . . . make certain she's—"

"Oh, of course," Willis said and graciously motioned Ian out of the room, apparently oblivious to any underlying tension.

Ian hurried up the stairs and approached the bedroom quietly. He found Wren sitting on the edge of the bed, crying so hard he feared that her emotion would trigger her labor.

"Oh, my darling," he said, sitting beside her and wrapping her in his arms.

"I couldn't bear t' lose ye, Ian," she muttered. "I couldn't. I'll live without ye for a time if that's how it needs t' be. I will! But I pray t' God that He will bring ye home safely t' me and our babies. I cannot bear t' lose ye."

"Everything will be all right, my love," he whispered and attempted to dry her tears, but in his deepest self, he felt once again as if he were lying.

Chapter Two
Wondering

In every practical respect, the dinner gathering went well. The meal was delicious and the company delightful. Ian couldn't deny that he felt great joy in having been reunited with the man who had been an instrument in God's hands to bring the gospel into his life. But the entire situation was so interlaced with irony and poignancy that by the time their guests left, Ian just felt exhausted. Still, he helped put the kitchen in order and helped put the children to bed. Then he walked through the house to make certain all the lamps were extinguished and the doors locked. He thought of Wren having to take over this little nightly ritual, and he felt a literal pain in his heart.

Ian climbed into bed next to Wren, and that pain in his heart seeped through every part of him. How could he leave her? How? It felt impossible! Implausible! Unconscionable! But at the same time, the very idea of *not* doing what he'd been asked to do by a prophet of God seemed even more so. How could he ever face such a perplexing dilemma and find peace?

Ian snuggled up close to Wren's back in a way that had become second nature to him. How could he even sleep without her in the same bed? How could she sleep without him? Since the day they'd exchanged vows, they had become so closely integrated into each other's lives that it felt as if they'd become one soul. Or perhaps they always had been. Perhaps in some heavenly realm they had already been connected somehow, and once he'd laid eyes on her in mortality, a part of his spirit had known that they needed to be one in all things. Being fully united with Wren in every aspect of life seemed as natural as rain falling from the sky or seeds growing from the earth; it was as if their being together was as much a part of God's plan as the existence of fire and water, sand and sky.

As if his soul mate had felt his feelings and read his thoughts, Wren said with a tremor in her voice, "How can we bear it, Ian?"

"I don't know," was all he could say.

She further proved that her thinking was the same as his when she added, "But how can we not be willing t' do it?"

"I don't know," he said again.

Wren rolled onto her back, and Ian's hand ended up on the mound of her belly. His eye was drawn momentarily to the curtain fluttering with a pleasant evening breeze. He then looked directly at Wren's face, even though he could only see the outline of it in the shadows of darkness.

"It's breaking my heart, Ian, t' even think of letting ye go . . . t' even think of getting by without ye . . . and t' wonder for who knows how long if ye're safe and well, or if . . ." Her voice broke, and her hand tightly gripped his shoulder. "Or if . . . something horrible has happened t' ye, and . . ." She pressed her face to his chest. "What if ye don't come home at all, Ian? What would I do? How could I bear it?" She lifted her face to look at him. "I *couldn't* bear it, Ian. I *couldn't*!"

"Nor could I," he said, hearing a crack in his own voice.

Wren cried for a few minutes, as if she had to simply let it out. Ian held her and shed a few tears of his own more silently. Her emotion settled into a tormented quiet while Ian slowly eased his fingers through her hair over and over, memorizing the feel of it. She shifted to her side, and he rolled onto his back, urging her head to a comfortable and familiar place on his shoulder. He tightened his arm around her to ease her closer, his other hand settling again over her belly where their baby waited to momentarily come into the world.

"But Ian," she said, putting a hand to his face. "I cannot forget the way I felt when God let me know that we should come t' America . . . that this would be where we would find His true gospel." She leaned up on her elbow to look more directly at his face. "And He let ye know the same. Ye could never deny it. *I* could never deny it!"

"No, I cannot deny it."

"Then if God is asking us t' do this thing, how can we *not* do it?"

Ian thought about that for a minute. "I know that Joseph is a prophet, Wren. I do! I could never deny *that*! But he said that we each needed to learn for ourselves that this call comes from God. I can't do this, Wren, unless I know for myself that it's right. It's not that I don't trust Joseph or believe in him. It's just that—"

"Ye don't have t' explain. I know what ye mean. And ye're right. We must pray t' get our own answers. We must know that it's right the same way that we knew we needed t' leave Scotland and come here. It's the knowing in yer heart that will make it possible t' get through the difficult moments."

"Every moment will surely be difficult."

Wren laid her head on his chest. "Yes, it surely will be." She sighed. "We already know that it's inevitable, don't we." It wasn't a question. "If we know Joseph is a prophet—and we do—then what he asks must surely come from God."

Ian had to gather great courage to let the words come through his lips. "Yes, we already know that it's inevitable. But . . . I need to feel it for myself. And so do you. You're right, Wren. We need to feel it the way we felt the need to come here. Without that personal conviction, I cannot have the strength to do it." His voice cracked again. "I'm not sure I have the strength anyway. Without knowing that God is with me, I could *never* do it. *Never!*" He wrapped his arms tightly around her. "I don't know how to leave you, Wren. I don't. Nothing short of divine providence could make doing this possible."

"Amen!" she muttered and snuggled closer to him.

Following more silence, Ian said, "I don't want to do it, Wren. Does that make me a faithless man?"

"No, Ian. A faithless man would *not* do it, would not be willing t' do it at all. It doesn't take courage t' do something if ye're not afraid, and it doesn't take faith t' do something that's easy. Ye're a man of great faith, Ian. And I love ye for it."

"I love you too, Wren," he whispered and kissed her brow. "You are an inspiration to me."

They said nothing more and eventually drifted to sleep, Ian's final conscious thought being that he hoped Wren wouldn't soon go into labor, now that he knew the baby's birth meant he would have to be preparing to leave. He couldn't believe it!

Ian woke up to find Wren beside him with little Donnan sleeping between them. He hadn't heard the baby fussing in the night, or Wren getting up to deal with him, and he felt bad that he hadn't. But he did take advantage of the opportunity to just look at them and take in the beauty of mother and child. With her little son sleeping close beside her, and her pregnant belly, she was the personification of motherhood, a beautiful representation of this sweet aspect of what God had created a woman to be. Her dark hair strewn over the white bed linens added to the fineness of her beauty. He tried to memorize the image, then he slid to his knees beside the bed and silently poured his heart out to God, telling Him he wanted to do the right thing. He wanted to heed the Prophet's call, he wanted to be a faithful man, but he could not deny his internal struggle over this thing that he was being asked to do. He asked, pleaded, begged for his own personal witness that this was what God required of him. *I'm not seeking for a sign,* he prayed. *I don't need a sign on which to base my faith, Father. But Thou hast taught Thy children through the scriptures the doctrine of witnesses . . . that in the mouth of two or three witnesses Thy word shall be established. I only ask that I might have a further witness that will give me the strength to do what Thou would have me do . . . and to be all that Thou would have me be.*

Ian went on to pray for the health and protection of his family and those in his household, especially Wren through her forthcoming childbirth. He prayed for all of the usual things he prayed for, then he returned to his plea for strength and understanding, and to know for himself that what he was being asked to do was the right step to take, for himself and for his family.

He brought himself reluctantly out of his prayer when little Donnan started to stir. Ian picked him up and quietly took him out of the room, hoping that Wren would be able to sleep a while longer. With little Donnan in his arms, just hinting at coming awake, Ian peeked into Gillian's room and could see that she was still sleeping. He took little Donnan into the nursery where his crib was located. Since there was also a rocking chair there, he sat and rocked, watching his son come awake in his arms, holding the moment close. He felt as if he were taking in each simple experience, etching them somehow more deeply into his memory to hold on to through the journey ahead. He found it strange that his spirit had accepted the need to do what had been asked of him, even though he couldn't say he knew for certain that it was right. He thought of what Wren had said about his faith. She had many times told him that he had more faith than he thought he did. He didn't know about that, but it did occur to him that in spite of being overcome with the absolute horror he felt at the absurdity of leaving his family behind to embark on a potentially hazardous journey, he was—at the very least—*willing* to do it. He hoped that counted for something.

It didn't take many minutes for Donnan to become fully awake and full of his natural wiggles. Ian changed his diaper and got him dressed. He peeked in again on Gillian and found her coming awake. He sat on the edge of her bed and let little Donnan crawl over her to help her along, which made both of the children giggle. Ian laughed at their antics and again assigned his mind to grasp the moment and hold on to it firmly so that it could be recalled with clarity. He helped Gillian get dressed for the day, guiding her through her attempts to try to do much of it on her own. He wondered what adventures of her growing independence he might miss during his absence. He wondered how long he would be gone. Then he forced his mind to the present and took his children downstairs to find Patricia already preparing breakfast and Ward playing with June on the braided rug near the fireplace—although there was no fire, because the house was already at a pleasant temperature and destined to become hot in the next few hours.

Ian greeted his friends in his usual pleasant manner and received the same warm greetings in return. Practically speaking, everything appeared normal. But he could feel that the sobriety of their moods matched his own. He knew they all needed to talk, but he thought it best to wait until Wren could be a part of the conversation. Wren appeared just a few minutes later while Ian was setting dishes on the table and Patricia was just finishing up the griddle cakes she had made.

"Oh," she said to Ian as he crossed the room to greet her with a kiss, "ye got the children up and dressed. Bless yer soul! What would I ever do without ye?" She said it casually in a way she'd said such things to him many times. But the irony of her words struck them both at the same moment. Their eyes met, and hers filled with moisture before she looked away. He knew she was trying to hide her tears, but then realized they had overtaken her too strongly to be hidden.

Patricia noticed and paused in her efforts to put the food out on the table. Ian put his arms around Wren, and Ward said, "I hear sniffling. Which woman is crying?"

"It's my wife," Ian said.

More sniffling preceded Patricia saying, "It's your wife too."

Ian looked up to see Patricia dabbing at her eyes with her apron. Ward came to his feet and reached out a hand toward the sound of her voice. She eased into his arms, and the two couples stood there for a long moment, mutually and silently contemplating the changes ahead.

Patricia's ability to keep life on an even keel broke up the tearful reprieve when she said, "Let's eat while the food is warm, and then I think we all need to talk this through. Enough with quietly pretending that we're not all having a . . ." her voice cracked, "a dreadfully hard time with this."

Ian situated Gillian on her chair, and little Donnan onto his lap, the same way that Ward held June on *his* lap. For not being able to see, he was amazingly adept at feeding his little daughter safe-size tidbits of food. Patricia helped here and there, and they were all peripherally aware enough of the situation to be certain that everything was as it should be in regard to things he couldn't see. The griddle cakes and warm maple syrup were delicious, and everyone commented on that fact more than once, but no one said a word about Joseph's visit the previous day, or the company they'd had the previous evening. No one talked about the weather or the garden or the happenings about town. Everything that was normally a part of the breakfast-table experience was completely absent. Everything had changed. And no one knew what to say.

Again Patricia exerted her ability to take the lead and announced as she stood to clear the table, "As soon as this is cleaned up, we need to all sit down in the parlor and have a nice long talk!" She said it like a mother speaking to her children, but Ian was grateful that *someone* around here could speak up at all. "Ian, if you'll look out for June, I'll have Ward help me clean the dishes." She nodded toward Wren. "I think you need to sit down and put your feet up. You look terrible."

"How kind of ye t' say," Wren said facetiously. Everyone chuckled, but it lacked enthusiasm.

When the gathering in the parlor commenced, with the children surrounded by plenty of toys to keep them busy, Patricia took the lead and said, "I think we all know what we have to do and we know why, but I think we need to talk about it. We can't ignore it, and we can't hide from it." She took a deep breath and added, "I'll go first." Before she could say another word, tears came to her eyes and she pulled her handkerchief out of her apron pocket. She sniffled and dabbed at her eyes while she talked about how horrible it felt to think of Ward leaving, her worry for him, her wondering how she would manage. Then she went on to express many of the same feelings that Ian and Wren had shared. She knew the gospel was true and she knew Joseph was a prophet. Despite all that she had lost and suffered in her life, she knew God was with her and He had richly blessed her. She finished by saying, "I will not risk the blessings of eternity that I am working so hard to attain by throwing a tantrum now and insisting— as I would want to do—that my husband stay here and keep me company, instead of having him go out into the world and do the work the Lord would have him do." She sniffled again, then blew her nose. "There. That's all I have to say for now. Who's next?"

"I'll go next," Wren said, and basically repeated the same feelings and convictions that Patricia had expressed. Her personal experiences had been different, but her testimony and strength were very similar to Patricia's.

When Wren had had her say, doing her own share of sniffling and dabbing at her eyes, Ward said, "Well, Ian, I don't know about you, but I think I am especially humbled when I compare myself to the amazing faith of these great women."

"Amen," Ian said, wanting to add that he felt humbled by *Ward's* faith as well. But he didn't comment further.

Ward went on to express fears and concerns that were more consistent with what Ian felt. Of course, it was the man's perspective, and it was also the view of having to leave home, face uncertainty, and endure the hardship of the journey while continually wondering if everything was all right with those they loved most. Ian was grateful to Ward for being able to put into words things that Ian had trouble articulating. Ward also talked about the need for each of them to prayerfully seek out a personal witness that this call came from the Lord—clarifying Ian's feelings that there wasn't any doubt about Joseph being a prophet, but it was simply a necessary process that would enable them to have the strength to do what needed to be done.

"Have any of you received that witness?" Ian asked.

His question was greeted with silence, which at least helped Ian feel a little better in knowing that he wasn't the only one struggling to reach that point. But at least they all agreed on the way they were feeling and what they believed needed to happen—what they needed to be praying for. Still, that didn't change the inevitable reality. It was evident they all believed that the witness *would* come, and he and Ward *would* be leaving their families and traveling back to their homeland for an indeterminate length of time. He figured their belief in the fact that it would happen showed some measure of their faith. He only hoped that their faith could carry them through, and that he *would* get the witness he needed to give him the strength to do what was being asked of him.

The gathering broke up, and the day ambled on as any typical summer day—at least as far as caring for children and home was concerned. The mood continued to be understandably sober, and not one of the adults had much to say. But the cooking and housework and weeding in the garden all went on as if nothing had changed. While the children were napping, Ian was glad to have Ward join him in the yard. Ian had often teased him about how ineffective he was at weeding when he couldn't see the difference between the good plants and the bad ones, but he always appreciated Ward's company while he worked at it. Ward sat nearby on the ground while Ian knelt in the pea patch, wondering with each weed he pulled how his wife was going to manage to care for the garden *and* the household *and* three children, including an infant. Of course, Patricia would be here, and it was a blessing for the two women to actually live under the same roof, especially under the circumstances. But Patricia wouldn't necessarily be any better at chopping wood or other such duties that a man was more prone to do. Ian just *hated* the idea of leaving these women on their own. Of course, there were men in the neighborhood, friends they knew from church, who would offer support and help if needed. But it just wasn't the same. And Ian *hated* it!

"I think we need to start talking about this, my friend," Ward said, as if he could smell the negative thoughts coming from Ian's head. The man couldn't see, but he had a sense about the emotions of people around him that was downright uncanny.

"I agree," Ian said, grateful for the comfortable relationship that had existed between them right from the start.

Ian and Ward had met by nothing short of divine intervention in a tea shop in Liverpool, and Ian had known from that very first meeting that they would be a significant part of each other's lives. Neither of them was afraid to say exactly what they felt, and they had a way of helping each other keep perspective when things were tough. Or more accurately, Ward helped keep Ian on the right path, since Ian always seemed to struggle more with holding on to his faith than did Ward. Ian had witnessed Ward lose more than one loved one and come through it with a remarkably positive attitude, even while his grief was consuming him. He knew for a fact that Ward leaving Patricia and June behind would be no easier for him than it would be for Ian to leave Wren and his own children. But Ward was strong and firm in his convictions, and he was a continual inspiration to Ian—a fact that left him completely unprepared to hear Ward say, "I don't think I can do this."

Ian leaned back on his heels, his dirty hands suspended midair as if they'd been frozen.

"Yes, you heard me correctly," Ward said, even though he could not see Ian's pose or expression.

"How do you do that?"

"Do what?"

"Practically read my mind when you can't even see me."

"You became *very* silent," Ward said. "So, are you disappointed in me? Are you going to tell me I need to muster up some faith and courage and press forward like a man?"

"No," Ian said, sitting on the ground and brushing the dirt from his hands. "I'm going to tell you that I'm glad to hear you express exactly what I'm feeling. You're always the strong one. I don't—"

"Where you came up with that, I can't imagine," Ward interrupted. "I'm the *strong* one?" He let out a cynical laugh. "I have seen you go through some terrible things, my brother, and you have always remained stout of heart and firm in your convictions."

"Now I *know* you're blind. Either that or you just weren't paying attention."

"Or maybe you just keep your feelings to yourself a little too much. And maybe I do the same. Has that ever occurred to you?"

Ian couldn't deny that it *hadn't* occurred to him.

"I admit that I've been given great strength to get through the hardships in my life," Ward said, "but I didn't necessarily come to it easily. You don't know how many weeks I cried at night when I was alone after we lost Bethia. And the same with my mother. I can put on a brave face just like you can. But I don't think I can do this . . . leave here . . . leave *them*. I don't think I can make that journey again . . . and then again to get home."

"I feel the same way, Ward; I do. But at the same time . . ." He couldn't finish the sentence.

"I know," Ward said and hung his head in a gesture of despair. "We both know Joseph is a prophet. We both know that others have sacrificed more than this. And while I was not the personal recipient of hearing about the gospel from a missionary, I heard about it from you, and I would not know what I know and have what I have if it had not been for those two men making that great sacrifice."

"Exactly," Ian said. "It keeps going back and forth in my mind. How can I do it? How can I *not* do it?"

"I don't know the answer to that question," Ward said.

"You told Joseph you would go," Ian reminded him.

"So did you," Ward said. Ian sighed, and silence filled many moments before Ward asked, "Are we liars, then? Are we cowards?"

Ian thought about that for many more silent moments before he answered firmly. "No, we're human. And somehow we've got to overcome these . . . painful human emotions we have and . . . find a way to do this."

"Somehow?"

"You know there's only one way that's possible. And that's the only possible thing we can do. We have to put our trust in the Lord."

More silence. "I don't know if I can," Ward said with a resignation Ian had never heard before. Then he shook his head and closed his eyes, which seemed unnecessary for a blind man. "I have *never* let my lack of eyesight keep me from doing my best to live like any other man. I have *never* used it as an excuse. But I want to use it now."

"And what excuse do I have?"

"Besides the need to take care of me, you mean?"

"I can take care of you either at home or abroad."

"And what if something happens to *you*? What would I do then? A man with no sight, utterly alone in a strange place? What would I do?"

Ian couldn't answer, so more silence followed the question. What could he possibly say? Ward's concerns were completely well-founded. It would certainly take a great deal more faith for him than it would the average man to embark on such an endeavor. Then a thought occurred to Ian, and he hoped saying it aloud would be more positive than negative. "When you made the decision to come to America with your mother, you must have wondered the same thing. She didn't survive the journey. But by then you had *me*. If God has asked you to do this, He will surely take your unique needs into consideration and not leave you alone in the dark. We just have to believe that we'll both come back safely. If we couldn't believe that, we could never bear it."

"I'm not sure we can anyway," Ward said, then he sighed. "But you make a good point. I admit that I *did* wonder what would happen if Mother were not there to help me. In fact, we talked about it a number of times. We decided together that we just had to go forward."

"And yet . . . religion was not a part of your lives at that point. It's as though you were acting on faith even though you didn't understand what faith meant. Isn't faith simply moving forward with something even when we don't fully understand why?"

"Partly, yes," Ward said. "But when I left England with my mother, she was the only family I had, and I was bringing her with me. Now I'm being asked to leave my family behind. I don't know how to do that. What little communication we might be able to share with our loved ones would be . . ." He shook his head and almost sounded angry. "Well . . . with moving around like nomads, and with it taking so many weeks for letters to cross the ocean, what point would there be in even trying?"

"I don't know, Ward. I can't answer that. I don't know what to say."

"I don't expect you to have the answers, friend," Ward said. "I know where I need to go for the answers, I just . . . have to get over feeling angry about this before I can move forward."

"Yes," Ian said, "I know what you mean."

"At least that makes us not quite so alone. If you get any great inspiration on how to make this more bearable, please let me know."

"No, *you* let *me* know," Ian said and stood up. He took Ward by the hand and helped him to his feet. "Let's go inside. It's getting hotter out here by the minute."

"Yes," Ward said, "but if we go inside, we'll find our wives either crying or not making any sound at all. In my world, that kind of silence is torturous. I far prefer my wife's lovely chattering over the silence."

"Amen," Ian said and put Ward's hand on his shoulder so that Ward could walk beside him and not collide with any unseen objects. They were comfortable with the routine, and neither of them gave it a second thought. But Ian thought of how much easier it was to help guide Ward through the steps he took when they were at home in familiar territory, where he knew the location of obstacles. Ward knew all the pathways through the house and around the yard as long as he got his bearings, and he even knew his way around town somewhat—at least enough that guiding him was easy and took very little effort. But Ian recalled during their journey to Nauvoo how difficult it had been for Ward to be in unfamiliar places, and how much more careful he'd needed to be. It seemed that Ian couldn't do *anything* without making comparisons related to their impending departure. He didn't want to think about it *at all,* but he couldn't think of anything else.

That night Ian lay in his bed and stared upward through the darkness, praying in his mind for the witness he needed, for the strength to do what had to be done, or for some miracle to occur that would bring Joseph to their door with the announcement that it had been a mistake and they didn't have to go after all. He knew the third option would never happen. He simply had to keep praying for the first two so that he could face this and survive it, and so that his sweet Wren could do the same.

Ian only knew that he'd fallen asleep when he was awakened by an abrupt nudge at the same time he heard his name spoken in an urgent whisper.

"What's wrong?" he asked, still not fully coherent enough to consider the most likely reason.

"The pains have started, Ian," he heard Wren say, and his mind suddenly became very alert. He sat up abruptly and made a panicked noise but her hand came to his arm with a soothing touch, and her voice was calm as she said, "It started quite a while ago, but it's getting more regular now. I think we'll know when it's time t' send for the doctor, but I . . . don't want t' be alone. I need ye t' help me through."

"Of course," he said and got up to light a lamp, although he set the wick low so that it would only offer a dim glow. "You should have awakened me as soon as it started."

"I wanted ye t' get yer sleep," she said, then laughed softly. He'd not heard her laugh since Joseph's visit. "Ye're going t' need it."

"I'm not the only one," he said, pretending that he would actually be here to help her deal with nighttime diaper changes and feedings.

Ian helped Wren get as comfortable as possible with some pillows behind her back and one beneath her knees, then he sat beside her on the bed and put his arm around her shoulders while he held her hand tightly in his. "Everything's going to be all right, Wren. It will be."

"Whatever happens," she said, "we'll get through it."

"Of course," he said, hating the fact that *whatever happens* included a number of frightening possibilities.

Minutes of silence passed while he was aware of her pains by the way she tightened her hold on him and then relaxed it. Then, with no warning, she said, "Ye mustn't worry about us, Ian."

He looked at her, confused, and she looked as if he should know what she was talking about.

"When ye leave here . . . with Ward," she clarified and he almost wanted to get angry with her for bringing it up. "Ye mustn't worry about us while ye're away. We'll be fine, ye know. All will be well. There are so many here who help care for one another. Ye're not leaving me alone; I'll never be alone." Tears rose in her eyes. "I'll only be without my one true love." She pressed her forehead to his. "Our needs will be met and all will be well. Ye mustn't worry. Only think of me missing ye as I know ye'll be missing me."

"Every hour of the day," Ian muttered and tightened his hold on her, wondering how he could ever bear it.

Chapter Three
The Key

Somewhere in the midst of Wren's grueling labor, Ian had a feeling sweep over him that caught him completely by surprise and actually took his breath away. He knew immediately it was what he'd been praying for, and the very fact that his prayers had been answered gave him a deep peace and comfort he could never describe. But he had a tiny moment of wishing his prayers *hadn't* been answered. If he'd never received that personal witness, he might have been able to talk himself out of going. Now he knew. He knew beyond any doubt that it was right for him to leave his family and do as the Prophet had asked. In the time it took for his heart to beat twice, his thoughts and feelings were filled with a plethora of information that swept over him like a warm, comforting wave. He could never repeat all of what he'd seen and felt in his mind and heart simultaneously, but he knew that everything would be all right, and that going on this mission was the right path for his life. The most important point that stood out to him was a distinct impression of taking Wren in his arms upon his return, of holding her close and closing the gap between them that this journey would create. It was an image that he knew would carry him through.

Ian became distracted by Wren's ongoing labor, but he kept getting glimpses in his mind of the impressions he'd seen and felt, and he couldn't help but thank God for answering his prayers, even while he was praying that all would go well with the delivery of this baby. It occurred to him that if Wren were alive and well to greet him when he returned home at some point in the future, then she would surely survive this childbirth. But he couldn't help worrying about the baby. Then suddenly it was over. He heard the baby's cry from the other room. A few hours later it was comfortably confirmed that the baby was healthy and strong, but it was also evident the birth had taken a toll on Wren. The doctor assured them she would be fine, but she needed to get a great deal of rest, and be patient with allowing herself to recover. She'd given birth three times in four years, and her body had good reason to be tired. Ironically it occurred to Ian that if he was gone for many months, possibly a year or two, there would be no concern about her getting pregnant again for quite some time.

With the afternoon sun emitting an uncomfortable warmth into the room, Ian sat by Wren's bedside, holding his new little daughter in his arms. Wren smiled weakly toward him, and he took her hand while keeping the baby secure in his other arm. They shared a long gaze, then firmly decided on naming the baby Anya Wren—Anya after Ian's mother. He told Wren he would write a letter home and tell her right away.

"Or ye could just tell her when ye see her," Wren said.

"What?" Ian asked, startled by the comment.

"Ye're going back, Ian," she said and got tears in her eyes. "I don't envy the journey, but I envy the thought of going back t' Brierley . . . t' our beloved Highlands. It will surely be a great blessing t' ye . . . and t' yer family—a blessing that will help make up for the sacrifice."

Ian could only give her a faint smile. He felt suddenly choked up. Joseph had said to *return to his homeland.* Why had going back to Brierley not occurred to him? Ward's homeland was England, but Ian's was Scotland. They were both on the same island, far across the Atlantic. And of course he would go back to Brierley! And perhaps he could finally share with his family the full depth of joy he'd found through the gospel. He'd written to them about it. But this would be different. So different! For the first time since Joseph had issued the call, Ian actually felt the tiniest bit of hope that something good could possibly come out of this.

"Ian," Wren said, her voice weak and fading with fatigue, "I must tell ye something."

Ian felt an inexplicable dread in hearing her words, and he wondered what it might be. Perhaps hoping to put it off, he said, "You should rest. We can talk later."

"I'll rest, but I need t' tell ye this first." Ian leaned closer and gave her his full attention. "During the labor . . . during the worst part of it . . . my prayers were answered." He saw tears leak from her eyes. With the placement of her head on the pillow, some tears ran over the bridge of her nose and others into her hair. He knew already what she was referring to, and he understood the feelings of dread. Just as with his own personal witness that leaving his family was the right thing to do, there was a poignancy in the reality of what it meant.

"What prayers?" he asked as if he didn't know, squeezing her hand at the same time to encourage her.

"In my mind . . . I saw ye coming back t' me . . . and I knew that it was right for ye t' go, and that all would be well with us while ye're gone. I can't say how I know it. But I know ye understand. I know that ye know what I mean."

"Yes," Ian said and bit his lip while he fought back the hot tears stinging his eyes, "I know what you mean, Wren, and . . . my prayers were answered too. I . . . saw the same; felt the same." With his admission, the tears become too strong to hold at bay and they trickled down his face. "I don't know how to leave you, Wren." He glanced at the tiny infant in his arms. "To leave our children." He looked back at Wren. "I don't know how to do it, but I know that I must. I know that it's right . . . that it's . . ." He squeezed his eyes closed and more tears came. "I know that it's what God wants me to do, and I must heed the call."

"God will give us both the strength we need t' get through this, Ian," she said with a conviction that warmed his heart, but it didn't necessarily soothe his fears or make him any less prone to believe that he was incapable of actually going through with it.

Ian simply nodded and said, "You need to rest, my darling. You've worked very hard today."

Wren's eyes shifted to their new daughter, and she smiled. "Our little Anya is beautiful, isn't she."

"She is," Ian agreed.

With that declaration, Wren closed her eyes and almost immediately fell asleep. Ian sat where he was with Wren's hand in his and the baby cradled in his arm. Now that Wren wasn't watching him, he let the tears flow more freely. Having a child born would be cause enough for a man to shed some tears, but the forthcoming separation from his family threatened to break his heart. He told himself he needed to pray, that relying on God was the only way he could ever do this, but the only words he could bring to his lips were simply, "God, please give me strength."

* * * * *

Through the next few days, Wren drifted in and out of sleep, struggling with pain and weakness. Ian did all he could to help with the baby, but he found he was more useful with the other children. He knew their needs and could keep them entertained and cared for. Patricia was a great blessing in assisting Wren and helping care for the new infant. Ian was inexplicably grateful for her, and for the comfortable closeness she shared with Wren. But he could hardly observe their interaction without wondering how the two of them would manage everything completely on their own, especially for so long.

Joseph and Emma Smith came by to check on Wren and the new baby, bringing with them a lovely meal for the whole family, and a little quilt for the new arrival. Emma visited with Wren and Patricia in the bedroom while Joseph sat with Ian and Ward in the parlor. The children played on the floor while the men chatted comfortably and Ian tried to ignore the tension he felt in knowing that Joseph would surely bring up their pending departure. He *did* bring it up, but there was genuine compassion in his voice when he asked, "How are the two of you feeling about this endeavor?"

Ward admitted, "It's difficult, but I know it's right." Ian was surprised, since Ward hadn't said anything to him about having received his own witness. But then, Ian hadn't told Ward that *he'd* received a witness. Perhaps neither of them had wanted to be the first to admit to it for reasons that were difficult to express. "And Patricia knows it too," Ward added.

Ian then admitted that both he and Wren had experienced similar feelings. They all talked about it for a while, then Joseph and Emma departed with well wishes. Once they'd left, Ian realized he had no choice but to accept that he and Ward would be leaving in three days' time. Ignoring it now would only leave them less prepared. They needed to pack their things and make certain their households were in order and that their wives had their needs met as much as it was possible.

Once the children were down for the night, Ian sat on the bed and held Wren close to him while they cried together—not for the first time.

"I want t' write ye letters," she said, "but how can I? Ye can send letters t' me because I'll always be here, but where do I send letters in return?"

"I don't know," he said. "If we're to be in any one place for any particular length of time, I'll write and let you know. Joseph told us we would know where we needed to go, and how long to stay, and when to come home. He told us the Spirit would guide us and we would know. It all feels so dreadfully uncertain to me, but I suppose that's all part of trusting in God. I might not know where I'll be—or for how long—but God knows."

"Indeed," she said. "God knows. We must both trust in that."

The following morning Ian woke up with an idea that he believed was inspired. He mentioned it to Ward in passing just after breakfast, then Ian went into town with the hope of finding just the right thing. He was delighted to find the perfect solution in the first shop he visited, and he bought out all that they had. He gave half of what he'd purchased to Ward, and took the other half to his bedroom where Wren was feeding the baby.

"What have ye got there?" she asked, noting the stack of four leather-bound books that he had.

He set them down and handed one of them to Wren, who took it with her free hand as he explained, "It's blank inside. This is where you can write your letters to me, Wren. Write to me every day." He sat on the bed and leaned toward her. "Write every detail of your days, of the things the children are doing. And when I come back, I will be able to read all of your letters, and it will give me back everything I'm missing by not being here." She got tears in her eyes, and he hurried to finish explaining his idea. "I will do the same," he said. "I've got two for each of us, and we'll buy more if we have to. I will write to you every day in this book and tell you of all my experiences. You'll be able to read it when I return, and you will know all the things that my memory isn't big enough to hold through the time that we're apart."

"Oh, it's a lovely idea!" Wren said, setting the book on the bed beside her to lovingly caress its cover, then she opened it and thumbed through the blank pages with fondness.

"I'm certain it was inspired," he said. "It will hardly compensate for not being able to share one another's company, but . . . it will help."

"Indeed," she said, looking up at him, "it will help."

The following day the temperature outside rose and it was especially hot. Ian found himself sweating while he struggled to get the children to calm down for their usual afternoon nap. He'd made certain they ate some lunch while Patricia had been bathing the baby, but he'd not eaten yet himself. He was hoping to eat with Wren, and she'd been asleep most of the day after having been up in the night a great deal with the baby. Once the children were finally settled down, Ian peered quietly into his own bedroom to see Wren sitting up in bed with little Anya sleeping close to her side. A lunch tray with food enough for two was also on the bed.

"Patricia said ye'd not eaten yet," Wren said, "and she knew ye'd check on me before ye went downstairs."

"Am I so predictable?" Ian asked.

"Indeed ye are, Ian Brierley," she said with a little laugh. But it was a weak laugh, not at all like her normal self, and he felt worried for her. The doctor had said more than once that everything was fine and she just needed time, but time was something Ian didn't have. The time left before his departure was now being measured in hours, and each one that passed brought them closer to saying good-bye.

"Before we eat," she said, "I have something for ye."

"Do you?" he asked, sitting close to her.

Wren opened her hand, and he could see a long, simple silver chain with a key on it. She lifted the chain into both hands and put it over Ian's head, then she held the key up in front of his face. "This already belongs t' ye. It's yer key t' the front door of our home. Its literal purpose is to open that door when ye come back, but I want ye t' wear it and not take it off until ye're able to use it again. When ye see it, when ye feel it next t' yer heart, I want ye t' think of home, but I also want ye t' remember that this is also the key t' my heart. Ye've had my heart for many years, Ian Brierley, and ye'll have it forever."

Ian nodded but couldn't speak. Wren opened a couple of buttons on his shirt and tucked the key underneath the fabric where it hung directly over the center of his chest, directly over his heart. She closed the buttons, kissed him quickly and said, "Let's eat."

They chatted in a comfortable way while they shared lunch as if there would be no gap in their ability to do so each and every day. After they were finished eating, Wren reached out her hand toward Ian, saying, "I need t' say something that ye might find strange, but I need t' say it."

Ian took her hand and moved closer to her so that he could face her directly. "When ye leave," she said, and tears rose immediately into her eyes. Ian had to fight to maintain his composure, certain if he started crying he'd never be able to stop; he would likely regress to his childhood and cry like a lost little boy. Wren cleared her throat and started again, as if she were finding it difficult to form the words. "Ye said that ye planned t' leave very early in the morning . . . before dawn."

"That's right," he said. "You know that's when the coach leaves to head east."

"I know, and . . . I just want t' say that . . . I want t' be asleep when ye leave." She closed her eyes and droplets of tears appeared on her lashes. Ian's heart began to pound when he realized a plan for his actual departure was being discussed, and the nature of her request made it clear how much she had thought about it, and how difficult it was for her. He felt some comfort to know that his leaving would be as hard for her as it would be for him, but at the same time, he didn't want to see her suffer or endure heartache for *any* reason, and it was difficult to witness her grief. She sniffled and went on. "I want t' share our farewells before we fall asleep t'gether. And we can be in each other's arms . . . the way we always are. And then . . . ." Her tears increased, and she whimpered without opening her eyes. "Then I can imagine that yer being gone is just a dream, and one day I'll wake up and it'll be over and ye'll be with me again."

Ian couldn't speak without betraying his own vulnerable emotions, but he drew her into his arms and held her close, letting her cry unrestrained against his chest. He was willing to honor her wish, and he knew that she knew he would, even without anything more being said.

He just didn't know how he could do it. He thought of men going off to war. It was a tradition of humankind nearly as old as the world, and he couldn't deny his gratitude that battlefields were not his intended destination. He certainly had a much higher chance of survival given that single fact. But the emotions related to the situation were surely much the same, and at the moment it seemed unbearable.

After Wren had indulged in a good cry, Ian encouraged her to get some rest. He took the lunch tray to the kitchen and went outside to work on being certain that everything was in as good an order as it could possibly be before he left. Throughout the remainder of that day and into the next, emotion gave way to practicality. There was too much to do, and too many things that needed to be planned and discussed for any of them to have time to wallow in the potential loneliness of the future. Ian chopped wood most of the day, since it was the task that he most hated imagining Wren having to do in his absence. He had spoken to a few different neighbors, asking them to check in on Wren and Patricia, to see if any masculine tasks might need to be performed. But Ian felt an instinctive need to provide for the needs of his household as much as he could before leaving. Money was not an issue—for which he was deeply grateful—but he wanted to be able to do the things that his family needed done. It felt important to him to leave as much chopped wood and kindling as possible, ready and waiting in the barn, so that the women would not have to rely on the help of anyone else any more than was absolutely necessary. He also got as much feed for the horses as was practical to store in the barn, and set up the situation there so that it would be as easy as possible for the women to feed and care for the horses. Wren was good with the horses, and very comfortable with them. She'd grown up near a kind man who'd owned a livery, and he'd allowed her to use his horses frequently. Both women knew how to hook one of the horses to the trap, which would give them transportation should they need to go farther than walking distance. They also knew how to saddle one of the horses if need be. Fortunately, they lived close enough to the center of town that much of what they needed on a regular basis—including eggs and milk and other essentials—could be purchased easily enough. Ian was more glad than ever that they'd chosen to build their home in this location.

While Ian chopped wood, only taking a break here and there to check on Wren or help with the children, Ward talked through household plans with Patricia and Wren. His practical nature and keen awareness of the happenings of the household were helpful in guiding the women to put some plans and schedules in writing that would assist them in the coming months in handling the finances, keeping their property and belongings properly cared for, and making certain that every need was met. Neighbors had become aware of the pending call for Ward and Ian to leave, and many stopped by to offer their assistance and to bid farewell to the men. Wren and Patricia were grateful to be able to compile a list of people they could call on should needs arise. It didn't ease the inevitable pain of separation, but it did ease some of the associated anxieties.

More important than every temporal preparation was Ian and Ward's equal desire to leave their dear wives with a spiritual blessing. The two men had already received priesthood blessings to set them apart to this calling, and in those blessings they had been given many wonderful promises. Before supper on their final day at home, they all gathered together so that Ian and Ward could each give their wives a priesthood blessing. The Spirit was present and strong, and there was much peace and comfort in the power of the priesthood and all it represented. Ian thought of all the struggles they'd endured on their previous journey and wondered how it might have differed if he and Ward had had this power at their disposal then. He felt some comfort to know that there were many priesthood holders available to offer assistance to their families in this way if it was needed throughout the course of this mission.

On the final evening that Ward and Ian would be with their families, they all abided by an unspoken agreement to pretend that everything was completely normal. Perhaps, even as young as the children were, they feared that it might upset them to be made aware of the impending departure of their fathers. Even so, Ian felt certain the children could surely sense the underlying tension.

Putting the children to bed was painfully difficult for Ian, but he hugged them and kissed their little faces as if the bedtime ritual was the same as it had always been. He waited until they were asleep before he sat by their bedsides and spoke softly to them of his love and devotion to their young lives, to the sanctity of family, and to the gospel that meant more to him than anything. He touched their wispy hair and pressed gentle kisses to their little brows before he went to his own bedroom to find Wren preparing for bed. With her desire to have him leave while she slept, he knew their good-byes were at hand. She was still mostly bedridden from childbirth, and he sat on the edge of the bed close to her once she'd gotten comfortable, leaning against pillows behind her back.

He took her hand and looked down before he found the courage to look at her directly. "I've been imagining this moment for days . . . wondering what to say. But how does a man put years' worth of thoughts and feelings into a few words?"

"There's no need," she said. "I know how ye feel."

"I know you do, but . . . I still have to say that . . . I love you, Wren." He tightened his hold on her hand and leaned closer. "You must never forget that. No matter what happens, no matter how long this goes on, you must never forget it!"

"I won't. Of course I won't," she said and started to cry, but since he was about to cry himself it wasn't a surprise. "And ye must remember the same, Ian. Ye must!"

"And you must remember, Wren, that there is only one thing more important to me than my love for you, and it's the only reason I'm doing this. My devotion to God is the *only* thing that could take me away from you like this. And you must know that you will be in my heart every hour of every day."

"I do know it!" she said, leaning forward to wrap her arms around his neck. "As ye will be in *my* heart."

Ian held her close for long minutes, then touched the tears on her face before he kissed her, and kissed her, and kissed her. He finally drew away to douse the lamp and crawled into bed, knowing that his bags were packed and his clothes all laid out for his predawn departure. He snuggled up close to Wren, loving the feel of her warmth close to him, trying to memorize the feeling the way he'd been trying to memorize a thousand aspects of the everyday life he shared with his wife and children. He couldn't help but consider yet another irony in the fact that Wren had recently given birth and it would not be possible or appropriate for him to share the kind of intimacy with her that a husband and wife would have naturally shared prior to such a lengthy separation. They still held each other close and soaked up the nearness of being together. They talked and cried and shared long stretches of silence, neither of them having much to say. If it hadn't already been said numerous times, it simply went without saying. There was no question or doubt between them in regard to the love they shared. The history between them, the depth of their feelings, and their hopes for the future were all in perfect alignment. They were like the sun and the moon, the stars and the sky, music and lyrics, ocean and sand, poetry and pen. One could not exist without the other. But somehow they would have to; or at least they would have to exist with an unfathomable distance between them. They each took comfort in knowing that they were living beneath the same sun and sky. The same moon would shine down upon them, and the same stars would glitter above them. But an ocean would lie between them, and they could only try to reach across it with their minds and their hearts, their thoughts and their feelings, and offer each other the kind of love and peace and comfort that could never be achieved with the physical senses. It would have to be something deeper and stronger than that, something miraculous and impossible to understand. But they both had to believe that such a miracle was possible, that with God *nothing* was impossible. Otherwise, they would never be able to face this separation.

They both finally slept despite their resistance. Ian woke to the sound of the baby crying. He got up to change little Anya's diaper, thinking it would be the last time he'd have the opportunity to perform such a simple task in regard to her care. He took her to Wren to be fed and left the lamp burning low so that he could just lie there and watch her, the baby at her breast, as beautiful as a rare and precious work of art. He touched her face and spoke quietly to her, knowing that the day ahead would surely be more difficult than any day Ian had ever endured in his life. He thought of the deaths of loved ones, some of them accompanied by great trauma, and he felt sure his perspective was distorted by the pain of the present. But *in* the present, nothing felt as hard as this. After the baby had gone back to sleep, he kissed Wren on and on, as if doing so could put off the inevitable indefinitely. Only the exhaustion of childbirth and nightly feedings finally lured her back to sleep, and he knew she'd not wake again before he left. He held her close but didn't sleep himself. He only soaked in the experience and tried not to think too hard or feel too much. When he knew it was nearly time, he got up and quietly got dressed. He spent a few minutes with each of his sleeping children while they remained completely oblivious to the impact of what was happening. Gillian had been told that her papa was leaving, but she could likely only comprehend it in the context of his previous departures, such as going into town for errands, or spending a day working on the temple. He returned quietly to his own bedroom and watched Wren sleeping until he could hear sounds downstairs to indicate that Ward was likely ready to go and waiting. He pressed a kiss to Wren's face that was far too gentle to wake her, then he forced himself to leave the room. He was only a few steps into the hall before he turned around and went back for one more glimpse and one more kiss to her sleeping, angelic face. Then he doused the lamp and left the room, hurrying down the stairs before he had a chance to change his mind. He went directly outside to avoid watching Ward share his final embrace with Patricia. He was barely holding on to his composure and wasn't about to tempt it to falter. A minute later Patricia guided Ward out onto the porch and put his hand on Ian's shoulder. They exchanged a firm gaze, as if she were officially putting her husband into his care. Then she closed the door.

"And so we're off," Ward said with false enthusiasm as Ian stepped off the porch and headed up the street, with Ward matching his gait. In Ward's free hand he carried a bag that held the minimal necessities a man would need for traveling, and Ian had the equivalent in a bag with a shoulder strap. In his hand he carried a portmanteau that contained nothing but books—several copies of one book in particular. It was heavy and it took only a few minutes of walking before he had to alternate hands in order to avoid having his arm ache. But his reasons for taking so many copies of the Book of Mormon were personal, and he was willing to do whatever it might take to carry the burden. That book had changed his life, even though he'd not taken the time to actually speak to the missionaries who had sold it to him. In Ian's mind, he imagined a person waiting for every single copy he carried— even if these people didn't know it yet. He imagined angels compiling a list of names and guiding him to be in the right place at the right time to be certain that each and every copy was delivered as it was meant to be. He also imagined bringing the portmanteau home empty, and how light it would be to carry when he knew that his mission had been completed. Or perhaps he wouldn't bring it home at all. All he had to bring home was himself and the key he wore over his heart.

They didn't have to walk very far to arrive at their destination, where the driver of the hired carriage took their luggage and tied it firmly to the top of the carriage, beneath an oiled canvas that would protect it from the weather. Memories of the journey to Nauvoo tightened Ian's heart as he watched them do so. It was a carriage accident during a terrible rainstorm that had taken Ward's mother from them. Ironically, all of their luggage that had been tied to the top of the carriage had remained undamaged and even dry. Ian forced his thoughts from the memories of Millie's tragic death and instead imagined his precious luggage remaining protected all through the journey so that each book could end up in the right hands.

Inside the carriage, Ian and Ward sat next to each other, across from a middle-aged couple heading east to visit their daughter's family. The strangers had very little to say, and their presence prevented Ian and Ward from saying much of anything to each other. As the carriage rolled forward, Ian felt Ward take hold of his forearm in a firm, almost painful grip. He'd held on to Ian's arm that way many times while Ian had helped guide him from place to place, but Ian knew the implication of his grip now, and it was difficult not to give in to his temptation to cry like a baby. Instead he gripped Ward's arm in a similar manner, silently telling him that their thoughts and feelings were the same. Then Ian tried not to think about what he was leaving behind. He tried instead to focus on what might lie ahead.

He couldn't think about the journey. It felt long and hard and he couldn't even try to imagine the miles they had yet to cross without inducing memories of their reverse journey and all the losses and hardships they'd experienced. So Ian imagined instead what it might be like when they arrived in England. Where would the Spirit guide them? What kind of people might they meet? What miracles might they see come to pass? Eventually he would make his way back home. He'd discussed with Ward whether they should start in Scotland

and work their way down the island toward London, or instead do it the other way around. They had both felt that they should sail to London, focus their attention in that tremendous city until moved upon to go elsewhere, and Ian's home in the Highlands would be their final destination.

Through their days of traveling east by carriage, Ian kept his mind focused on their destination and their purpose for this endeavor. On the occasions when they would spend the night at an inn to get a good night's sleep—as opposed to just dozing on and off through the night in a jostling carriage—Ian would indulge in thoughts of home and how desperately he missed his babies and his precious Wren. Sometimes he just couldn't hold back the tears. He did his best to cry them quietly since Ward was generally sleeping in the same room. But he suspected that Ward was doing the same thing. Neither of them said much to each other about home or missing their families. It was as if speaking about it would only make it more painful. So they talked about the weather and the scenery, and they frequently read together from the Book of Mormon, since Ward's only means of reading was for Ian to read aloud to him. The words of the book gave them comfort and the means to fill in the spaces of silence. But during the times when silence was inevitable, when the dark of night and the quiet of a strange room was almost haunting, Ian could do nothing but think of home and wonder if he was missed as much as he was missing them. Prayer was his only possible remedy for his ailment, and he could only fall asleep when his thoughts were consumed with silent conversation with his Maker, pleading for his own heart to be comforted, and for his family to have peace and comfort in every possible way during his absence.

* * * * *

Wren came reluctantly awake to the sound of the baby crying and struggled to orient herself enough to get up and see to her little daughter's needs. Even though she was physically capable of doing so, she couldn't deny her weakness and exhaustion that made it clear that this was *all* she was capable of doing. She rolled over carefully, still brutally aware of the lingering pain of childbirth, but she didn't get her feet to the floor before the reality struck her. She gasped and reached toward the other side of the bed, only to find it empty and cold. He'd done as she'd asked. He'd left while she slept. He was gone, and she had no idea how many months—or years—it might be until she would find him sleeping there beside her again. The growing volume of the baby's crying shocked her back to the present reality. She lit a lamp and tried to hold the tears back until she could manage them, but they blurred her vision while she changed the baby's diaper, and she could barely see to get back into bed to nurse the baby. Once she was lying on her side with the baby at her breast, she allowed the tears to come fully, and she sobbed without restraint until it seemed to disrupt the baby's eating. Wren managed to keep her tears more silent and controlled until little Anya was back to sleep, then she wrapped her arms around Ian's pillow and cried while the light of day trickled slowly into the room. Her tears gave way to a quiet shock, not unlike how she'd felt when she'd lost a loved one to death. She reminded herself that Ian was alive and well and he *would* come home to her. But that was so long from now, and the miles were growing between them even at this moment. Exhausted as she was, she couldn't go back to sleep, even though the house was quiet. She became utterly lost in that quiet until she heard noises to indicate that little Donnan was awake. Wren pulled herself together and crossed the hall to find him standing in his crib, squealing with excitement when he saw her, oblivious to the departure of his father. But his happiness made her smile, and she was glad for it. She urged him to lie down so she could change his diaper, and she was able to get him dressed since he was old enough to cooperate somewhat with the process. But she was under strict orders not to lift him, and she simply needed to give him some toys and keep him entertained there in his crib until Patricia came. Wren glanced at the clock and knew it wouldn't be long.

Gillian ran in to the room and greeted her mother with a hug and laughter similar to her brother's. Gillian was able to help keep Donnan entertained, and Wren knew she could send Gillian to get Patricia if she needed her. But Gillian climbed into the crib with her brother and the two of them played delightfully until Patricia arrived a few minutes later with June in her arms. She set June down in order to get little Donnan out of his crib, then she took all of the children with her downstairs to prepare breakfast, insisting that Wren go back to bed and stay there. They'd all agreed this was how it needed to be until Wren got her strength back. She knew that pushing herself too quickly might only cause more damage and increase the amount of time that Patricia would need to carry the majority of the burden of work in the house while their husbands were gone. But Wren hated feeling useless, and she especially hated this situation. And she'd only been awake and without Ian less than a few hours. She reminded herself to have faith and trust in the Lord. Then she reminded herself that if she *didn't* have faith and trust in the Lord, she wouldn't have let Ian go. She reminded herself to rely on the comfort that only God could give her, and she focused her attention on prayer until the baby woke up again, needing attention.

Patricia surprised Wren when she brought breakfast up to the bedroom. Wren's meals had been delivered to her room since she'd given birth, since the doctor didn't want her going up and down the stairs just yet. The surprise was that Patricia had brought her own meal as well so the two women could eat together.

"The children have eaten and they're playing across the hall," Patricia said, and Wren could hear noises to indicate the truth of this. "But I refuse to eat alone. Therefore, wherever you're eating, I'm eating with you."

"I wholly agree," Wren said, knowing a prolonged pattern was being set in motion.

As they ate they talked a little about their feelings, then they agreed *not* to talk about it too much when they were both prevented from being able to eat due to the onslaught of tears.

Days passed according to the same routine while Wren felt only a gradual improvement in her health that left her infuriatingly impatient. Patricia was kind and helpful and never showed the least bit of irritation at being entirely in charge of the household, including three children. Wren was mostly able to care for herself and the new baby on her own, but occasionally she even needed Patricia's assistance in that regard. She could only tell her friend each day how grateful she was and take good care of herself so that she could cease being an invalid as soon as possible and do her part.

Neighbors and women from the Relief Society checked in regularly to see that they were all right. Brother Peters from down the street hauled wood in to the house every few days, and he even helped care for the horses. Sister Hibbert and Sister Sutherland picked up groceries for them, insisting they would do so until Wren was back on her feet. Sister Waterton came to the house and watched the children a couple of times so that Patricia could walk to town and get some things they needed. Other sisters in the Relief Society brought meals in occasionally to assist with the workload, and Emma Smith herself dropped by to see how they were coming along. In every practical respect, they were coming along fine. Their needs were being met, and they were doing well—except that Wren and Patricia missed their husbands so desperately that they could scarcely breathe if they thought about it too much. Emma offered compassion in that regard that was likely more deeply empathetic than that offered by any other woman they had spoken to. While she didn't expound on her own feelings and experiences with her many separations from Joseph, it was evident from the kind words she offered, and the very look in her eyes, that she knew *exactly* how they felt. If anything, what Wren and Patricia were enduring was likely not even close to the hardships that Emma had experienced, and knowing a little about things that Joseph and Emma had suffered through—together *and* apart—gave Wren strength. And she told Emma so more than once.

The heat of summer intensified and became difficult to endure, some days more than others. The women often preferred playing with the children on the lawn in the shade of the trees as opposed to being in the house, which seemed to hold on to the heat during the day. Wren was gradually becoming able to do more around the house and with the children, and it was rare that she and Patricia didn't spend nearly every waking minute together, working side by side to do all that needed to be done and sharing a common bond that gave them much to talk about. But even when they didn't speak at all, there was a quiet understanding between them that made the loneliness almost bearable.

Occasionally, the close quarters shared by the two women, the stress of several young children, and the emotional strain brought on by their husbands' absence created some tension or mild discord between Wren and Patricia. But neither of them was prone to speak unkindly to the other, and such moments generally passed quickly and were resolved without too much effort. Overall, they were both deeply grateful for the other's company and assistance. They agreed that they didn't know how they would have managed otherwise.

Each night before putting the children to bed, they all knelt together, and the women took turns praying verbally. They expressed gratitude for many things, and asked for blessings on behalf of many people they cared for. But above all else they prayed that their husbands would remain safe and healthy, that they would be successful in their endeavors, and that they would return home to their families when the time came, as strong and full of vigor as they had been when they left.

Chapter Four
Miles

Ian found the endless days of traveling by carriage exhausting. In comparing this journey to the last one, when they'd been traveling the other direction, being without Wren and Gillian was an obvious difference—and one he hated. Ward couldn't make that comparison, since he'd met Patricia after they'd arrived in Nauvoo. But his mother had been with them through most of the journey, until the accident that had caused her death. He and Ward were able to travel at a faster rate than they had before, given that they weren't as concerned with comfort as they were with just getting to their destination as quickly as possible. When they'd been traveling in the company of women and a baby, it had been entirely different. The other great difference Ian noticed was the heat. They'd traveled in the late spring before; now it was well into summer, and the heat was utterly miserable at times. Trying to sleep in the carriage involved its own brand of misery, but at least the nights were cooler and balanced out the annoyance somewhat.

Hardly a minute passed when Ian didn't think of his sweet Wren and their beautiful children. But he tried very hard to keep his thinking carefully placed in a part of his mind that wouldn't allow him to fully feel the ache of missing them. Each mile they traversed was a mile of added distance between them. He could only long for the day when he would be traveling in the other direction, and each mile would bring him closer to home. For now he could only focus on the purpose of his quest and do his best to trust that God would care for his family and bring him safely back to them when the time came.

Ian knew they would be arriving in New York City sometime the following day when Ward said to him, "Of course we'll book passage to England as soon as we arrive, but we'll likely be spending a few days in the city before we leave."

"That's likely, I suppose," Ian said, bored with the scenery outside the carriage window. He actually hadn't thought about it, but he hated the thought of any delay in getting to their destination. Every day that he wasn't working to get those books—and the message the book represented—delivered to the right people,was simply a day away from his family.

"That's good, I think," Ward said.

"Why is that?" Ian said, turning more toward him.

Ward looked toward Ian as well, his expression astonished. Even though he couldn't see, he had a way of still delivering some form of a glare when he wanted to. "My friend, the travel has addled your brain."

"That is highly possible," Ian said, unable to deny that he felt bone weary and intensely deprived of good sleep.

"We lived in New York City for several months," Ward said, as if Ian didn't know.

"Yes," Ian drawled.

"And I distinctly recall your telling me more than once that you were saddened to think that you would likely never return to this city. And now you are."

Ian allowed that to penetrate his clouded brain. When enlightenment struck him, he gasped. "Good heavens!" he said and firmly gripped Ward's forearm in a way that had become a habit of silent communication between them through the course of their journey. It seemed to mean, *Are you thinking what I'm thinking?* Or sometimes it meant, *I'm grateful to have you by my side and not be in this alone.* In that moment, Ian clarified his gratitude. "It's a good thing one of us is thinking clearly. Thank you, my friend. Strangely enough, I suddenly feel glad to be arriving in the city, when I was dreading it before."

"Many difficult things happened while we were there," Ward said with compassion.

"Yes, it was without doubt a difficult time," Ian agreed. He thought of the horrible illnesses that Wren, Ward, Millie, and Gillian had all endured. He thought of the endless waiting and wondering through months of seemingly fruitless efforts to discover the whereabouts of the Mormons, and then preparing to make that journey west to Illinois. But the crowning moment of difficulty during their stay in New York was the death of Ian and Wren's newborn daughter, their beautiful little Joy. She had lived only minutes after her birth, and the memories of those minutes were some of the most difficult of Ian's life, followed by the memories of grieving that he and Wren had shared. They'd both come far in making peace with the loss of their little daughter, but it would always be a tender spot in his heart. Added to the difficulty of losing little Joy was the fact that her grave was in a city they were leaving, and he'd had no reason to believe that he would ever return there. But now he was. The idea of visiting his daughter's grave was poignant at best, but it still gave him a strange sense of comfort, perhaps even a mild dose of compensation for the miles he'd traveled.

A related thought occurred to him, and he said to Ward, "We didn't go through the town where your mother is buried."

"No, we didn't," Ward said.

They'd simply taken hired carriages going east and Ian hadn't given any thought to the particular routes beyond just getting to the ocean so they could sail to England. He now felt it was important to declare, "Then we must certainly make a point to go that way when we return. It would only be proper to stop and visit where she rests."

Ward gave a sad smile and turned away, as if he could see the view out the window. Ian considered, not for the first time, how boring the journey must be for Ward when he couldn't see the scenery. Even though Ian often found it tedious, at least he had *something* to look at as the miles passed by. "That would be nice," Ward said. "And it will be nice to pay a proper visit to your dear little Joy."

"Yes, it will," Ian said, and more miles passed in silence.

The carriage made a stop where Ian and Ward had time to eat a proper lunch, then they were off again with other passengers sharing the ride, which made it more difficult to converse freely with each other, although Ian and Ward had been taking advantage of fellow passengers to practice being more conversational. They had privately discussed how they were never going to be able to share the gospel if they remained silent among strangers. Ward had initially been more bold in initiating conversation. He had become very good at using his blindness as a conversation tactic. "Forgive me," he would say, "but I'm blind and the only way I can become acquainted with my fellow passengers is by conversing with them." He'd then follow with questions about where they were from, where they were going, and he'd move smoothly into questions about family members, which gracefully eased into the value of loving relationships. Stepping from there into a gentle statement about the love of God for His children was easier with some people than others. Some people became very reticent at the mention of God, but others remained open and friendly. Ian had learned a great deal from observing Ward, and he'd become more comfortable with participating in the conversation. When people asked Ian and Ward about their home and their destination, they'd both become very forthright about admitting that they'd left their families behind because they felt very strongly about sharing the gospel of Jesus Christ with the people of England and Scotland. So far, they'd given away two Books of Mormon. And for those who weren't interested in the book, Ward had come up with the idea of at least giving people a card with their names and address in Nauvoo. He'd purchased some stationery at one of their stops, and had prepared several small cards already sealed in envelopes. Of course, Ian had needed to do the writing, but they'd worked together to compose a brief but sincere testimony of Christ as the Savior of the world, and an invitation to write to them at this address in the future if they ever had questions or would like to keep in touch.

Today it became quickly evident that the new passengers had *no* interest in any conversation whatsoever. Ian and Ward could do nothing but remain politely silent and accept that not everyone would be open to what they wanted so very much to share. In fact, in this instance, they were more likely to have their message shunned than embraced. But they would never find the people seeking the message if they themselves didn't actively seek out those whose hearts were prepared to listen.

Arriving in New York City spurred many memories for Ian, and many of them were not pleasant. But as he and Ward indulged in some reminiscing, they were able to remember the good times they'd shared here. Ward talked a great deal about his mother. She had enjoyed the city life, and she had confessed to her son many times that sharing their travels and living quarters with Ian and Wren had been one of the most delightful times of her life.

"You never told me that before," Ian said.

"And now I have," Ward declared with a little laugh.

Once they had a place to stay in the city, they took a cab to where they could make arrangements for their passage to England. They had previously discussed whether they should sail to London or Liverpool, the latter being where they had departed from a few years earlier. They had both agreed that London felt right. There was a little more debate between them on the accommodations they should get onboard the ship. They were both well-to-do enough that they could afford cabins that offered more space and privacy than the majority of the passengers who would be gathered in the steerage. Ward had argued that being more closely involved with the other passengers would give them more opportunity for sharing their message. Ian had argued that there was more likelihood of being exposed to sickness in such circumstances, and if they didn't protect their health, they would never be able to do what they had been called to do. They also needed to do everything in their power to return home safely to their families. In the end, they both agreed to pray about it until they could come to an agreement that was inspired through the personal revelation of the Holy Ghost. Only the night before arriving in the city had Ward admitted to Ian that he believed they should get cabins on the ship. "No matter where we sleep, we can interact with the other passengers as much as we choose," he said.

"What a wonderful idea," Ian said, and they'd both laughed.

Now that they'd actually booked their passage and they had a place to stay in New York until their departure in three days' time, Ian's greatest desire was to acquire a lovely bouquet of flowers and take it to his daughter's grave. But since it was nearly evening, they decided to have a relaxing supper and see to that endeavor in the morning. Having once lived in this city made it easy for them to find their way around, and with Ward's hand placed on Ian's shoulder, he could walk just to the side and slightly behind Ian, and it was comfortable and easy for them to walk the busy streets.

Following a fine meal, they retired to the room they'd rented with the hope of a good, long night's sleep, which they could both use. The room was not nearly the quality they might have paid for if they'd been traveling with their wives, but it was adequate and they were glad to not be trying to sleep in a moving carriage.

The next morning over a simple breakfast, they expressed gratitude to each other over the fact that they *had* gotten a good night's sleep, then they speculated over what their wives and children might be doing. Such speculations never lasted long, however, before they lapsed into the silence of missing them, and they were mutually unable to speak until one of them found the means through which to change the subject.

After breakfast they walked up the street to find a flower shop, following the directions of a friendly woman who worked at the hotel where they were staying. Ian took a great deal of time choosing a variety of blooms that he then had the florist put together for him into a bouquet. He tried to imagine what Wren would choose, and he thought of how he would write about it in the book of letters he was already writing in nearly every day. Ian told Ward in detail about the different colors and unique appearance of each flower, while Ward took in their fragrances with extra sensitivity. They argued lightly over one that Ward reported had a terrible smell, but Ian liked the way it looked and declared that Joy in her spiritual state could likely not smell the flowers, but he would like to think that she could see them.

When the flowers had been purchased and tied together with a lovely pink ribbon, Ian hired a cab that took them to the edge of the cemetery where little Joy was buried. He asked the cab driver to wait, but told him it might be a while. Ian was glad to pay the man for his time, because this felt inexplicably important to him. Again he thought of writing about it and of Wren later reading it. Perhaps it would be at least as important to *her* to know that he did this on their behalf. Even though it had been years, Ian went directly to the correct place. He let out a soft, emotional cry when he saw the gravestone, as if a part of him might have hoped it had all been a bad dream and he hadn't really left the remains of his infant daughter here in this place that was so foreign to the home they'd now found. But there it was, engraved in stone. *Bethia Joy Brierley.* There was only one date; she was born and had died on the same day. The information, however minimal, told the story of her brief life. But most people passing by would not know that this child had been called Bethia after her aunt who had led a troubled life and died a tragic death. Nor would people realize that this child would have been called Joy every day of her life because her parents had taken one look at her and had believed that she would live to bring them joy. Any passerby wouldn't realize that the name Brierley was not the name her father had been given at his own birth, but a modified version of it. The official changing of his surname had been a big step as he and Wren had chosen to become Americans. MacBrier had sounded so distinctly Scottish. And while Ian was proud of his Scottish heritage, he wanted his descendants to have a name that would make them feel like Americans. Brierley was the name of the home where Ian had been raised, the residence of the Earl of Brierley for many generations. Ian's brother, Donnan, was now the earl, since the passing of their father a few years earlier. And here on this tiny gravestone, obscurely placed in a cemetery far from Scotland, and far from Illinois where her family resided, no one would pass by and read it and realize all that it represented. But *Ian* knew, and it both warmed and saddened his heart. He knelt beside it, and Ward knelt there with him.

"Show me," Ward said, and Ian guided his hand to the stone where he could feel the name and date carved there, and he took his time to feel it carefully.

"It's very beautiful," Ward said.

"Yes, it is," Ian said, brushing away some dirt and dead leaves from around it.

"Do you remember the story Joseph told us about his brother Alvin?"

"I do," Ian said. "What are you referring to specifically?"

"That he knew when his father died that Alvin was there to greet him . . . that they were together. It will surely be that way, Ian. We know it will. You will surely have your little Joy again."

"Yes, I believe that's true," Ian said. "If I didn't believe it, the pain would be unbearable." He chuckled with no humor. "Even in believing that I'll see her again, it's often felt unbearable. I cannot comprehend how it might feel to believe that death is the end."

"There are many people in the world who *do* believe death is the end," Ward said and put a hand on Ian's shoulder. "That's why we're on our way to England, my friend."

"Yes," Ian said and chuckled again, a bit more lightly. "We might actually be able to convince one or two of them that death is *not* the end."

"We just might," Ward said.

They both sat on the ground and stayed there for a long while, even though the sun had risen higher, and it had begun to get uncomfortably warm. Ian felt reluctant to leave, but thoughts of writing about it in a letter to Wren helped motivate him to get back to their hotel room and get busy doing so. They weren't back five minutes before Ian sat down and began to write of the morning's experience. He wrote about it in the journal he'd brought with him, and he wrote about it again in a letter for Wren. While she would never know where to send letters to him, he could send letters to her, and he delighted in imagining her reading them. He'd already posted two letters along the way, but this one was longer, filling in some details he'd omitted previously due to being in more of a hurry, and he wrote a detailed account of the flowers he'd purchased and his feelings in visiting the grave of their daughter. He imagined Wren crying when she read the letter, but he hoped her tears would have as much joy in them as sorrow—and he told her so. He felt good about recording the events of his adventure in the book as well as in letters he would mail, just in case any of his letters might not make it to her. At least then the experience would be preserved, and perhaps someday it might have some meaning to his children and grandchildren—or perhaps simply in his own reminiscing when he became older.

Ian and Ward left to get some lunch in a café nearby, then returned to the hotel room, where Ian finished his letter and his journal writing. He then took dictation from Ward so that he too could send a letter to his wife, and also record his experiences in a journal. They'd joked about how much time Ian would spend writing during the course of this journey, since he was doing so on Ward's behalf as well as his own. But Ian was fine with that, and they both felt it was important to have their experiences preserved in writing.

The following morning they mailed their letters right after breakfast, then they spent the day getting some things that would make their journey more comfortable and hopefully less tedious.

That evening, once they'd eaten some supper, they called on friends they'd had in the city. Shona had come from Scotland with Ian and Wren, initially for the purpose of helping care for Bethia since she had some sensitive needs. Following Bethia's death, they had met Ronald and Shirley aboard the ship. Shirley had graciously served as a wet-nurse for little Gillian, and Shona had become very attached to Shirley and her children—so much so that she'd decided to stay with them in New York City when Ian and Wren went west to Illinois. Ian and Ward were fortunate enough now to find Ronald, Shirley, and Shona all at home—and all thrilled to see them. The house was crowded and noisy with the number of children in the large family, but they still had a good visit as long as a certain topic was avoided. There were mixed reactions when Ian explained that they had joined the Mormon Church, but the mixture ranged from negative to indifferent, so neither Ian nor Ward said any more about that. The only explanation they gave regarding the reasons for their journey to England was an assignment related to their church, but they also explained that they planned to visit family while they were there.

Ian was pleased to know that Shona was doing well, and that she'd met a young man who intended to marry her in the fall. Shona had always wanted a family of her own, and Ian knew that Wren would be pleased to hear this news. He encouraged Shona to write a letter to Wren, and she promised to do so. They had exchanged a couple of letters soon after they'd settled in Nauvoo, and Wren had written to tell Shona where they were, but they'd not had any contact since then.

That night Ian felt satisfied that he'd done everything in this city that he needed to do, and he was glad to know they would be sailing the following evening. He enjoyed a pleasant night's sleep, knowing this bed was far more comfortable than what would likely be provided for him on the ship. The next morning, since they had some time on their hands, Ian asked Ward if he would mind accompanying him one more time to the grave of little Joy. They did so and then wandered the city a bit before going aboard the ship to get settled in before they sailed with the tide. The cabins were tiny, with narrow beds and barely enough room to move, but they *were* private and Ian was grateful for that. Ward's cabin was directly next to Ian's, and he could knock on the wall if he needed help with anything during the rare times they wouldn't be together, mostly when they were sleeping.

Settling into the inevitable weeks at sea, Ian began to miss his family even more. He tried all the methods he'd used up to this point to focus on the purpose of his journey and imagine the joy of his return. He prayed and struggled to put his faith in God to comfort his sorrow. But it seemed there was simply a certain amount of sorrow that insisted on being felt and acknowledged. Ian was especially grateful for the privacy of his cabin when he often couldn't hold back tears while he was trying to go to sleep. He started speaking aloud to Wren, imagining that somehow his spirit might connect with hers across the miles and she would hear the words of his heart. He wondered how many miles exactly that had become, and he wondered how long it would be until he could see her and hold her in his arms again.

* * * * *

Wren hurried home as quickly as her feet would take her. On each arm she had baskets of wares that she'd purchased in town, but it was the letters she held tightly in her hand that made her heart quicken with excitement. She'd been tempted to sit down right there on the street in front of the post office and read her letter, but she'd restrained herself, wanting to read it in the comfort of her own home, where she could cry her eyes out if necessary and not become a spectacle. She also wanted Patricia to have her own letter and would have felt badly if she'd indulged in the pleasure of receiving a letter from her husband even minutes before Patricia had that same pleasure.

"Patricia!" she called, coming through the back door into the kitchen, where Patricia was stirring something at the stove and the children were playing nearby. Little Anya was in her cradle, contentedly looking around, and Wren knew that any minute now her contentment would cease and she would demand to be fed. Patricia turned to look at Wren just as she set the baskets down on the table. "Letters!" she said, holding them up. "I have letters!"

"Oh!" Patricia gasped and wiped her hands on her apron before she reached out to take hers as if it had been spun from gold. They'd received letters twice before, and always there was one for each of them at the same time. They were always both written in the same hand, since Ian wrote the letters Ward dictated to him. Patricia quickly noticed evidence on the envelope that Wren had noticed when she'd picked them up at the post office. "They're from New York City."

"Which means they've probably sailed by now," Wren said.

"Which means it will be a good, long while before we get another letter," Patricia added, and the women embraced each other and wept a little, each clutching the unopened letters in their hands.

In almost perfect unison, they sat down near the table, took a deep breath, and carefully broke the seal on their letters. They always read them first in silence, and then aloud to each other, sharing every detail. Since Ian was helping Ward write his letters, they had agreed before the men had departed that they wouldn't ever put anything *too* personal in them.

As Wren looked at the date on the letter and then glanced at the calendar on the wall, her suspicions were verified. Ian and Ward would have been at sea many days by now. But every day of his absence was a day closer to his return. The statement had become somewhat of a motto that she recited to herself frequently. She took her time reading the letter, savoring every word. Ian described in detail his visit to their little daughter's grave, and he offered a full description of every flower in the bouquet he'd left there. Wren couldn't keep from weeping to imagine such a moment. She wished that she had been there to share it with him. But then if she started making wishes, she would wish that little Joy had lived. And she would wish that Ian was here with her instead of sailing across the Atlantic, getting farther and farther away from her by the minute.

Wren was also pleased to hear that Ian had visited with their friends in New York City. But again, she would have preferred to be with him. She knew, however, that they never would have made such an arduous journey simply to chat with friends and visit their daughter's grave. Ian never would have returned to New York City if not for his fulfilling this call. In her heart she knew it was right. And she knew that heeding the commandments of God in all things was important above all else. She would not risk losing the blessings of eternity by holding back any evidence of her commitment or devotion to God here and now. But knowing something was right certainly didn't make it easy. And so far, through the weeks that Ian had been gone, every waking moment was difficult.

Wren found great comfort, however, in reading from the scriptures. They were full of stories of hardship and sacrifice, and the blessings that came from doing the right thing—even when it was difficult. Wren also found strength—and great humility— in associating with the Saints here in Nauvoo. There was hardly a resident in this fair city who hadn't endured some form of unspeakable suffering for the sake of their beliefs. Wren didn't have to look far to find people who had suffered far more than she had, and she even became acquainted with women who had either previously been left alone while their husbands had served missions, or were currently in that situation. Wren gleaned comfort and wisdom from associating with other women who shared her convictions, and she also found opportunities to reach outside herself and give aid to those who were much worse off. The Relief Society organization for the women of the Church was starting to blossom in a way that gave structure and purpose to the innate desire these women had to serve and lift one another. Wren and Patricia had enjoyed becoming a part of such a great cause. Wren still didn't feel entirely recovered from her most recent childbirth experience, but she still sought out opportunities to serve that were within her limitations, and she looked forward to feeling better so that she could do more. Doing for others was a good way to keep her mind off her own loneliness and misery in Ian's absence.

On that particular day, with a new letter in her hands, Wren felt a little less miserable but no less lonely. Interspersed with caring for the children and performing the usual daily tasks around the house, Wren and Patricia both spent the day rereading their letters, silently and aloud to each other, analyzing and speculating together over their husbands' experiences and how things might be going for them now. Patricia had been born in America and had never seen the ocean, nor had she sailed on a ship. Wren related details of her own experience in crossing the Atlantic to come to this land, and together they tried to imagine how it might be for Ian and Ward. Even though they knew it would be many weeks before the men arrived in England, and many more weeks after that before letters could make it back across the ocean and many miles of land, they still anticipated the day when more letters would arrive. In the meantime, they were determined to keep busy, continue praying for their beloved husbands, and live each day with the hope of being reunited.

* * * * *

It didn't take Ian long to recall how much he disliked sea travel. Of course, memories of Bethia's tragic death at sea didn't help. He could hardly stand on the deck of the ship without recalling how his sister-in-law had flung her over the side, certain that doing so would bring her the peace of mind she'd been desperately seeking. Bethia had suffered with an ailment of the mind that had been a continual challenge for herself as well as those who loved her and were committed to caring for her. Perhaps Bethia's jumping into the ocean and subsequently drowning *had* brought her to a place of peace. But Ian still hated the memories. He'd gone in after her and had miraculously been able to find her, but it had been too late.

Ian struggled hourly to keep his mind from bad memories and difficult thoughts, but the battle never proved to be easy. He and Ward spent time every day mingling with the other passengers, simply seeking to be kind and helpful rather than trying to approach anyone too quickly or boldly with the message they wanted to share. Over time, they found that their reasons for traveling to England came up naturally in conversation as they got to know people better, and some asked questions that motivated further discussion. Some people made it clear they weren't interested, but others were obviously intrigued, and Ward and Ian gave away a few copies of the Book of Mormon, gratified in knowing the books were being read.

When Ian and Ward were not visiting with other passengers, they spent time reading from the scriptures and discussing important principles. They knew that the more educated they became on doctrinal and spiritual matters, the better prepared they would be to answer questions and engage in stimulating conversation that might lead people to an interest in discovering the truth for themselves. With Ward's inability to read, they naturally always studied together, with Ian reading aloud, stopping frequently to talk about what they were reading and what it meant.

Beyond the simple daily routines of eating and taking care of their personal hygiene, the only other activities they engaged in were writing letters to their wives, as well as keeping a record of their experiences in their journals. Ian spent a great deal of time each day with a pen in his hand, and he acquired permanent ink stains on his fingers. Between his own letters and journals, and Ward's as well, it seemed there was always something to be written. But he didn't mind. In fact, he enjoyed it simply because he could imagine Wren and Patricia reading every word he wrote—whether in letters they might receive during this separation, or in the journals they would be able to read after they were all reunited.

They encountered a couple of storms at sea, one mild and the other fairly severe. The tossing of the ship made Ian feel more vulnerable and weak than he'd ever felt in his life. He could only sit with Ward while they prayed, both aloud and silently, that they would be preserved to return home safely to their families. They talked about the stories in the Bible that indicated the Lord's power over the elements, and Ian knew their lives were entirely in God's hands.

An alarming breakout of illness occurred among the passengers in steerage, and again Ian became excruciatingly aware of his human vulnerability. He and Ward both prayed diligently that they would be spared from the illness, especially when daily burials at sea began taking place. All passengers were cautioned by the captain to remain quarantined from other passengers as much as possible, and only fit and healthy crew members were allowed to handle the food preparation. Ward admitted to Ian that the Lord had surely known this would happen, and their having private cabins was certainly protecting their health so that they could remain healthy and fulfill their mission.

Despite storms and illness, they arrived safely in London on a gray, dismal day that left the city so thick with fog that it was difficult to even know that a city existed beyond the sound of their own voices. Ian and Ward left the ship with their minimal possessions and their portmanteau of books, not certain where to go or how to find accommodations. After asking for directions or suggestions a few times from passersby, Ian was surprised to find himself on a street that felt familiar to him.

"I know this place!" he told Ward, who exhaled with relief. For all that Ian felt misplaced and confused, he couldn't imagine how Ward felt to be blind and utterly reliant on a man who was utterly lost. "I wandered this area quite a bit during my prodigal days. On the chance that nothing's changed too much in five or six years . . . I know of a place we might stay."

"Was it five or six?" Ward asked, holding firmly to Ian's shoulder as they moved along.

Ian thought about that for a moment. "Actually *less* than five. Incredible how much life can change in so short a time."

"It *is* incredible," Ward agreed.

"I must admit that I'd wondered about finding places I once knew here in the city, but I was so confused back then that I wasn't sure I could, so I didn't mention it."

"What you really mean," Ward said in a humorous tone, "is that you were so drunk back then that you didn't think you could remember it."

"Thank you for reminding me," Ian said with light sarcasm. "Yes, that's what I mean." He stopped for a moment and looked around, noting the fog was not quite so thick here as it had been when they'd left the ship. "But here we are. I actually know where we are."

"It would seem God is looking out for us," Ward said.

"Yes, it would seem that He is," Ian agreed as they turned down a familiar street, hoping to find that the only place where he'd found a little bit of sanctuary back then would still be here, and that it would still be owned by one of the few people who had been truly kind to him when he'd been so lost and miserable.

Chapter Five
The Note

Ian was not entirely surprised to walk through the door of a pub called The Copper Kettle and be struck by its quaint familiarity. He *was* surprised to immediately see a familiar face behind the bar, and to realize that this woman recognized him the same moment he recognized her. Edith was old enough to be his mother, and large enough to be his mother two times over. He knew her to be a kind and pleasant woman who, simply out of the goodness of her heart, had more than once let him sleep off his liquor in the safety of the pub. She'd encouraged him many times to leave London and go home to his family. When he'd finally taken her advice, he'd not taken the time to come and tell her good-bye, nor to thank her for all she'd done for him. Since the main floor of the pub served food and drinks and the upper floor had rooms for rent, he knew that Edith could help him now. And he was glad to be in a position to properly express his appreciation for her kindness in the past.

Edith gave him a long gaze and set down the towel she'd been using to dry her hands. It was a quiet time of day at the pub, and there was no one else in the room except for a couple of men sitting together and talking quietly on the other side of the room.

"I don't remember yer name, Scottish Boy." It was what she'd always called him. "But I remember yer face. Lor' bless me, ye've come back."

"I have," he said. "And I remember *your* name, dear sweet Edith. I think you kept me alive more than once."

Edith came around the bar, and Ian dropped his bags while she hugged him as if he were a little boy and not more than a head taller

ANITA STANSFIELD

than she. "Lor' bless me!" she said again, looking him up and down. "'Ow many years 'as it been?"

"Four or five . . . thereabouts," Ian said.

"And ye've got a friend with ye," she said. "A fine gentleman like yerself, t' be sure. What might yer name be, young man?"

"I'm Ward," he said, reaching out a hand in a way that drew Edith's attention to the fact that he couldn't see.

"Yes, Ward is blind and not ashamed to admit it. Ward, this is Edith, a fine woman who runs a fair establishment."

"A pleasure, Edith," Ward said, and the woman shook his hand exuberantly as if they were making a business deal that greatly excited her.

"Any friend o' the Scottish boy would be a friend o' mine," Edith said.

"It's our hope that you have a room available," Ian said. "And we've got good money to pay up front."

"Oh, this means ye're staying a bit, then," Edith said with glee. "Ye might liven th' place up a bit. I've got a room indeed, and it's m' finest. I'll give ye m' special rate that I only gives t' special folks."

"No need for that," Ian said. "I'm just glad to have found you and to know we have a place to sleep tonight." He nudged Ward and added, "And we can be sure to get no finer-tasting food in London than right here." To Edith he asked, "Do you still have Raoul working in the kitchen?"

"I do," Edith said. "Yes, I do." She gave Ward a manly kind of slap on the shoulder and said, "'E's got a foul temperament, that Raoul, but 'e's a fine cook t' be sure. 'Is shepherd's pie and lamb stew bring folks 'ere from all o'er the city."

"Then it seems we've certainly found the right place," Ward said.

Edith got a key from a drawer and led the men up the stairs and to the third door on the left. Ian was pleased to see a tiny parlor—the emphasis on *tiny* since it barely had room for the two chairs and little table that were situated near a little fireplace. But two doors opened off the parlor into two separate bedrooms. These rooms were also very small, but certainly adequate, and Ian felt as if God had reserved the place for them and sent angels to lead them here. His being so far from home didn't feel quite so ominous in that moment. He had evidence that God was watching out for them, and had guided them to familiar surroundings in which to move forward in their work here.

Ian expressed his approval of the room to Edith, which delighted her. Then she asked, "'Ow long might th' two o' ye be stayin'?"

"We're not sure exactly," Ian said, "but it will probably be a while . . . if that's all right with you." He finished with a wink and a smile toward their hostess. Since he and Ward had discussed their plans and prayed about them, they both felt confident the Lord wanted them to remain in London for a significant amount of time. It was a big city with many struggling souls, and there was surely much work to do here and many opportunities for service.

Edith just laughed and left them to settle in, declaring she'd have water sent up for washing and that Raoul was working on a chicken pot pie for the lunch crowd and she'd be sure to save them some.

Once Ian was alone with Ward, he explained the appearance of the room while guiding him through a typical exploration of the doors, the windows, and the furnishings, so that he could get his bearings. Ian helped Ward settle into the bedroom that would be his, and set out his belongings in a way that allowed Ward to easily find what he needed. Ian then settled into his own little bedroom before he announced to his friend with some delight, "Now that we're settled here for a fair amount of time, we can write letters to our wives, and perhaps even get some in return."

"What a wonderful thought!" Ward said.

"And since Edith is someone I know and trust, even if their letters miss us, I know I can get her to send them on to Brierley, or return them to Illinois."

"Then write letters we must!" Ward said, and they sat down together at the little table while Ian assessed that they would likely have to go out that afternoon and purchase more ink and paper. But since he knew this part of the city, even with fog heavy in the streets, he knew where to go and how to go about it. For the first time since he'd left home, he actually felt like he could handle this endeavor. Grateful as he felt, he suggested to Ward that before they started their letters, they should kneel and pray together. They thanked God for their safe journey, and for being preserved from any harm or illness. They thanked Him for leading them to this place, for helping meet their needs, and, as always, they prayed that their home would be protected and their families comforted during this time apart. When they had spoken a hearty amen, they sat again at the table, and Ward began to dictate his thoughts to his wife while Ian took pleasure in acting as his scribe.

* * * * *

Wren loved Sundays; it was undoubtedly her favorite day of the week, even though getting herself and her babies dressed for the Sabbath meeting and getting there on time could be exhausting. But she loved gathering with the Saints. She loved singing the hymns, especially those that had been written expressly for the Latter-day Saints, singing praises for the glory of the restoration of the gospel in this dispensation. While singing such glorious hymns, Wren's mind would often wander to the years she'd spent attending church meetings in Scotland, glad to be there but always feeling a vague sense of uneasiness, as if something were missing or not quite right. And she'd felt somehow odd, or perhaps even wicked or dissident for simply having such feelings. Once Wren had read the Book of Mormon and had come to know for herself that it was true, she'd had even more trouble going to church, knowing that the fulness of the gospel was elsewhere and out of her reach. And then the local minister had treated the situation of Bethia's pregnancy with such outward disdain, behaving in a blatantly *un*-Christian manner. They had left Scotland soon after that, knowing that Bethia—with her mental illness *and* her unexplainable pregnancy—could never remain in that community and feel safe or accepted. Of course, no one had known that Bethia's husband had actually been alive—for reasons that were still difficult to understand—and therefore her pregnancy *was* legitimate. But it had all been far too complicated to ever explain to anyone without causing a tremendous stir in the community that never would have settled. Still, Wren believed that any man whose position in a community was to represent God would have been—and should have been—compassionate toward Bethia and her situation, no matter *what* the explanation might have been. After that, Wren had not attended church at all. In New York City, Ian and Ward had attended some different church meetings, but she'd had no desire to attend a meeting where the truth was not being taught.

There had been many blessings that had come into Wren's life after finally arriving in Nauvoo and being able to live among the

Saints. But most precious to Wren was simply being able to attend a church meeting on the Sabbath and know that the truth was being taught, and that she was worshiping among people who shared her beliefs and would behave—for the most part—in a Christian manner. No one was perfect, and she knew well enough that these people had faults and weaknesses among them the same as any other people. But most of these people were here because they had deep convictions in regard to the gospel of Jesus Christ, and many of them had made significant sacrifices in order to be among the Saints and worship freely. So Wren sang the hymns with all the energy of her soul, lifting her face heavenward as she did, adding a prayer in her heart as she sang that God would know of the depth of her praises to Him, and her gratitude for being in this place at this time.

Throughout the meeting Wren couldn't help thinking of Ian. She always did. The question continually hovered in her mind, *What would this moment be like if Ian were beside me?* And that question was always followed by, *I wonder what Ian is doing right now. Is he safe and well? Does he miss me as much as I miss him?* On that last count she had no doubt, whatsoever. As for the other, she could only pray for him and try to send her love across the miles with the hope that some miraculous means might make it possible for him to feel it, wherever he was, and whatever he might be doing.

Near the end of the meeting, a thought occurred to Wren, seemingly out of nowhere. Her mind went to Ian's own miraculous experience of having the Book of Mormon come into his hands through missionaries who had made sacrifices to leave their homes and families and share the gospel on the other side of the Atlantic— just as Ian was doing now. Almost simultaneously, she thought of Ian meeting Brother Tyler, and of the things he'd said about his missionary companion, who had passed away soon after his return. Wren felt a little out of breath with the way so many thoughts had come into her mind seemingly all at once and with a certain amount of force, as if they were determined to be heard and acknowledged. The crowning thought, the seeming purpose of the experience, was recalling that Ian had found a note inside the Book of Mormon he'd purchased from a stranger that day in London. And in that moment, Wren knew she needed to return that note to its rightful owner.

When Wren and Patricia returned home together, it always took a while to get the children settled, then they worked together to put on a meal since everyone was hungry. Patricia was an excellent cook, and she was skilled at leaving the oven just so with something or other roasting there, or a pot on the stove that held a simmering delight so that they could eat soon after their return. Wren helped her finish up the meal preparations, then they sat together to eat, praying over their food with an emphasis—as always—on asking God to watch over and protect their husbands, and to guide them to those who needed the message they had to share.

While they ate and worked together to keep the children happy and under control, Wren told Patricia about the note that Ian had found tucked inside the copy of the Book of Mormon that he had purchased years ago from a missionary in London. Patricia was excited over the apparent assignment Wren had been given, and considered it somewhat of an adventure. She offered to watch the children that very afternoon so that Wren could call on Brother and Sister Tyler and inquire over the whereabouts of the widow of Brother Tyler's former missionary companion. Wren seemed to recall that his name was Brother Givan, and that his widow had remarried. Nauvoo had many residents, but she hoped that Brother Tyler would still know the whereabouts of Brother Givan's family.

Wren went to her bedroom and dug out that original copy of the Book of Mormon, the one that she and Ian had both read in order to gain their testimonies. They had then loaned it to Ward and his mother so that she could read the book to him, and they too had come to their own convictions through their reading. In time they had acquired more copies from which to read and study, and this one, in its worn condition, had been put into a drawer, cherished as one of their most prized possessions due to all it represented in their lives. Wren had imagined passing it down to her children and grandchildren as something of an heirloom. Wren opened that treasured copy now, allowing it to fall open to the place where a note had been tucked between two pages. She picked up the handwritten note to read: *"How beautiful upon the mountains are the feet of those who shall hereafter publish peace." Never forget that you will be in my every prayer while you travel so far to serve the Lord, and to publish His peace. May your feet be guided in your journey, and may you come home safely to my arms when your work is done. Yours eternally, Beatrice.*

It took Wren a few minutes just to read the whole thing since she was so overcome by tears that she did more sobbing and wiping her eyes than she did reading. Once she was able to read it through, she read it over and over. She considered the story behind the note. A husband and wife separated for the sake of spreading the gospel, a sacrifice that had ultimately brought the gospel to Ian, and subsequently to her. And sweet Beatrice Givan, waiting and wondering—just as Wren was now—through the long months of her husband's absence. And then to have him return home ill and never recover. The very idea broke Wren's heart. She couldn't imagine how she might face such a sacrifice herself. Being without Ian, temporarily, felt unbearable every day. But she was holding on to the hope that he would return healthy and strong and they would be able to move forward together through this life. The thought of having to give up her husband completely—at least for the duration of this life—would surely break her spirit completely. She couldn't even imagine! And she couldn't imagine how she could face Beatrice Givan and return this note to her without presenting herself as a blubbering fool, utterly falling apart and likely becoming unable to speak at all. Of course, she didn't have to do it today. She simply had to visit Brother Tyler and gather some information about Beatrice Givan. She could call on Beatrice—if doing so was ever possible—on another day when she was more composed.

Wren looked at the book in her hands, noting that some passages had been highlighted—apparently by Beatrice, and obviously referring to the phrase of scripture she had quoted in the note. Ian had told Wren that he wondered if this particular copy being sold to him had been a mistake, because it had obviously belonged to one of the men he'd met in London. At the time, he'd not had any reason to believe he could ever return it to its rightful owner. But now it *was* possible. It had to be! Surely Wren would not have received such strong revelation if it were *not* possible. Then it occurred to her that perhaps she wasn't just supposed to return the note to Beatrice, but perhaps she needed to return the book to her as well. The thought of giving up this particular copy provoked a pang in her heart. But she had to consider all that Beatrice had given up, and returning the book to her felt like a petty contribution to this woman's life. Determined to follow through on her assignment in whatever way the Lord would have her do it, Wren dried her tears and got herself ready to go and visit Brother and Sister Tyler.

Knowing the children were in good hands, Wren harnessed the trap and drove it to where she knew Brother and Sister Tyler lived. She felt nervous as she approached the home and secured the horse, but she said a silent prayer and reminded herself that she was acting on inspiration; surely she would be blessed and guided.

Sister Tyler answered the door and immediately showed a smile of recognition. "Sister Brierley!" she said as if they were long-lost relations. "A delightful surprise, indeed. Come in. Come in."

"Thank ye," Wren said and stepped inside, hearing the door close behind her. She realized she couldn't remember this woman's first name, then wondered if she'd ever been told.

"Willis," Sister Tyler called toward the other room. "Come and see who's here to visit!"

"I don't need t' take too much of yer time," Wren said. "I simply wondered if—"

"Well, hello there, Sister Brierley," Willis Tyler said with enthusiasm equal to his wife's. "This *is* a lovely distraction, now isn't it, Arla."

Arla, Wren noted. Her name was Arla.

"Indeed it is," Arla said. "Please sit down."

"Thank you," Wren said, and they all took a seat in the parlor.

"Tell us, then," Willis Tyler said, "how you and your household are coming along with the men gone abroad."

Wren looked down and forced back any temptation to get emotional. She knew these people had perfect empathy for her situation, but she had no desire to complain or get emotional, and she focused on the purpose of her visit.

"We're doing well," she said. "Of course we miss Ian and Ward very much, but we've been very blessed."

"I'm glad to hear it," Willis said.

"So glad to hear it," his wife echoed.

"And what can we do for you today?" Willis asked. "If we can help in any way, we'd be glad to know of it."

"Yer kindness is appreciated more than ye know," Wren said. "Our needs are being met very well; thank ye for asking. It's a great blessing t' know there are good people such as yerselves that we can call on if needs arise."

"You certainly *can* call on us," Arla said with conviction. "It would be an honor and a pleasure to do anything we could to help you through."

"I concur with my wife completely," Willis added.

"Ye're very kind," Wren said, finding it more difficult to maintain her composure, mostly because she knew their offer was sincere and from the heart, and she knew there were many others here in Nauvoo who were equally willing and eager to help if needs arose. She found great comfort each and every day in knowing that in spite of Ian's absence, she would never go without help and care should problems arise.

"I've come t'day hoping that ye can give me some information. I know ye told us about the man who went t' England with ye . . . Brother Givan."

"That's right," Willis said.

"And did ye say that his widow had married again?"

"That's right," he said again.

"I wonder if ye know where I could find her. I've felt impressed that I need t' share something with her." A thought occurred to Wren that took her off guard. What if she had not connected the events together correctly in her mind? Perhaps the Beatrice who had written that note was *not* the widow of Brother Givan. She realized that she hadn't even recalled the first name of Brother Tyler's wife until a minute ago. How would she be feeling right now if she'd found out that *her* name was Beatrice? It wasn't, which made her think she was more likely on the right path than not, but she had to ask. "Is Sister's Givan's name Beatrice, by chance?"

"It is," Arla said. "Beatrice and I were very close while our husbands were away, as you can well imagine." Wren nodded. "We didn't live under the same roof as you and Sister Mickel do, but we saw each other often and helped each other through. When our husbands returned and Brother Givan was in such a sorry state, I . . ." Arla sniffled and dabbed at her eyes with her fingertips. "I almost felt guilty for having my husband back healthy and strong, when hers was so ill. And then when he died . . ." Her words faded, and she fought back more tears.

"It was a dreadful time," Willis said, his eyes taking on a distant look, and Wren wondered how it might have been for him to have served a mission with this man and then to lose him like that. They surely must have been very close and shared a deep bond.

Wren felt bad about the melancholy mood she had provoked. "I didn't mean t' stir up unpleasant memories for ye," she said. "I only wonder if ye could help me find Beatrice. Ye see, the copy of the Book of Mormon that my Ian purchased from ye in England had a note tucked inside that obviously belonged to Brother Givan. It's signed with the name *Beatrice*. Of course, before we came here, we would have had no way of knowing the connection. But it just occurred t' me this morning that this woman should have that note, and I feel that I need t' give it t' her."

Wren noted then that Willis's expression had altered during her explanation. He was clearly recalling something with growing enlightenment. "I remember," he said, "how we had no copies of the book left except our own, and we had both decided we would gladly give them up if we were compelled to do so. After your husband purchased that copy, Brother Givan mentioned that he should have first removed the note from his wife." Willis's sadness over Brother Givan's death became completely replaced by an apparent joy that glowed in his expression. "What a remarkable thing, that you would now have that note in your possession. I do remember his mentioning it more than once . . . quite clearly. How very remarkable!"

"Ye can help me find her, then?"

"Of course we can!" Willis said.

"I do believe we should *all* pay Beatrice a visit right this very moment," Arla declared, and Wren's heart responded with a nervous excitement. "Do you have the note in your possession?"

"I do," Wren said, thinking that she wouldn't have brought it with her if she hadn't believed that delivering it today might not be a possibility. Still, she couldn't help feeling some trepidation. How did one go about facing a stranger with the intent to share something so personal and dear?

Wren waited only a minute while Arla put on a bonnet and Willis grabbed his hat. Since Wren's trap was there and harnessed, the three of them squeezed into it, and Willis graciously took the reins. Wren thought how she missed having a man with her to do such a simple thing as taking the reins, then it broadened into a deeply metaphorical thought. She missed having Ian there to take the reins in many aspects of life. But then, here she was, sitting next to Arla, who had once been without her husband for more than two years. The very nearness of these people who had endured and survived this experience gave Wren an abstract kind of comfort that warmed her heart.

As Willis drove, he explained that Beatrice had married a farmer, and they lived on a farm in one of the Mormon settlements that lay on the outskirts of the city of Nauvoo. It wasn't the first time that Wren had been to one of these settlements. She knew the Saints were numerous, and the city and surrounding areas were dominated by people who shared her faith. She was glad now to have Willis and Arla actually going with her, as opposed to simply trying to find Beatrice's home on her own according to someone's directions. They chatted pleasantly as they went along, and Wren felt an increasing gratitude that Ian had encountered Willis Tyler before he'd left, so that she could have their company and their assistance now. Surely God's hand was in these matters more than she could ever comprehend.

Willis and Arla began reminiscing about the time when Willis had been away doing missionary work. They each spoke of the situation from their perspective in a way that made Wren feel both sad and deeply validated in her own emotions. She heard Willis talking about the miracles that he'd witnessed during his time in England, and of the people who had found the gospel through his efforts. She heard him express his joy in knowing he'd been able to make that contribution to building the kingdom, and Arla expressed a comparable joy in having contributed simply by supporting him and caring for everything at home in his absence. Wren felt the glimmer of a new perspective. Would a day come in her life when the joy of what was being accomplished would outweigh the current heartache she and Ian were both enduring for the sake of this work?

She recalled words from a message given at church earlier that day. Its principle was clear. Sacrifice brings blessings. Surely that would be as true for her and Ian, and for Ward and Patricia, as it had been for Willis and Arla. But then Wren thought of Beatrice Givan—now married to someone else—and she couldn't imagine that *her* sacrifice could have ever given her enough joy that she would ever believe it was worth it.

They finally arrived at a lovely farmhouse surrounded by white-washed fences, with horses lazily grazing like moving, breathing orna-mentation that added to the beauty of the home. Willis secured the horse and helped the ladies step down from the trap. Wren still felt nervous, but less so when she realized that Willis and Arla knew this woman and could handle introductions and offer some explanation for their visit. She couldn't imagine just knocking on the woman's door and trying to explain her visit and intentions when they'd never seen each other before.

A boy in his teens answered the door, and Willis introduced himself as if he knew who the boy was but didn't expect the boy to know *him.* When the boy went to get Beatrice, Willis explained quietly to Wren that he was the son of the man that Beatrice had married, and so Willis and Arla had never known him personally beyond a passing introduction a couple of years earlier.

Wren got a good look at Beatrice as she came up the hall toward the open door where they were standing. She was average in height, slightly plump, with graying brown hair and a pleasant countenance.

"Willis! Arla!" she said with warm enthusiasm and embraced them both, holding to Arla for a long moment, as if they were silently exchanging memories of the trials they'd endured together.

"It's so good to see you, Beatrice," Arla said as she eased back from their embrace but put her hands on Beatrice's shoulders.

"It is at that!" Beatrice said, then turned her eyes questioningly toward Wren. Arla put an arm around Wren's shoulders, as if to draw her into their circle of friendship. "This is Wren Brierley."

"Sister Brierley," Beatrice said and took her hand in a friendly manner. "A pleasure to meet you."

"The pleasure's mine," Wren said and was glad when Arla continued, which saved Wren from having to explain why she was there.

"If we could sit for a few minutes, Sister Brierley's story—and the reason for our visit—is something I believe you'll appreciate."

"Oh, of course. Of course," Beatrice said and guided them into a spacious but cluttered parlor. In spite of the excessive amount of items in the room, which implied that a great deal of family activity took place here, there was a warm, comfortable feeling that encompassed Wren as she took a seat next to Arla on a sofa. Willis took a chair, and Beatrice sat on a smaller sofa across from the two other women.

Wren wasn't sure how this might go from here, but Beatrice made it easy when she said, "So, tell me about yourself, Sister Brierley."

"Please call me Wren," she said.

Beatrice nodded and smiled. "You're from Scotland? Is that the accent I hear?"

"That's right," Wren said. "We arrived in Nauvoo just a couple of years ago. The thing is . . . I must tell ye . . . that my husband Ian was in London at a time when he was very lost and troubled, and it was Brother Tyler here—and yer own husband—that put the Book of Mormon int' his hands and sent him home, and eventually brought us here."

Beatrice put a hand to her heart, as if just hearing that much had created a physical warmth there that overflowed into her countenance and gave her a mild glow, accentuated by the subtle glisten of moisture in her eyes.

"My husband—Ian—crossed paths with Brother Tyler on the street early in the summer, and recognized him from that encounter. He then shared yer story with us, and . . . I want t' say how much . . ." Wren's voice cracked, and she wasn't sure how to go on without becoming utterly overcome with tears. Then a quiet voice in her mind whispered the idea to her that perhaps another woman's tears might give Beatrice some kind of additional comfort or understanding. As if given permission to cry, Wren let her own tears flow with her words. "I want ye t' know how grateful I am . . . we are . . . for yer sacrifice . . . and yer husband's sacrifice . . . in making it possible for us t' have the gospel in our lives. I know that what ye've suffered is something I can't understand. I can only offer my condolences for yer loss—even though it's been some years now—and tell ye how grateful I am."

When tears trickled down Beatrice's face, Wren felt a little less self-conscious about her own tears. She reached into the satchel she'd brought with her to retrieve a handkerchief at the same moment that Beatrice pulled her own handkerchief from her apron pocket. A quick glance toward Willis and Arla showed that Willis's countenance was filled with compassion and that Arla was a little teary herself.

"That means more to me than I could say," Beatrice muttered and wiped the tears from her cheeks. "Since Willis and Arla have been such good friends to me, I feel that I can be candid and say that . . . losing my dear Harold was surely the most difficult thing that's ever happened to me." Her tears increased while she looked so intently at Wren that their spirits seemed to connect in some silent, inexplicable way. As a result, Wren shed even more tears. As her compassion for Beatrice deepened, she couldn't help wondering how she would feel to be in this woman's position, and she prayed even in that moment it would never come to that. "And to be truthful," Beatrice went on, "it's the knowledge of the love we share that gets me through the days."

Wren found the comment interesting in light of the fact that Beatrice was now remarried. Beatrice had no qualms about explaining, as if it were a fact so taken for granted in her life that it was easy to discuss—even with a relative stranger. "Reginald, my good husband at present, is a fine man and he cares well for me and my son. I care very much for him, and his children have become like my own. I love them dearly. We were in a position to help each other since he'd also lost a spouse to death. But we both know that our marriage is one of practicality. We share many common bonds, but our hearts are with the ones we've lost. We are grateful to know that we can be with those loved ones again. I'm certain, as he is, that God will work all things out once we get to the other side. Surely God would not give us such feelings without purpose to them. If we are meant to be happy in heaven—and we surely are—then we must certainly be with those we love most."

Wren listened and nodded, attempting to comprehend a deeper layer of this woman's sacrifice. If her husband had not answered the Prophet's call to serve a mission, he would not have become ill and passed away. And now Beatrice and her eternal soulmate were separated by the veil between life and death for the remainder of Beatrice's mortal life. Of course, Beatrice was being cared for, and she was surely a blessing to her current husband and his children. But Wren wondered what it would be like to be married to someone with whom there was an absence of the deep, abiding love that she and Ian felt for each other. She wondered how many people in the world were in such marriages—based on practicality and mutual respect. Of course, she knew there were likely many marriages based on much worse than that. But considering Beatrice's situation made her appreciate all she *did* share with Ian. She could only pray that he would come home safe and healthy and she would not be denied his presence in her life through the remainder of her mortal existence.

"I'm certain you're right," Arla said, softening the intensity of a moment that was so highly emotional for both Beatrice and Wren.

Silence followed while the women attempted to gain their composure, then Willis said, "Wren here has something for you. It's something that I recall Harold talking to me about, but I never dreamed something like this would happen." Wren was grateful for Willis's explanation, especially when it became evident that it was taking the burden from her shoulders of having to tell the story while she was in a such a highly emotional state. "You see," Willis went on, "we had both decided that we needed to be willing to give up our own copies of the Book of Mormon when we ran out. Seems that Harold's personal copy is the one that ended up in Ian Brierley's hands, and . . ."

Beatrice gasped as she realized the implication of what Willis was saying. She looked intensely at him, then at Wren. "He told me . . . before he died . . . that his copy of the book had been sold to someone in London. He . . . apologized. I told him it didn't matter, but . . ." She didn't seem to know how to finish.

Wren reached into her satchel and brought out the worn copy of the book. She let it fall open to the page where the note had been kept all these years. Beatrice gasped again, then put a hand over her mouth as if she might otherwise burst into audible sobbing. Wren kept the book open to that page but lifted the note with her fingers and held it out to Beatrice. "We never believed we would find the owner of this note. Ian never even knew the names of the missionaries he'd encountered in London."

Willis added with the hint of a crack in his voice, "Harold told me he wished he'd gotten the note from you out of the book before it was put into someone else's hands. He told me that note had kept him going during the hard times. It seems a miracle to me that it's coming back to you now."

"A miracle indeed," Arla said, dabbing at her eyes.

"Oh," Beatrice said, finally able to remove her hand from her mouth. She took the note with trembling fingers and read the words she'd written to her husband so many years ago. "Oh!" she said again and put a hand to her heart. "It's as if his spirit is with us here now, letting me know that it's all going to be all right."

"That's a lovely thought," Arla said, becoming more emotional. "I've no doubt it's true."

"Oh, thank you, Wren!" Beatrice said, holding the note to her heart. "Thank you so much! It means so very much to me to get this back . . . and to know that my Harold being where he was made such a difference in *your* life."

Wren nodded. "I know the Spirit guided me here today . . . and thanks t' Willis and Arla, I was able t' find ye." She held the Book of Mormon, still open, toward Beatrice. "Ye should have this back." Even as she said it Wren almost felt her hands shaking at the thought of letting it go, but she knew it was the right thing to do.

"Oh, no!" Beatrice said. "The note is enough. I'm certain that particular copy of the book must have great meaning for you. You must keep it."

"But . . . it was his, and . . . if I were in yer place, I would surely want t' have—"

"Truly, Wren," she said with a warmth in her eyes that implied they had been friends for years, "I mean it when I say that the note is enough, and I want you to keep the book."

Wren drew the book to her chest, closing it as she did. Unable to explain what this meant, but wanting to be gracious, she simply said, "Thank ye, Beatrice. This copy of the book *is* very precious t' me, but . . . I want ye t' know that with all that ye've sacrificed, I just wanted ye t' have the . . ." Wren was unable to finish.

Beatrice nodded with an understanding smile. "The note is enough," she repeated. "I will treasure it always, and the way that you brought it back to me." She stood and opened her arms, inviting Wren to do the same. They embraced and held to each other the same way that Beatrice and Arla had done when they'd first arrived, as if they were silently sharing a bond, with a mutual understanding of each other that required no words of expression.

Chapter Six
Hour by Hour

Wren returned home in time to feed her baby before Anya became too unhappy following a lengthy nap. While she did so, Patricia sat nearby, and Wren shared with her the remarkable experience that had occurred. They both marveled anew at the guidance of the Holy Spirit in their lives, and the evidence of the hand of God in the tender details of their experiences. They talked openly about their fears in regard to their husbands remaining safe and healthy, but committed themselves anew—to God and to each other—to strive to have faith and remain positive, holding to the belief that all would be well and they would all be reunited when this mission was completed.

* * * * *

On a beautiful autumn day, Wren and Patricia decided at breakfast to go out together with all of the children and walk into town, instead of having one of them stay at home to watch the children while the other went to buy whatever items they needed. They were anxious to see if there was any mail for them at the post office. Since neither of them had received any mail from anyone for any reason for many, many weeks, stopping at the post office seemed somewhat ridiculous on most days. But how could they not stop and at least see? They never knew when something might finally arrive from their husbands.

Wren and Patricia took their shopping at a slow pace, amazed that the children were actually being quite well behaved and seemed to be enjoying the outing. They had lunch at a little café, then stopped at the post office last of all before heading home to put the children down for their afternoon naps. To their astonishment and delight, a thick letter was waiting for each of them, and the postmaster wore an excessively big smile when he handed them over, as if he'd been anticipating the moment with delight. After having to tell one or the other of them so many times that there was no mail of any kind, he seemed to find some personal pleasure in being able to finally deliver the best surprise that Wren or Patricia could receive. And he declared that it was especially pleasant to see them both together for such a moment.

The two women stood outside the post office for a long moment, each just staring at the letters in their hands as if they'd been sprinkled with some kind of fairy dust that might at any moment emit some magical spell that would bring their husbands home to them.

"We must wait t' read them at home," Wren declared.

"Yes, we must," Patricia said, and the women hurried home as fast as it was possible to go with three small children and a baby. They both became almost giddy with laughter before they got home, then it took them a few minutes to make certain the children were settled and content enough for them to be able to sit down and read with as few interruptions as possible. They sat down together at the table in the kitchen, as if it had become a practiced ritual—even though this was only the fourth letter they'd received in more than that many months. It seemed only fair that one of them should not have the opportunity to read her letter before the other; they were in this together. Following a firm gaze engendered by their deep bond of friendship, they each sighed in unison and opened their letters, reading silently with the anticipation of reading them aloud to each other after their initial, private reading. They each reached for their handkerchiefs at about the same moment as the tears inevitably came.

"Oh!" Wren said, unable to contain herself and hold back the information, even though she felt certain the *same* information would be in Patricia's letter eventually. "They're settled in London and will be there long enough that we can write letters that they will likely receive."

"Oh!" Patricia said, a pitch higher than Wren had said it, then they both jumped off their chairs and jumped up and down a bit, much like little girls, before they hugged each other tightly and sat back down to finish reading, their silence a stark contrast to the outburst that had drawn the curious attention of the children for just a moment.

They each read their lengthy letters through silently two times, and then aloud to each other, having to pause occasionally to deal with the children and see to their needs. Beyond eating and taking care of absolute necessities, the entire day was filled with soaking in every word their husbands had written, then they began straightaway to write lengthy letters in return. They knew it could take days to write letters that they would consider adequate to catch up all that Ian and Ward had missed. If they'd anticipated being able to send letters, they might have been more prepared, but they had all assumed that the men would be living like nomads and never be in one place long enough to receive mail. But now their husbands both felt strongly impressed by the Spirit that they were to remain in London until they felt equally impressed to move on. *There are many needs among the poor and destitute of this city,* Ian had written. *I'm certain we could focus our attention here for many months and not be lacking any opportunity to serve or to share the gospel message.*

Wren loved knowing that her husband would be in the same place long enough for them to share some frequent communication. She also loved reading his words and their indication of changes taking place in him. His previous letters had certainly given information about their journey and experiences, but they had also been very much filled with a stark longing for home and repeated expressions of his personal struggle to do what had been asked of him. In this letter, it was still clearly evident how much he missed her and the children, but he had enthusiasm for the opportunities before them to do good and make a positive difference in the lives of people who were in need of what they had to share.

Wren took great delight in writing to Ian about all of the little things the children were doing, of the simple happenings in Nauvoo, and of her ongoing love for him. She told him of her experience of meeting Beatrice and returning the note to her, and that Beatrice had since come to visit. Wren told Ian she thought she and Beatrice would become good friends. She also told him that she had received a letter from Shona that she'd written following Ian's visit to New York City, and that she'd also received a letter addressed to him from his mother. They had agreed prior to his departure that Wren would answer any such letters on his behalf with the vague explanation that he was traveling, engaged in some responsibilities to do with their religion. Wren reported now that she had done so, and she summarized the news his mother had shared in the letter she'd sent to him.

Wren did her best as she wrote to remind Ian of home and how very much she missed him, but not to weigh her letter down with details or feelings that might encourage his own longing to be there. She told him how proud she was of him for the work he was doing, and how she could feel his enthusiasm for the work in his letter. She encouraged him to take advantage of every moment and every resource he had with him to do the Lord's work, and that he would surely be blessed to have his needs met.

As she wrote down that thought, Wren felt strongly impressed to go to the Bible and find words she'd read there in the past. She frantically searched for the right passage, then laughed aloud with delight when she found it. She carefully copied it down, feeling a calm assurance that at some particular moment in the future, it might give her husband the strength and guidance he would need.

Always remember, my darling, what it says in Mark, chapter 6. "And he called unto him the twelve, and began to send them forth by two and two; And commanded them that they should take nothing for their journey; no scrip, no bread, no money in their purse: And he said unto them, In what place soever ye enter into an house, there abide till ye depart from that place."

Wren reread the words from the scriptures that she had carefully copied, feeling quite satisfied, then the impression came to her that there was more she needed to find in the Bible and copy down, another passage that was equally important. Again it took her some time and careful searching to find it, and she was glad to be doing this at a late hour, which allowed her the peace of sleeping children to concentrate and focus. Once more she felt delighted to find what she knew was right, what she knew she had been guided to on Ian's behalf. And once again she felt a joyful peace in knowing that a day would come when Ian would need these words. She knew it as surely as if she'd heard an audible voice whisper it into her ear. But she didn't need an audible voice. Her heart knew the truth of her love for Ian as surely as it knew the truth of the gospel. And her heart knew how to discern the voice of the Lord when it spoke to her in its still, small, but undeniable voice. She knew that Ian could hear that same still, small voice. And knowing that gave her more comfort than anything else. Between her letters and the guidance of the Spirit, her husband would surely be given all the strength and encouragement he needed.

And also remember, she wrote, *the wonderful words of the Savior in Matthew, chapter 6. "Therefore I say unto you, Take no thought for your life, what ye shall eat, or what ye shall drink; nor yet for your body, what ye shall put on. Is not the life more than meat, and the body than raiment? Behold the fowls of the air: for they sow not, neither do they reap, nor gather into barns; yet your heavenly Father feedeth them. Are ye not much better than they? . . . Consider the lilies of the field, how they grow; they toil not, neither do they spin: And yet I say unto you, That even Solomon in all his glory was not arrayed like one of these. Wherefore, if God so clothe the grass of the field, which to day is, and to morrow is cast into the oven, shall he not much more clothe you, O ye of little faith? Therefore take no thought, saying, What shall we eat? or, What shall we drink? or, Wherewithal shall we be clothed? . . . for your heavenly Father knoweth that ye have need of all these things. But seek ye first the kingdom of God, and his righteousness; and all these things shall be added unto you. Take therefore no thought for the morrow: for the morrow shall take thought for the things of itself."*

Four days after receiving their letters from England, Wren and Patricia walked together to the post office with the children to mail very thick letters to their husbands. Each woman held a prayer in her heart that the letters would arrive intact and that they would find their recipients safe and well.

Throughout the following weeks, Wren and Patricia kept busy with caring for their household and their children, and also remaining involved with the Relief Society in its ongoing efforts to help those in the community who were struggling. On a number of occasions they worked together to take a meal to a family in need, and they often tended children in their home to assist an ill mother. Wren was usually working on some kind of sewing project to offer a piece of needed clothing for a man working on the temple, and Patricia used her excellent baking skills to provide fresh bread or biscuits to the workers or to a family in need.

Beatrice came more than once to visit, and Wren quickly grew to love this woman and her easy way of offering support and encouragement in matters where she had great personal experience. Wren also went to visit Beatrice once on her own, and another time with Patricia and all of the children. Beatrice and her kind husband seemed to take great pleasure in the children, and it proved to be a delightful outing.

In spite of all the busyness of life, Wren and Patricia always found the time to write and send many letters to their husbands. Knowing that there was a place to send them, they were eager to offer words of encouragement and details of life at home that might help their husbands feel a little less cut off from their home and families. Beyond their continual prayers, it was the best they could do to support the missionary efforts of these men they loved so dearly. Every hour of every day, Wren did everything she could to care for her family, serve where she was needed, and be a distant support to her husband. And every hour she took a moment to imagine what it would be like when he came home to her. It was the hope of that moment that kept her going.

* * * * *

Ian and Ward quickly settled into their new accommodations and found them rather pleasing, all things considered. Their first order of business, after mailing off lengthy letters to their wives, was to get out on the streets and go wherever the Spirit might guide them. They prayed together before leaving their rooms. With breakfast in their stomachs and each carrying a couple of copies of the Book of Mormon in bags slung over their shoulders, they walked the streets of London, Ward holding tightly to Ian's shoulder to be guided to take the same steps, and to go whichever direction Ian might feel inclined to go. During the morning they approached a few people on the streets, but their efforts at conversation were met with rudeness and even a couple of hearty threats.

They sat together on some stairs near the river to eat the lunch that Edith had packed for them, then they prayed again and pressed forward. It was dark before they finally conceded that the day had not afforded them any success, but they would surely need to meet with many failures in order to find those whom the Lord had prepared to receive their message.

"No one ever said it would be easy," Ward said, as if he'd not said it dozens of times before.

Exhausted and hungry, they headed back toward the inn, ready to call it a day, knowing they had many more days ahead that could either bring success or more intense discouragement such as they both felt at the moment. After they'd had some supper and were both settling in for the night, Ward suggested that perhaps they should try the approach of preaching in the streets, as the missionaries had been doing when Ian had found them. Ian appreciated the concept—and its personal connection to his own experience—but he didn't feel drawn to the idea. He didn't know—and readily admitted to Ward— if his hesitation was because of his own lack of self-confidence, or if it just wasn't the right thing to do at that time. When he asked Ward if *he* felt ready to stand in the street and preach a sermon, Ward admitted that he was equally hesitant. They prayerfully determined that for now they would keep combing the streets and approaching people according to what felt right, minute by minute, hour by hour.

Sometimes the only thing that got Ian through a day was the thought that every hour he spent engaged in this work was an hour closer to being able to return home and be with Wren and the children again. If not for that beacon before him in his mind, he wasn't sure at times how he would make it through the hours of disappointment and discouragement.

As they made their way back to the inn after another fruitless day, Ian and Ward tried to count how many days they'd been in London, but neither of them knew for sure. They knew they'd mailed thick letters to their wives once a week, and they'd mailed three letters now. They speculated on how many weeks it might take to receive letters in return when it took a ship approximately six weeks to cross the Atlantic each direction. The time when they might possibly receive any word from home felt forever away and added to their mutually disheartened state.

Ian decided to take a different route home, but he didn't mention it to Ward, figuring he wouldn't notice the difference since he couldn't

see the *normal* route home. He was a little taken aback to turn a
corner and find himself in a long, dark alley. He knew being in such a
place, especially at night, was neither safe nor smart. But he felt more
compelled to keep moving forward as opposed to turning around to
go back and find a safer route.

"It's too quiet," Ward said. "We're walking a different street than
we usually do."

"You're too perceptive for your own good," Ian said. "I felt like we
should go in a different direction."

"Fair enough. But next time *tell* me we're going a different direction."

"And spoil the adventure of your figuring it out for yourself?" Ian
countered and chuckled, wishing his lightness could ease his concern
for being where they were and wondering what purpose might be
served by such a detour. His cynical self wondered if their getting
robbed and beaten might serve as some lesson in humility. But he
preferred to avoid such a lesson and instead be humble by choice. So
he humbly asked God to guide his steps and keep them safe.

Ian kept walking and praying. Suddenly, he heard a sound that
made his heartbeat quicken, and he wondered if he should just take hold
of Ward's arm and run. He heard it again and instead stopped to listen.

"What's wrong?" Ward asked in a whisper.

"I don't know," Ian whispered back.

He turned and looked every direction, seeing nothing, no one.
Then he looked down and to his left. His already quickened heartbeat
began to race, and he felt almost physically ill as all of his senses
abruptly took him back to another time in his life, as swiftly and
surely as if he'd traveled through time and he were now standing
above himself, looking down at his mirror image from years earlier,
huddled in an obscure alleyway in London, lost and oblivious to the
potential dangers of being in such a state and in such a place. It was
too dark to even discern this man's hair color or anything about his
features. To Ian, he only looked like a mirror image of himself, and he
stared for long moments, dazed and bewildered while he attempted to
take into his spirit what seemed to be a deep and powerful message.

"What's happening?" Ward whispered.

"It's me," Ian said.

"I don't understand," Ward said.

"Forgive me," Ian said, coming back to the present. "There's a man here. He appears to be passed out drunk." The man groaned as if in response to hearing voices. Ian added, "Or close to it." He sighed. "I just had the strangest moment . . . of remembering myself . . . so much like this. I'm certain we were led here. We must help him."

"Of course," Ward said eagerly.

Ian guided Ward's hand to the brick wall at the edge of the alley so that he had something to touch to help him get his bearings. Ian then went to his knees beside this man, who was curled up against the wall. He nudged the man and said in a loud voice, "Are you all right, good man? Can we help you?"

The man groaned again and halfheartedly resisted Ian's intrusion on his drunken stupor. Once Ian realized the man was dazed but not unconscious, he put an arm around him and hoisted him to his feet, his effort meeting with only mild resistance.

"We're going to help you," Ian said more than once. "Just lean on me and we'll get you someplace safe." The man began to be more cooperative, and Ian was able to guide Ward to stand on one side of this man so that he could help support him. Ward was blind, but he was strong, and Ian was able to be eyes enough for all three of them as he walked slowly and carefully out of the alley with a barely coherent drunk man staggering between him and Ward. Ian had to verbally tell Ward where to step in many cases, but they managed tolerably well to get this man back to the inn where Edith declared that she'd begun to worry about them.

"You don't have to be our mother, you know," Ian said to her, although he knew that she was well aware of his appreciation for the way she kept track of their comings and goings. Edith herself had boldly declared no interest in the book they were promoting, but she had expressed respect for their efforts.

"Think o' th' trouble ya'd be in without me," Edith said lightly but with her focus on the man Ian was guiding to a chair. "And what stray dog 'ave ye brought in with ye now?"

"Not unlike myself a few years back," Ian said to her.

"Now that's true, fer certain," Edith said.

The man was barely managing to remain in the chair, not even keeping his head upright. Ian knew he needed to sleep off the liquor before they even had hope of having a conversation. Edith didn't have any rooms available that night, so Ian had Ward help him guide the man to his own bed, where he quickly became lost in unconsciousness. Ian slept on the floor nearby with an extra blanket and pillow that Edith had provided. And he slept securely, knowing that he might have done something to keep one other human being a little safer that night.

The following morning, Ian and Ward ate breakfast in their room. They sat in their tiny parlor with the door open to the room where the stranger was still sleeping, on the alert for the moment when he would finally come around. After praying for guidance in dealing with the man in the other room, Ian read aloud from the scriptures, and they worked some on writing in their journals. When they began hearing indications of life from the bedroom, Ian moved the chairs so they were situated on both sides of the bed. And there they sat, waiting for the object of their charity to come awake.

Ian felt a repeat of last night's dreamlike experience of watching this man and seeing a previous version of himself. Taking himself back to that time in his life, he felt some actual fear at the thought of what *could* have happened to him during those many months in London. He felt that same fear in wondering where his life might be if he hadn't acquired that Book of Mormon; if he hadn't gone home, made amends, married Wren, gone to America. His entire life seemed hinged on those experiences in London that had preceded waking up in an alleyway, startled out of a drunken stupor, and then wandering aimlessly to the street where Mormon missionaries were preaching. He had long ago come to recognize the hand of God in those events. Even the helpless wandering of the streets all that time seemed a necessary part of his life's experience, a tumultuous tutorial that had prepared him and humbled him sufficiently to truly *hear* what had been preached that day, and to be drawn to having that Book of Mormon come into his hands. Ian prayed that now in this place and this time he could be an instrument to help this man turn his life around. He reminded himself that he could not make decisions for this man, nor could he take away his free will. Perhaps this would lead to nothing but more disappointment. Perhaps, after all that Ian and Ward could do, this man would return to his drunken ways and a life of waste and despair. But at least Ian would know that they'd tried. And maybe, just maybe, they *could* make a difference to this man. He was surprised at the amount of hope he was placing in this man, and they didn't even know his name, or anything about him. But the stranger was coming around, and they would soon know more.

Ian and Ward patiently watched and waited while this man was lured toward consciousness. They could tell that the bright, late-morning sun coming through the window was obviously offending the man by the way he turned away from it, moaning with indications that his head was hurting. Ian knew *exactly* how he felt, and he commended Ward for not have *any idea* how he felt.

Suddenly the man bolted upright in the bed and looked back and forth between the two men on either side of him as if they might immediately end his life. "Who *are* you?" the man demanded. "And where *am* I?"

"We found you in an alley last night," Ian said. "And we brought you here to keep you safe until you were sober." The man looked confused, and Ian asked, "What do you remember?"

"After my fifth drink at the corner pub, nothing . . . to be truthful."

The man's speech indicated that he was educated and refined. He was not of the lower classes.

"I know exactly how you feel," Ian said. "In fact, I've been in your exact position."

"What?" the man said, still seeming overtly concerned. "Waking up in a strange room with men who claim to have dragged you out of an alley?"

Ian chuckled. "Not that *exactly*, but . . . certainly passed out drunk in an alley . . . many times. It's not a safe place to be, my good man, and therefore not conducive to your well-being."

The man looked dubious, then his headache seemed to assert itself past his fear of the situation. He groaned and leaned back against the headboard of the bed. To fill the silence, Ian said, "My name is Ian Brierley, and this is my friend, Ward Mickel."

"Hello," the man said passively, but didn't offer his own name.

"I'm originally from Scotland, and—"

"Now, that's not terribly difficult to figure," the man said with light sarcasm, in reference to Ian's accent.

"And Ward is from England. Although we both now officially reside in Illinois." The man looked confused, and Ian clarified, "In America, right next to the Mississippi River."

The man made a disinterested noise. "So what brings the two of you all the way from the Mississippi to drag me out of an alley?"

Ian chuckled, and Ward said, "That is a question we would love to answer, my good man, as soon as you've had a chance to freshen up and get some breakfast in you."

The man took a closer look at Ward, and Ian said, "Yes, he's blind, but don't tell him I told you."

"How quaint," the man said, unimpressed with Ian's pathetic attempt at humor. "I'd like to say something about the blind leading the blind, but perhaps I shouldn't."

"Perhaps not," Ian said.

"I *can* hear," Ward said, and the man let out a chuckle at last. "Might we know your name?" he added.

"Hugh Montgomery," the man said. "Do you think I could get a cup of coffee?"

"Of course," Ian said and left to go downstairs and get some. He knew Edith always had a pot on the stove. He returned a couple of minutes later to hear Ward asking Mr. Montgomery where he was from, but Mr. Montgomery ignored the question and gratefully took the steaming cup of coffee, cradling it in his hands as if it could save him. Ian knew it might help the effects of his hangover a bit, but there was only one thing that could truly save him. With any luck— and the hand of Providence—this man might be willing to hear what they had to share and be receptive to it.

Ian allowed him a long minute of peace with his coffee before he said, "So, may I ask why a man like yourself is getting blind drunk and passing out in an alley in this part of town?"

"You may ask, but I don't know that I care to tell you." Mr. Montgomery looked hard at Ian and added, "Why did a man like *yourself* get blind drunk and pass out in an alleyway in this part of town? I assume it was this part of town."

"It was, and I'm glad to answer that question. I was hiding. Lost. Wandering. Does any of that give us something in common?"

"It might," Mr. Montgomery said, but with a begrudging glare. He sighed loudly. "Listen, I'm grateful for your kindness and I am happy to pay you for any inconvenience or—"

"We don't want your money, Mr. Montgomery," Ward said. "And it was no inconvenience; none of any consequence anyway. We would very much like to talk with you about something that has made a tremendous difference in our lives; something that has given us a great deal of happiness. It's not our wish to simply keep you safe one night of your life. We would like to share something with you that could *change* your life, something that could give you the answers you're looking for."

"What makes you think I'm looking for any answers?" Mr. Montgomery countered.

"If you're not, maybe you should be," Ward said with equal assertiveness.

"I'll tell you what," Mr. Montgomery said. "You boys get me some breakfast and give me an hour to cope with this headache, and I'll listen to what you have to say."

He said it with arrogance, as if he would do anything just to get what he wanted and get out of here, but Ian eagerly said, "It's a deal," and went downstairs to get Mr. Montgomery something to eat.

Ian kept a running tab with Edith, even though he knew she was giving him discounts, and she knew that he in turn was paying her extra to compensate for all the special attention she gave to him and Ward. She now seemed somewhat emotionally invested in the new visitor, and curious over the state of his health. She was thrilled to put together a breakfast tray for the guest and did it quickly and with gusto. Ian took it up to Mr. Montgomery, and they left him alone to eat. A while later Edith had warm water sent up for the guest to wash with, and Ian took the tray of used dishes and the empty buckets down the stairs in order to save Edith or one of her employees from having to come up and get them.

Ian and Ward were both sitting in the little parlor, reading together, when Mr. Montgomery appeared, not looking too terribly disheveled, especially considering the state in which they'd found him the previous evening, and also taking into consideration the fact that he didn't have any clean clothes and was therefore still wearing what they'd found him in. Now it was even more evident that he was a well-dressed man—which added to the mystery of his reasons for being in this part of town, but it also left Ian relating to him even more. The eerie feeling that he'd come upon himself deepened further. He asked himself in that moment why the son of an earl had ended up in the seedy part of London; then it occurred to him that perhaps telling his own story to this man might be the best place to start, and perhaps the most effective—given their possible commonality regarding certain aspects of their lives.

"Very well, gentlemen," Mr. Montgomery said, "I'm ready to hear what you are so intent upon telling me."

Ian motioned him toward a third chair they had brought in from Ward's bedroom. The room was very small, which made it necessary for the three of them to sit fairly close together. But Ian liked that. It seemed conducive to what he hoped to accomplish. Mr. Montgomery, however, scooted his chair back as far as it could go, and then leaned back and folded his arms in a gesture of some kind of self-protection. Ian was all right with that, as long as the man was willing to listen. Perhaps the tactic of rescuing people and giving them a meal might prove a good means of bribery to get people to listen. Maybe they were on to something.

"Very well," Ian said. "I would like to start by telling you a little about myself and how I was once drinking myself into oblivion in this part of the city, and my friend Ward here can share with you whatever he might feel inclined to share."

"I'm all ears," Ward said, completely serious, but Mr. Montgomery chuckled.

"I was raised in the Highlands of Scotland," Ian began. "My father was an earl, and I came from a good family. I never wanted for anything, least of all love and support from my parents and friends. I had no reason to feel the need to leave home, but I felt the need nevertheless. It was like a sickness in me. I couldn't shake it. In fact, it was part of the reason I started drinking. Then a friend of mine was killed in a terrible fire. I blamed myself for his death. So I left. I left without any explanation to my loved ones beyond a cursory little note. I ended up here in London, wandering the places in the city where it was easier to hide and wallow in my drunkenness and misery. The good woman who runs this inn likely saved my life a time or two, but she was one of very few people I encountered who showed any kindness toward me at all. I kept thinking that I should go home, but I couldn't bring myself to do it."

Ian paused to note that Mr. Montgomery was listening, but his countenance was mostly bored. There was a tiny spark of something in his eyes, however, that gave Ian hope that his story wouldn't fall on deaf ears.

"One day I woke up in an alley, terrified more than usual to realize where I was and that I couldn't remember how I'd gotten there. Later that morning, I happened to wander into a small crowd gathered on the street, where two men were teaching out of a book of scripture."

Mr. Montgomery's countenance darkened. "Preaching, you mean. You mean *preaching*. This is about religion, isn't it!" He said it with anger, and Ian saw Ward's countenance falter.

Ian knew he had prayed for guidance in this conversation, and he felt sure his prayers had been heard when he simply said, "You agreed to hear what we have to say. If you'll just sit in that chair a short while and hear what we have to say, we'll not bother you any further. Fair enough?"

Mr. Montgomery thought about it for a minute; his anger faded slightly into a forced patience before he said, "Fine. I'll listen."

"What I heard these men say," Ian began again, "went into my heart as if God Himself had forced the words directly there. I knew that I needed to get home. But I also felt compelled to purchase a copy of the book these men had been teaching from. I bought the book and I started home. Truthfully, an hour after I'd bought it, I wondered why. I went home, put the book in the bottom of a closet, and completely forgot about it until some months had passed and I was dealing with some especially difficult matters. I remembered the book very suddenly, as if it had called to me. I started reading it that very day, and I cannot deny that the principles and concepts I read in that book completely changed my life. Over time, I came to understand my compulsion to wander, my feelings of being lost, and the way that God had guided me that day to get the answers I needed."

Ian felt compelled to lean more toward Mr. Montgomery, and he spoke with all the conviction he felt over the matter. "I must tell you, sir, and I cannot hold myself back when I tell you. I must tell you that I know that God loves His children, and that you and I are among those children. I absolutely felt a power beyond my own guiding me to where I found you in that alley last night, Mr. Montgomery. I don't know how or why, but I know that God's hand is in your life. He knows how you've been suffering. He has the answers that you've been actively seeking."

Ian stopped to consider what had just come out of his mouth and was a little astonished by his own boldness. Who was he to say that this man was suffering, that he was actively seeking answers? But he couldn't deny that the words had come from a source beyond his own thinking, and he was not going to dispute any inspiration, especially now, after so many weeks of praying and seeking to be able to make a difference in someone's life.

Ian allowed silence to settle in the room, but it settled uncomfortably. Mr. Montgomery looked away, seeming to have a sudden aversion to eye contact. He looked at the floor, then the wall. He cleared his throat, then finally looked again at Ian. There was no defiance or impatience in his expression; he looked more like a child trying to get out of doing a distasteful chore. But there was something indefinable in his eyes that gave Ian the hope this man had just the tiniest piece of his heart open and receptive to what he was trying to tell him.

"So, what is it you want exactly, gentlemen?" Mr. Montgomery asked.

Ian jumped quickly at answering the question. "If I give you a copy of the book that changed my life, will you read it?"

"Is it boring?"

"Depends on how you approach it, I suppose," Ward said. "I for one never found it boring."

"Nor I," Ian said.

"So, you're implying that I'm a boor who would not be able to appreciate fine literature?"

"You are certainly not a boor," Ian said. "And fine literature . . . well, the definition of that is relative, is it not? Just promise us you'll read it. Read it instead of drinking . . . just for a few days."

Mr. Montgomery thought about it. "I suppose I could do that."

"Do you need to stay here with us so we can make certain you keep your promise?" Ian asked.

"I don't need a nanny, thank you very much," Mr. Montgomery said.

Ian asked more gently, "Do you have a place to stay?"

Mr. Montgomery sighed and again looked uncomfortably toward the floor. "For another week or two," he said and came to his feet. "Where is this book you're talking about?"

Ian had it nearby and handed it to him. Mr. Montgomery looked it over but didn't so much as crack the cover.

"Will you tell us where to find you?"

"Besides in a nearby alley?" the man asked with self-deprecation. "I know where to find *you.*" He moved toward the door and added, "I'll read it. I promise. Believe it or not, I'm a man of my word."

"I believe it," Ian said.

"Why?" Ward asked.

"Why what?" Mr. Montgomery asked.

"Why are you willing to read it? A few minutes ago you said you had no interest in—"

"If this book ends up being worth reading," Mr. Montgomery said, "I might actually be willing to answer that question. Good day, gentlemen." He opened the door, then turned and said, "Oh, and . . . thank you . . . for your help . . . and for breakfast. It's nice to know there are still decent people in the world."

"Take good care of yourself," Ian said, and Mr. Montgomery left.

"A colorful morning," Ward said lightly. "A break from the same old routine, if nothing else."

"Indeed," Ian said. "Let's hope it turns out to be more than just a break from the same old routine."

"Let's hope," Ward said.

Chapter Seven
Unto the Least of These

The following day Ian suggested to Ward that the situation with Mr. Montgomery had given him an idea. While Mr. Montgomery appeared to be a wealthy man in a difficult situation, there were many impoverished people on the streets of London; people who were in difficult situations through no fault of their own. Ian felt that perhaps they might have success in taking the teachings and example of Jesus from the New Testament quite literally and be able to share the gospel of Christ by living its most basic principles.

Ward was thrilled with the idea, and the two men sat down to speak with Edith about the possibility of converting a barely used storage room at the back of her inn into a place where Ian and Ward might bring people who were down on their luck. They could have a good meal, perhaps spend the night, and then they would see what they could do to help them get back on their feet. Ian and Ward agreed to pay all expenses so that all Edith would have to do was provide the room and be willing to cook a little extra food each day. She was so fond of Ward and Ian that she could hardly say no, but she actually showed some enthusiasm for the project.

Edith's enthusiasm waned a bit when she found the back room of the inn full of a number of people down on their luck. She insisted that no one would be eating there without first cleaning up, and she was glad to provide warm water and soap and towels to do so. When more help was needed in the kitchen to handle the extra load, Ian spoke to some of the more able-bodied people who were in need of help about working in the kitchen in exchange for the meals they were receiving. The truly humble and grateful were more than glad to do so. The not-so-humble-and-grateful were soon on their way, having no interest in having to listen to religious preaching as the price for being given some decent meals and a chance of something better.

Edith gained some enthusiasm for the project when she began to see changes taking place in people's lives. Over the weeks, a number of people took hold of the message that Ian and Ward had to share, and they were able to find sufficient work to earn passage to America. It became a common cycle for Ian and Ward to find someone in need on the streets, bring them to Edith's for a safe place to sleep and some decent meals in exchange for a little work in the kitchen. Ian and Ward would teach these people the message they had, and those who could read were given a Book of Mormon if their interest in it was sincere. Ian and Ward began performing baptisms at a regular pace, and then the newly baptized members would do everything they could to get to America. Therefore, Ian and Ward were also regularly helping people arrange passage and seeing them off.

The joy that Ian and Ward both felt in the work they were doing was something they found difficult to express, even to each other. But they wrote of it in detail to their wives and recorded it carefully in their journals. Ian came to know more in his heart what it truly meant in the scriptures when it said, *For inasmuch as ye do it unto the least of these, ye do it unto me.* He also gained a deep love for the passage, *And if it so be that you should labor all your days in crying repentance unto this people, and bring, save it be one soul unto me, how great shall be your joy.* His joy was indeed great! In spite of how very much he missed his home and family, he could not deny his joy! Not that the work was by any means easy, and some days were very discouraging. He continually felt disheartened over the human condition on the streets of London, and he felt saddened each time their message was rejected. But there were precious moments interspersed with the difficult ones. There were people eagerly seeking a better way, longing to find answers of hope and joy. And Ian and Ward were in a position to guide people to those answers.

Winter was settling over London before letters arrived from home, but Ian and Ward each received two letters, with one of the two being very thick. The city felt less cold and damp, and the prospect of all things became brighter with letters from their wives in hand. Winter moved into spring while the established pattern of work continued, and letters began arriving from Nauvoo on a regular basis.

It was a warm day in April before Ian and Ward saw Hugh Montgomery again. He simply showed up at Edith's, informed them that he'd read the Book of Mormon and knew it to be true. He told them practically nothing about his situation except that he had no family left to speak of, and it was just as well because they would only be ashamed of him. He had squandered his inheritance, and his life had been in ruins when they'd found him that night in the alley. Now he had taken care of those matters in his life to the best of his ability, and he wanted to be baptized. He was ready to embark upon his own journey to a new land and a new life.

A few days after Hugh was baptized, he came to Edith's one last time to see Ian and Ward, and to thank them for how their efforts had changed his life. As he was leaving, Hugh handed a piece of paper to Ian, who unfolded it to see a name and address written there.

"My aunt," he said. "My only living relative, as far as I know. It's a lot to ask, but I'd like the two of you to pay her a visit."

"Why is it a lot to ask?" Ward inquired.

Hugh chuckled. "She's cranky and old and utterly intolerable. But if anything could make her happier, it's what the two of you could teach her. It's worth a try."

"Thank you," Ian said. "We certainly *will* pay her a visit."

"When do you sail?" Ward asked.

"This evening, actually," Hugh said. "I must hurry along. But I couldn't leave without saying good-bye . . . and thank you. Although simply saying *thank you* feels so trite."

"I know what you mean," Ian said, "but it's not necessary. Seeing you this way—and knowing how your life has changed—is more than thanks enough."

Hugh took hold of Ward's hand to shake it firmly, then they shared a brotherly embrace. "We will see you in Nauvoo, my friend," Ward said.

"Yes, you will," Hugh said. "I'll be anxiously awaiting your return."

Ian shared an equally warm handshake and embrace with Hugh, then they said their reluctant good-byes and watched him leave. Ian put an arm around Ward's shoulders and said, "We did well, my friend. By that I mean we did well at listening to the guidance of the Spirit and heeding it."

"I know what you meant," Ward said. "And yes, we did well. It all seems worth it in such moments, does it not?"

"It certainly does," Ian said. "Let's go and write letters to our wives and tell them all about Mr. Montgomery."

"Excellent idea," Ward said. "Although I think Mr. Montgomery might arrive in Nauvoo before our letters do."

"Either way, we should write some letters."

"Yes, I agree," Ward said. "But first, I think we need to visit Mr. Montgomery's aunt."

"Today?" Ian asked.

"We have some hours of daylight left. Why not?"

"Fine, then," Ian said and looked at the address. "I think we're going to need to hire a cab. We're not going to find her in *this* part of town."

They found the home of the elderly Mrs. Montgomery to be enormous and surrounded by a very high, ornate fence. Thankfully the gate was not locked, and they were able to get to the front door and knock. A manservant opened the door and looked at them suspiciously, but Ian declared with confidence that Mr. Hugh Montgomery had sent them to inquire after his aunt, since he was leaving the country.

Ian and Ward waited a ridiculously long time in a ridiculously ornate entry hall before the manservant returned and led them wordlessly to a stuffy drawing room. He opened drapes that emitted clouds of dust, then he left the room and closed the doors.

"I assume that to mean Mrs. Montgomery will see us," Ian said, guiding Ward to a sofa that didn't look nearly as dusty as the drapes—at least he hoped not.

"I assume," Ward said, and Ian sat beside him.

A minute later an elderly woman entered the room, and the men stood up. She looked as ornate as the entry hall and as dusty as the drapes. Ian wished that he could whisper to Ward that the woman was scowling and didn't look at all friendly, but he couldn't have done so without appearing rude. And Hugh *had* warned them that his aunt might not be pleasant.

"And who might you be?" the woman demanded.

"Your nephew sent us," Ian reported.

"Hugh?" she asked as if his name was distasteful to her.

"That's right," Ian said and hurried to give enough information to prevent her from kicking them out. "My name is Ian Brierley, and this is Ward Mickel. Ward here is blind, in case you're wondering and—"

"Blind?" she repeated with more curiosity than compassion. "How did that happen?"

"A mysterious medical condition," Ward reported. "It came on in my childhood."

"How very tragic," she said as if she didn't mean it.

She made no effort to sit down; therefore, the men remained standing as well, and Ian hurried to say, "Some months ago we found Hugh in a rather disagreeable state, and—"

"Drunk, you mean," she snapped.

"Yes," Ian said, "but we shared a spiritual message with him and he's not had a drink at all for months now. He's actually on his way to America to begin a new life, and he asked us to visit you and to share the same message."

"Not a single drink?" she asked with some skepticism.

"Not one," Ward said. "He's a changed man. You wouldn't know him."

"He came to see me," the woman said and finally sat down, motioning with her arm for the men to do the same. Ian sat, keeping his hand on Ward's arm to guide him to sit as well. "He told me he'd changed, but I didn't believe him."

"Why do you believe *us?*" Ward asked.

"You both seem like decent enough gentlemen," she said, but perhaps the real reason for her becoming more receptive came out when she added, "I've not had any company for going on a year now. Or is it two? Hugh only came by to aggravate me . . . until that last visit. He told me he'd changed, but I admit that I wasn't very trusting."

"We thank you for trusting us enough to hear what we have to say," Ian said.

"Who said I trust you?" Mrs. Montgomery asked.

"You're allowing us to visit with you," Ward said.

"Perhaps I'm just bored," she snapped. "Did you ever think of that?"

Bored or not, Ian only wanted her to listen to what they had to say. "Would you be willing, then, to hear the message we would like to share?"

"A spiritual message, you say?"

"That's right," Ward said.

"I've not been to church in nearly a decade. Don't like that new vicar, whatever his name is." She motioned her hand impatiently toward the men as if she were a queen granting them an audience. "Why not? I'm listening. What else have I got to do?"

"Very well," Ian said.

Ward said, "Thank you."

The two men went back and forth with their experiences in finding the gospel, their knowledge of the truthfulness of the gospel, and their desire for all people everywhere to have the peace that could be found through the Atonement of Jesus Christ. Mrs. Montgomery listened and asked an occasional question. She didn't become any less cantankerous during the visit, but she did agree to read the book and invited them to return in a few weeks. They set up a date and time and she called in her servant to tell it to him, insisting that when Ian and Ward returned, they would share supper with her.

After Ian and Ward had returned to their rooms that night, they speculated on the miracle of Hugh, a changed man, sailing to America, and they both felt hopeful that his aunt's heart might soften in time.

In the weeks leading up to their next visit with Mrs. Montgomery, Ian and Ward continued to actively do the work they'd been doing. When they *did* return to visit the elderly woman, she was a bit more pleasant than she'd been on their previous visit, and she had obviously done some reading in the book, but their efforts to steer the conversation toward anything of a spiritual nature were generally thwarted. They left her home with a good meal in their stomachs and an appointment to return, but not certain if Mrs. Montgomery had—or would ever have—any interest in the message they had to share.

With spring easing toward summer, the men pressed forward in their work, and their visits to Mrs. Montgomery's home became a regular and predictable occurrence. But despite her lack of interest in the message of the gospel, they felt it was right to keep visiting her.

Letters from their wives arrived on a regular basis, and they continued to mail letters home at least once or twice a week. They were both grateful to be in a position where such communication was possible, and they considered it to be a great, tender mercy from the Lord that helped ease the strain of missing their families. All in all, they could not deny that they had been very blessed, and as far as they were aware, all had been well with their families while they'd been away. They hoped that it continued to be that way for whatever amount of time they remained far from home.

* * * * *

Wren put the sleeping baby into her little bed across the hall from her own bedroom. She brushed gentle fingers over little Anya's head, admiring her soft blonde hair that was so much like her grandmother's, her namesake. She was growing so quickly and changing every day. Wren thought of all that Ian had missed, but she had to slam the door on that thought, knowing it would only lead to tears and heartache. She thought instead of the joy they would all feel when he returned and he could have the pleasure of reacquainting himself with his children—and with her.

Wren walked through the rooms of the other children, touching their little heads as well, doing her best to absorb the joy of being their mother without engaging in the sorrow she felt in the absence of their father. Assured that all was well, she returned to her own room, leaving her door open so that she could easily hear if one of the children awoke. She took up her brush and sat on the edge of the bed to brush out her hair with strokes that were especially long and slow. Her mind wandered while she systematically performed the habitual task. This was always the most difficult time of day. The quiet of sleeping children, the absence of Patricia's presence and conversation, the stillness of a slumbering neighborhood, and the darkness of night all combined to make these moments preceding her own sleep the hardest time of all. Each morning she came awake to the sound of at least one child needing her, and the distraction of motherhood was immediate. Through the day there was always something to occupy her time and distract her mind easily away from the continual pain of missing Ian. But here in these silent moments of late evening, Wren had nothing but her thoughts to keep her company. She was always torn between thinking of him too much or trying not to think of him at all. The latter was impossible when his place in her life was so deeply woven into her very existence that not thinking of him would be like not acknowledging her own consciousness, her own need to eat and to breathe and to live. He was always there in the back of her mind, hovering effortlessly among every trivial matter of daily life. But actively indulging in thoughts of him almost always led her down a path that brought her to tears and sometimes made her physically ache with longing. She always prayed for him, night and morning and many times in between. He always existed there in her mind, as if each moment of each day might be seen on his behalf while she was simultaneously seeing it through her own eyes. But to allow herself to mentally go to another time was often more painful than comforting. Still, she could hardly keep from doing so.

Wren often tried to get into bed quickly and allow the exhaustion of being a mother of three—who had not been allowed to sleep through the night since her motherhood had begun—to overtake her quickly and therefore prevent her from thinking too long or too hard about Ian. But tonight she felt reluctant to do so. Tonight, for some reason, she missed him so deeply that she wanted to do nothing but recall every memory of her life with him in intricate detail. She wanted to imagine his return and the grand moment when they would be in each other's arms again. She wanted to think of all the things they would do together when they were reunited as a family. Wren wanted to stay awake as long as humanly possible and bask in mentally bringing herself as close to Ian as it was possible to do with the thousands of miles that stood between them. She often imagined what it might be like to just be able to speak to him, to somehow magically hear his voice across the miles, and to have him hear hers. Oh, if they could only have a conversation now and then! How it would ease the intensity of her loneliness! But such magic was impossible, and all she could do was read and reread his letters, and get through each day with her memories and her hopes for the future. And in that moment, she indulged in them deeply, as if thoughts of Ian were a lovely pond of cool, refreshing water, and she could leap headlong into it, drenching herself completely and allowing it to soothe her every nerve. She could bathe in the sensation and mentally take it into her every physical sense as much as in her imagination.

Wren set the brush aside and just sat there, her eyes closed, her face lifted partially toward the heavens, as if that alone might bring her closer to him. She recalled the hundreds of nights that he had sat here with her on the bed this time of day, how they would hold hands and talk, how he might help brush out her hair, often pressing a kiss to her neck or the side of her face between strokes of the brush. She imagined the feel of his arms around her. The power of her own imagination took her breath away when it suddenly felt as if he truly *were* behind her. She felt a pleasant shiver, the exact sensation she would have gotten if he'd kissed a particular spot on the back of her neck. In her mind she could hear him laughing softly at her response. Wren was surprised at how long she was able to hold the sensation close to her, soaking in the comfort of her husband's love and reassurance, almost as if he were really there. She climbed into bed while the impression continued, and she fell asleep feeling as if she were comfortably wrapped in his arms.

That night she dreamt of Ian with such clarity that she awoke feeling as if they had spent a brief amount of time together. She had heard his voice and felt his embrace and embarked on her day certain that God in His mercy had given her the gift of such a dream to help ease this loneliness that could sometimes be almost crippling. Throughout that day and the next, Wren felt a little better than usual. The tenderness of her experiences—both while sleeping and awake— had assuaged her grief over Ian's absence and strengthened her belief that God's mercy was integrated intricately into this current situation. But the day after that, Wren began to feel a nagging uneasiness that clouded her mind with confusion and doubt. When she stopped to ponder the possible reasons, her heart was seized with such immediate and overwhelming fear that she almost went to her knees and was glad to be alone at the time to avoid having to explain to Patricia or anyone else what had made her gasp so loudly, and then to moan as her heart seemed to break in two at that very moment.

"He's dead," she muttered, hot tears accompanying her words into the open. That was why she'd felt him so close. That was why she'd dreamt about him so clearly. He was surely dead, and his spirit had been allowed

to be close to her.

Through the remainder of the day, Wren could hardly function. Patricia naturally took note of her condition right away and questioned her boldly. When Wren explained the entire situation and her belief over her reasons for feeling the way she did, Patricia immediately dismissed the possibility that such experiences would imply Ian's death. She pointed out with great wisdom that the scriptures taught very clearly—and she found the passages to strengthen her point—the methods for discerning whether or not something came from God or from Satan. She then talked Wren through her entire series of experiences and feelings, asking her to take note of how she had felt initially during what she believed to be a wonderful spiritual experience, and how she had felt once the doubt had started creeping in.

"But . . ." Wren protested, "of course I would feel horrible . . . t' realize my husband is dead and not coming back t' me. How could I possibly discern between such grief and anything that Satan might do t' confuse or upset me?"

"You can discern it by asking God to answer your questions in regard to this, and to offer you the reassurance you need to understand the source of your experience."

The principle made sense to Wren, but it didn't settle very well into the enormity of her present emotional state. She could admit, however, "Ye're a very wise woman, Patricia. I'll give what ye've said some thought and prayer."

Patricia assured Wren that she was always available to talk, and she also assured her that Wren would get her answers and be able to find peace. Wren thought as she heard the words that she would eventually be able to find peace over the fact that Ian was dead, but she tried to keep her mind and heart open as she went straight to her bedroom and to her knees that very moment and poured out her heart in prayer. She was grateful to Patricia for watching the children so that she could pray without interruption for a long while. She wept with a combination of her feelings of grief and her utter dependence on God to give her peace. One way or another, she had to find peace. She simply couldn't live with such pain and confusion in her heart. She finally ended her prayer and took over the care of her children, not feeling the evidence of any answers. However, she did feel a tiny spark of hope in believing that God *would* give her the answers she sought, and that He would give her the peace she needed—even if it took time.

Wren continued to pray and ponder and reexamine her feelings and experiences. Her answer didn't come all at once, but rather it came on slowly through the course of a day. As the day came to a close, she couldn't deny that she felt a warmth and peace inside of her that had not been present when the day had begun. And she simply knew that Ian was alive and well. She knew that Patricia had been correct in her theories over what had happened, and she simply had to press forward. Realizing that her experience truly *had* been what she'd initially believed—a sweet blessing from God to comfort her and give her strength—she felt a peaceful joy that swelled inside of her, a feeling so perfectly right and good that she knew Satan could *never* counterfeit such an experience.

When Wren received a letter from Ian, dated after the experience she'd had that she'd somehow misconstrued as having his spirit with her, she felt hugely relieved. As she prayerfully tried to understand what had happened and why, she concluded that somehow through the miraculous power of the Holy Ghost, God had given her that experience to give her strength and comfort. It was likely Satan's efforts in the course of opposition that had lured her away from the comfort of the experience and toward a belief that had caused her anxiety and grief. She came away from the experience more determined to have faith and trust in God—and in the feelings that God gave to her through the Holy Ghost.

Weeks slipped into months while Wren continued to rely on the Comforter in her life. She managed day by day to care for her home and children, live the gospel to her full capacity, and reach out to serve others with the means of time and energy she was able to give. The seasons changed, and the children grew. Little Anya took easily to walking and graduated quickly to running most of the time. She was continually difficult to keep up with and gave Wren a great deal of exercise. Little Donnan was also very active and busy, full of energy while chattering continually, even though Wren could hardly understand more than a syllable here and there. Patricia's daughter,

June, was a beautiful child with a strong will that often made them laugh in spite of it being a frequent challenge. June's stubborn nature made her—as Patricia declared—as challenging as Wren's three children put together. But the two women worked together to care for their children, and the four of them were as close as if they were siblings.

Gillian had just turned four and had merged into a stage of unusual maturity for a child her age. She was quiet and preferred playing by herself as opposed to being with other children. She had a vivid imagination and was often caught up in very dramatic play-acting with many imaginary friends. In spite of her playing so well by herself, she was frequently eager to assist with her younger siblings. She was actually very good at keeping them entertained while indoors. And when playing outside, Gillian could keep the little ones close by in the yard, rather than allowing them to run off into the nearby woods. Patricia commented to Wren once that Gillian was like a little sheepherding dog that ran back and forth and kept the three younger children from straying away, as if they were little lambs trying to wander from the fold where they were safe.

Gillian truly was a very good little girl, and Wren found her to be a great joy in her life. The irony of her actually being the child of Wren's sister occurred to her frequently, although Wren had never attempted to explain the situation to the child. As far as Gillian knew, she was as much a child to Ian and Wren as her younger siblings were. And that's the way Wren wanted it. She felt no less love for Gillian than she did the others, and she was grateful to have this tangible remnant of her sister.

Wren spoke often to Gillian about her father, and how he was traveling far away to teach people about Jesus. Gillian had memories of Ian that she would talk about in a surprisingly mature way, and she also had a very clear concept of who Jesus was and why He was so important to their lives. Gillian's speech was very clear for a four-year-old, and she articulated sentences more like an adult than a child. Because of this, Wren was able to have actual conversations with the child, who was full of curiosity about life and the world around them in a way that fascinated Wren. She kept a daily record of these conversations in her journal, always with the intent of preserving each memory to share with Ian when he returned. She also wrote each day of the antics of the other children, and of every joy and challenge that was worth noting. Wren never wrote such things without feeling joy at the thought of Ian one day reading what she'd written. However, she also grieved over the fact that he wasn't here now to share in such things as they occurred.

Late in the summer, more than a year after Ian had left them, Wren woke in the dark one night to be confronted with a serious concern over their oldest daughter. She came awake abruptly, her heart pounding, and realized that she'd distinctly heard a noise from across the hall. She waited and listened and heard it again. Her first thought was that they had an intruder in their home. She rushed toward the sound, only to find Gillian in her room, in the dark, taking toys and books down from her shelf and talking as if she were not alone. Wren lit a lamp to assure herself of what was happening, and felt a little stunned. She was most unnerved by the talking because of the flood of memories that came with what she was seeing. Gillian's mother had suffered from a dreadful disease of her mind. No one had ever been able to understand it, but Bethia had genuinely believed that there were people around her, people who existed only in her own mind. These people had names and could convince her to do horrible things. Bethia had almost always been uneasy and prone to strange outbursts. It had certainly crossed Wren's mind that such a thing might be hereditary; in fact, she and Ian had talked about it more than once. Of course, there was nothing they could do but hope that wasn't the case and simply take good care of Gillian no matter what. But Bethia's disease hadn't begun to manifest until she was nearly an adult. She'd always been a little odd, but never out of her mind until her later teen years.

Wren stood there in the bedroom observing Gillian's behavior now, and she wanted to drop to her knees and scream. Instead she took hold of the doorframe to steady herself, and she put a hand over her mouth until she could speak reasonably. Then she knelt beside Gillian and took the child's little shoulders into her hands. She looked directly into Gillian's face and spoke to her, simply asking, "What's wrong, darling? Tell Mama what's wrong."

When Gillian seemed to look right through her with a dazed expression, Wren realized this was *not* the way that Bethia had ever been. For all of Bethia's wild behavior, she'd never been unaware of Wren's presence. She felt even more afraid when she had to admit she had no idea what she was dealing with. Wren shook Gillian gently and said her name. After she did it again, Gillian came out of the stupor, immediately confused and upset, wondering what was happening and why she was not in her bed asleep. Wren helped Gillian put the toys away, reassured her that everything was fine, and tucked her into bed, laying beside her until she fell back to sleep. Wren lay there much longer, stewing over what might be going on, and how she might handle the situation—especially with Ian so far away.

Gillian's strange nighttime behavior happened twice more before Wren accepted that she could not solve this problem on her own. She spoke to Patricia about her concerns, who immediately recommended that Wren take the child to see a local doctor. "Perhaps she's just sleepwalking," Patricia suggested.

"Sleepwalking?" Wren repeated. She'd never heard of such a thing, but Patricia assured her that a friend of her brother's, many years earlier, had been known to do that very thing. This person would somehow get out of bed and wander around the house and do all kinds of things while actually asleep, and have no recollection of it once he awoke.

"Is such a thing really possible?"

"According to this friend, it is," she said. "As I recall, the doctor gave him something to help him sleep more deeply, and it stopped."

Wren took a day to ponder the idea, and also to pray about the situation. She felt good about taking Gillian to the recommended doctor. He declared that sleepwalking truly was an actual condition and that he *could* give her some medicine to help her sleep more deeply, but he cautioned that such medicines could become addictive or cause other problems. He suggested that it was more practical to just take some precautions to keep the child safe, and she would likely grow out of it. He suggested making certain that the doors leading out of the house were locked in a way that the child could not wander outside during one of her episodes, and to just make certain there weren't things around her room that she might trip over or hurt herself on when the situation occurred. Wren felt his advice was good, and the following day she had some new locks installed that were too high and complex for Gillian to unlock on her own.

Wren found it difficult to sleep while she worried that her little girl might start wandering around in her sleep and possibly get hurt. But exhaustion always overruled. Wren worked far too hard during the days and got far too little rest at night to not sleep eventually when the opportunity came. She needed her rest in order to keep up with her responsibilities. She considered sleeping in Gillian's room, but sleeping in the same bed with the child was too cramped and uncomfortable. She considered having Gillian sleep in Wren's bed with her, but Gillian insisted that she wanted to sleep in her own room. The child didn't seem concerned over the problem, and Wren finally concluded that she should just have more faith that God would surely protect her daughter, and she should not worry so much about it. She concluded that even though Ian was absent now, he would eventually come home, and it wouldn't be good for their daughter to be in the habit of sleeping in the spot where he normally slept.

Whenever Wren *did* wake up during the night—most often because one of the younger children was crying, needing a drink of water, or requiring some comfort—she always first peeked in on Gillian to be certain she was in her bed and sleeping soundly. Each time she saw her there, she breathed in the relief and thanked God for keeping her children safe.

Chapter Eight
The Rescue

Wren awoke on a morning in August to the sound of little Anya announcing that the day had begun. Her loud, happy noises expressed a desire to be lifted out of her crib, but Wren preferred hovering in her own bed for just a minute longer. The room already felt hot and stuffy, and she knew it would be another day spent sticky with sweat while keeping the children happy and the house under control. Wren finally put her feet on the floor, but, as was her habit, she went to Gillian's room first to peek in at her. Panic seized her every nerve to see the bed empty and no sign of the child in the room. It was rare for Gillian to wake up until the noise of the other children woke her, and then she always came to tell her mother that she was awake. A quick glance in the other children's rooms told Wren that Gillian was not there. She ignored Anya's demands and rushed down the stairs, telling herself that she would find her daughter contentedly playing somewhere else in the house, and surely everything would be fine. To Wren's horror, she entered the kitchen to see that a chair had been slid next to the door, which had been unlocked and left wide open.

"Oh no," Wren muttered beneath her breath and rushed outside. "No, no, no!"

She stepped out the door and called for Gillian as loudly as she could, but she heard no response. She ran the perimeter of the yard, peering into the woods, calling her name over and over, oblivious to the fact that she was only wearing a nightgown and that her feet were bare. She could hear Anya crying through an open window of the house and felt torn between the needs of one child and the needs of another who was missing and likely in danger. She clearly needed help and ran back into the house to get Patricia, who met her halfway across the kitchen.

"What on earth has happened?" Patricia demanded, obviously having heard Wren's shouting. She'd apparently been out of bed a while since she was already dressed and her hair was up.

Wren could point more than speak. "The door . . . the lock . . . the chair . . ."

"Gillian's gone?" Patricia asked. Wren nodded and started to cry. Patricia took hold of her shoulders and said with firm presence of mind, "You take care of your babies and get yourself dressed. I'll take June next door with me to get some help and we'll find her." Wren nodded but couldn't speak and couldn't move. "We'll find her!" Patricia repeated, shaking Wren a bit. "Hurry along now."

Wren was startled to hear Anya crying in the distance, and she hurried up the stairs, telling herself that what Patricia had said was true. They would find her! Surely they would find her! Patricia was going for help. They were surrounded by wonderful neighbors. The entire community of Nauvoo was known for rallying together to help in times of crisis. If any community could find a wandering child, it would be this one. But there were a lot of woods, and there was a very wide, deep river nearby. Wren refused to think for more than a moment of the possibility that Gillian had sleepwalked herself straight into the river and had then drowned in the swift current. The fact that Gillian's mother had drowned made that thought doubly terrifying. Wren focused instead on meeting the immediate needs of Anya and Donnan, who was also well awake by now.

By the time Wren had herself and the two little ones dressed, an abundant search party had been organized, and they were thoroughly combing the woods and surrounding area. At Patricia's suggestion, she and Wren carefully searched every inch of the house, making certain the child hadn't crawled under a bed or into a closet and was innocently sleeping under their own roof while strangers were out searching for her. Wren far preferred that scenario. She preferred to think that even though Gillian had gotten outside, she had come right back in and found a strange hiding place. But she was not to be found, and Wren had to force herself to stay calm and care for her other children while she trusted that those searching on her behalf would be led to her little daughter—and quickly. She doubted that she had ever prayed so hard in her life. She kept reminding herself that God knew where Gillian was, and He would surely lead these people to find her. But her efforts at being positive and rooted in faith were counterbalanced by imagining herself having to write a letter to her husband to tell him that their daughter had gone missing, presumably drowned in the Mississippi River. She imagined Gillian's little body washing up on the shore of some other town down the river; then she had to force her thoughts away from such wretched images and she tried to imagine instead how it would feel to hold little Gillian in her arms again once she was found. She kept listening and watching out the open windows, convincing herself that any moment a man would come running out of the woods with Gillian in his arms, declaring that she'd been found. But hours passed, and the search continued. Wren tried to remain calm and dignified, but she couldn't deny her gratitude for the women from the Relief Society who stayed with her and Patricia, helping with the children and taking over in the kitchen.

When the heat of afternoon was at its peak and Gillian had still not been found, Wren completely broke down and cried to Patricia. "I should have . . . locked her in the room with me at night. I should have . . . slept on the floor of her room . . . right in front of the door so she never could have gotten out without going past me. I should have . . . been more—"

"That's enough of that," Patricia insisted, putting her arms firmly around Wren. "Regret won't get you anywhere. They'll find her."

"How can you know that? You can't know that!"

"They'll find her," Patricia repeated gently, but Wren couldn't believe her.

Hours later, when Wren realized the sun was going down over the Mississippi, she felt near to despair. Some of the people around her were trying very hard to remain positive, but others were quietly behaving as if a death in the family had already occurred.

When the moment came that Wren had been imagining, she felt so spent that it took her several seconds to realize that what she was hearing was indeed real.

"I've found her! I've found her!" a male voice called, growing louder in volume as he came closer to the house from out of the woods. The jubilance in his voice could have never been an indication of having found her dead.

Wren rushed out the back door and saw a man emerge from the trees with Gillian upright in his arms, her blonde hair bouncing as he ran. Wren sank to her knees, weak from the intensity of her relief and gratitude. She muttered her thanks to God as Gillian was set down and she ran across the grass and into her mother's arms. "Oh!" Wren moaned, then sobbed, holding her daughter close. The experience was even more wonderful than she'd imagined, just as she was sure that having this turn out badly would have been far more difficult to face than she had imagined.

"Thank you so much!" Wren said, looking up over Gillian's head to the smiling man who had found her little girl.

"A pleasure, Sister Brierley," he said in a British accent.

"Have we met?" she asked. It was mildly difficult to see him with the way she was crying.

"Not yet," he said in a gentlemanly manner, "although I've certainly *wanted* to make your acquaintance. Hugh Montgomery." The name sounded obliquely familiar to Wren, but her head felt foggy from the strain of the day. And then Mr. Montgomery added, "Your husband baptized me in London." He smiled and spoke again before Wren could even catch her breath after such an announcement. "I'll help call in the search party and let everyone know she's been found." He nodded. "A pleasure meeting you at last, Sister Brierley."

"I'm grateful t' ye," was all Wren could squeak out as she watched him walk away. She sat there on the lawn for many minutes, just holding Gillian in her arms while the wonderful people who had been helping them throughout the day flocked around her, assuring themselves that mother and child had indeed been reunited. Finally Patricia suggested that Gillian must be starving, and a short while later Wren was sitting at the table in the kitchen, staring pleasantly at Gillian while she ate more than her father would have. Thankfully the sisters who had been in the house earlier had left a hearty supper for the family. Everyone was gone now except for those who actually lived in the house. Patricia was kindly getting the little ones ready for bed so that Wren could just be with her little daughter and try to comprehend the whole spectrum of her feelings since waking up that morning.

"As soon as ye've had enough t' eat," Wren said, "we need t' get ye a good bath. Ye must be filthy after being out in the woods all day like that. The water's heating on the stove."

Gillian just nodded and kept eating. Wren wanted to demand to know what had happened to bring on this drama, and she wanted to know how to prevent it from ever happening again. But she doubted that Gillian could answer those questions. She had likely awakened in the woods and been terrified. They certainly needed to talk about it, because Gillian probably needed to understand what had happened as much as Wren did. But for now, Wren just let her eat as she savored the pleasure of having her home, safe and sound. Now she could write to Ian and tell him the story, beginning with the happy ending so that he didn't have to wonder for even a minute if everything was all right at home.

Following Gillian's bath, with the other children sleeping soundly and the house locked up tight for the night, Wren was wondering how to talk to Gillian about what had happened, and even more importantly, how to prevent it from happening again. She couldn't call the whole town out to search for her daughter on a regular basis. And next time, Gillian *might* find her way to the river without having any idea where she was or what she was doing.

"Maybe ye should sleep with Mama t'night," Wren said right after she slipped a clean nightgown over Gillian's head.

"I'll be all right, Mama," Gillian said, as if she were the adult needing to reassure a child.

Wren tied the ribbon at the neck of Gillian's nightgown into a neat bow. "But ye wandered outside in yer sleep, little one. Do ye even remember leaving the house?"

"Yes," Gillian said matter-of-factly.

Wren was a little taken aback but simply asked, "Were ye asleep . . . like ye were the other times when I had t' wake ye up because ye weren't in yer bed?"

"I don't know," Gillian said after pondering it for a long moment. "I felt like I was asleep, Mama, but I remember going down the stairs and unlocking the door."

"How did ye do that?" Wren asked to test her and see if she *really* remembered.

"I slid the chair over to the door and stood on it to reach the lock."

"How did ye know how t' undo the lock? No one's ever taught ye how t' do that."

"The man showed me how."

Wren managed to cover a noise of shock with a stilted cough. Memories of her sister's unstable mind came rushing back, compounded into fear that this sweet child would have to suffer with the same malady throughout her life. "What man?" Wren asked, pleased that she was able to speak in such an even tone.

"The man who told me to come down the stairs and slide the chair over to the door." Wren nodded but said nothing. She moved from kneeling to sitting on the floor when she felt a little light-headed. Gillian seemed oblivious to her mother's growing emotion and kept talking. "He told me how to unfasten the lock, and he told me that if I went out into the woods, there would be a surprise waiting for me. After I was in the trees and couldn't find my way, I couldn't see the man anywhere. I knew then that he was a very bad man and that he'd wanted me to get lost."

Wren felt as if she would melt into the floor if she didn't keep her hands firmly planted at her sides to hold herself up. Memories of Gillian's mother following instructions from people who didn't exist echoed with deafening intensity in Wren's mind. How many times had she tried to calm Bethia down while she'd been actively engaged in an argument with imaginary adversaries? Wren couldn't begin to count! Bethia's life had been filled with struggle and suffering. How could Wren ever face seeing this sweet child go through the same thing to any degree? How could she? And how could she contend with discovering it now while Ian was so far away and unable to help and support her in this situation? She prayed silently, knowing there was no other source from which to find the strength she would need to take on whatever might be required to keep Gillian safe and as happy as possible. She thought of how she'd had to try to keep Bethia from interacting with other people, afraid that they'd notice something was wrong and have her forced into a dreadful asylum of some kind. She wondered if the people of Nauvoo would be tolerant of such a problem.

While Wren continued to pray silently as she searched for words to say to her daughter, Gillian voluntarily continued her story. "I got scared when I knew I was lost." This sounded very much to Wren as if Gillian had been awake, which was far more frightening than to think of her sleepwalking—for reasons she would have a great deal of trouble explaining to a child. "I almost fell in the river," she said in the same nonchalant tone, but Wren gasped. "I'm all right, though, because Mama was there and she told me to stop and turn around and go back the other way."

"What?" Wren demanded, her voice jumping out of what had a moment ago been a paralyzed throat.

"Mama told me to stop and go back," Gillian repeated as if Wren should fully understand what she meant.

Certain this couldn't mean what it seemed to mean, Wren thought as she resorted to obvious logic. Gillian had never been told that her real mother was dead. "My sweetheart," she said, "I'm yer mama."

"You are the mama I have in this world to take care of me, but my real mama is an angel."

Wren put a hand over her mouth, but it didn't stifle the whimper that escaped from her throat. "You don't need to cry, Mama. It's all right. My other mama is happy and safe, and she promised to watch out for me and keep me safe."

Gillian threw her arms around Wren's neck and hugged her tightly. Wren returned the hug, crying as she had earlier on the lawn when Gillian had come back into her arms. "It's all right, Mama," the child said again, then she let go and knelt by her bed to pray, as Wren had taught her to do. Wren gathered herself together to kneel next to her daughter, who prayed aloud with simple humility, thanking Heavenly Father for sending her *angel mama* to keep her safe. She prayed for her father who was so far away teaching people about Jesus, then she said her amen and climbed into bed. Wren kissed her on the face, told her how grateful she was to have her back safely, then she extinguished the lamp and went across the hall to her own room. She practically staggered to the bed and collapsed there, muffling her tears with her pillow, so overcome she didn't know what to think. She couldn't deny the miracle! Clearly Gillian's mother *had* saved her from falling in the river. It was too incredible for Wren to be able to fully grasp it with her mind. But her heart knew it was true. It *had* to be true! But what of the man that Gillian had followed down the stairs and out the door? How could that have any other explanation besides Gillian having inherited her mother's illness?

Wren finally forced herself to get ready for bed. She checked on each of the children, wondering how she could ever sleep while worrying that Gillian would once again be lured out of her bed by someone who didn't exist, urging her to wander into the woods. She recalled Gillian saying that her mama would keep her safe. Wren found great comfort in that. Bethia had apparently saved her daughter's life today. Knowing that an angel would watch out for Gillian when Wren had no awareness of a problem was a wondrous comfort indeed! But it didn't completely eradicate Wren's worry. Just before she crawled into her bed, she had the idea to get a ribbon and a little bell from a box of odds and ends in the back of a cupboard. The bell had once been purchased simply because Donnan had been fascinated with it while he'd been fussy and Wren had needed to finish her shopping. Now Wren tied the little bell to the door handle of Gillian's room, and she closed the door so that Gillian couldn't leave the room without that bell ringing. She wondered why she hadn't thought of it before. The idea felt inspired, but if it had been inspired before last night, they could have been spared today's drama. However, Wren thought, crawling into bed, if they hadn't experienced today's drama, they could not have experienced the miracle of knowing that Bethia had saved her daughter's life. Wren drifted to sleep thinking about that miracle, and trying *not* to think about the man who had led Gillian out the door and into the woods, only to leave her there, lost and wandering.

Wren was awakened twice in the night, once by Donnan and the other time by Anya. Each time she checked on Gillian by holding the bell to keep it from ringing while she turned the door handle. She found her daughter sleeping safely and sighed with gratitude and contentment before she went back to bed. When Wren woke to daylight, Gillian was still sleeping and Wren left her to do so, knowing she'd had a long day yesterday and she'd gotten to bed late.

Wren loved the normalcy of the new day in contrast to the previous one. She felt an acute sense of gratitude for her daughter's safety, and silently expressed that gratitude to God each time it occurred to her. She also felt a keen appreciation for the miracle that had saved Gillian's life. She thanked God for that as well. But intermixed with her gratitude was a deep concern for Gillian's mental health. And she asked God for guidance and discernment, and especially that He might give them another miracle and simply heal Gillian's mind so that she might not have to suffer the things her mother had suffered.

In the afternoon, while the two younger children were napping, Wren made a point to leave Patricia to listen for the little ones while she took a walk around the yard with Gillian, hoping to be able to talk to her some more about what had happened yesterday so that she could gain some insight and understanding that might help her know how to contend with this. For at least the thousandth time since Ian had left, she desperately wished that he was here to assist her in parenting their children. While she and Gillian walked slowly, hand in hand beneath the trees, Wren prayed silently and searched for the right words to use in speaking to a four-year-old about the strange events of the previous day. She decided to just come straight to the point.

"Yesterday was a very difficult day for us. Ye must have been frightened out in the woods all that time."

"I was a little bit, but Mama was with me. And she told me that Brother Montgomery would find me."

Wren stopped walking and looked down at Gillian. "Your mama called him Brother Montgomery? Before he found ye there?"

"Yes," Gillian said as if she couldn't understand her mother's confusion.

For a long moment Wren wondered if Gillian had heard Brother Montgomery mention his name following the rescue and had simply taken the opportunity to elaborate on her story in ways that weren't entirely true. Wren sat down on the grass and urged Gillian to sit where they could look directly at each other. Wren said with patience, "Ye understand the difference between telling the truth and telling a lie."

"I would never tell a lie!" Gillian sounded insulted.

"Good, I'm very glad t' hear it. I'd like ye t' tell me again what yer angel mama said about Brother Montgomery."

"She said if I sat and waited there under the tree that was kind of crooked that Brother Montgomery would find me there and take me home. She said that he was one of Papa's friends in London. She said that Papa found him in the dark when he was sick, and then Papa gave him a book, and then Brother Montgomery came to America on a boat, and it was like the boat that we came to America on. I was born on the boat, and my mama died on the boat. That's why you and Papa take care of me until I can be with my real mama again."

Wren was utterly speechless, and too astonished to cry the tears that seemed to be backing up in her head. Her little Gillian had just accurately stated facts about Ian's interaction with Brother Montgomery that Wren knew from Ian's letters, but she had never told them to Gillian. She'd also stated facts about her own birth and her mother's death that she couldn't have possibly known. Since Gillian had never specifically asked questions about where and when she was born, Wren had never talked about it. They were difficult memories for Wren. She'd always known that eventually Gillian would need to know the truth, and she had always believed that she would know when the time was right. Now Wren never had to dread telling Gillian about her real mother. She knew the truth, and she had taken it in with perfect ease. But then, being taught *any* truth by an angel would surely be easier to accept. She had to silently add the point that it would entirely depend on whether the person being taught actually believed in angels, or trusted what they had to say. Laman and Lemuel in the Book of Mormon certainly hadn't learned anything from the angels they had been privileged to see.

Gillian was oblivious to Wren's astonishment, distracted by a butterfly that was flitting around nearby. She jumped up and began to chase it, trying to catch it in her hands and giggling with each failed attempt. The butterfly finally moved on, and Gillian plopped herself down in Wren's lap. Now that Wren had been allowed a few minutes to gather her thoughts and try to take in the miracle unfolding before her, she was able to say, "Do ye know what a miracle is, my sweetheart?"

"Jesus does miracles," she said, equating the word with stories she'd been told from the Bible.

"That's right. A miracle is something that can't be explained as normal in the ways of the world. Only God can perform a miracle. So we know that when a miracle happens, God's hand is in our lives."

"Jesus is God," Gillian said.

"That's right," Wren said again. "Ye're a very smart young lady. And our Heavenly Father is God also."

"Heavenly Father and Jesus came to talk to Brother Joseph."

Wren laughed softly, wondering if the child's remarkable understanding of life, and her excessive maturity, would remain with her throughout the course of her life. "That's right," Wren said still again, then the blossoming of hope on behalf of Gillian's forthcoming life was dampened by thoughts of her concerns. She hugged Gillian tightly as if doing so might protect her from the possible illness in her mind that had already begun to manifest itself. Since the child was sitting still and seemed content for the moment on Wren's lap, she took the opportunity to say, "Could you tell me more about the man who told you to unlock the door."

"Mama said he was a *bad* man!" Gillian said with unusual vehemence. "He was a dark man!"

"Dark?" Wren asked, not understanding.

"Mama was light. The man was dark. Mama told me that I could see the dark and the light and I would know what was dark and what was light. The man was dark."

Gillian giggled at the sight of another butterfly. Or perhaps it was the same one come back to play some more. The child jumped up and began running about the yard while Wren tried to understand what had just been said. Realizing she only felt more confused, her fear for Gillian's well-being increased. When Bethia had been alive, one of the imaginary people in her life could have certainly been classified as *dark* or *bad.* There was some reassurance to think that if Gillian could see her angel mother, who would help protect her, and help her discern these things, then perhaps the disease could be more manageable for Gillian than it had been for Bethia. But it still deeply troubled Wren, and she wished once again that Ian was here to help her figure out what to do.

Certain that Gillian was not interested in any more conversation on the matter right now, Wren got pen and paper and started writing a letter to Ian in which she told him of the drama of the previous day and her concerns over the situation. She hated the fact that it would take so many weeks for him to receive the letter, and the same amount of time for his letter to come back to her. But given the possibility that the problem might not be any closer to a solution then than it was now, she earnestly sought her husband's advice. He loved Gillian as much as she did, and he'd also been keenly aware of Bethia's challenges. No one else knew the details of the situation better than Ian.

That night after the children were put to bed—the bell in place on the door handle to Gillian's room—Wren knelt beside her own bed and prayed fervently on behalf of her dear Ian, and on behalf of her children. She put extra effort and focus into asking for help and guidance in regard to this situation with Gillian. When her prayer was done, Wren felt inclined to read from the Book of Mormon. She'd already done so *before* her prayer, but she gave in to the inclination and picked up the book once she'd made herself comfortable on pillows stacked against the headboard of the bed.

Wren opened the book, thumbing idly through pages for a few minutes while her mind was anywhere but with a desire to read. She finally settled on a page, and almost immediately her eyes were drawn to phrases that seemed almost to be illuminated, whereas the rest of the page seemed to be only a blur of words. Wren had to read the words multiple times before their meaning sank into her heart with such force that she had to exhale a burst of hot air to counteract the impact. *And again, to another, the beholding of angels and ministering spirits; . . . And all these gifts come by the Spirit of Christ; and they come unto every man severally, according as he will. And I would exhort you, my beloved brethren, that ye remember that every good gift cometh of Christ.*

While Wren was trying to consider if the implication could be what it seemed to be, an impression came strongly to her mind, accompanied by the rush of a chill that warmed rather than cooled her. *Gillian is not ill. She has a wonderful gift that will always keep her safe. There is no need to worry. I will always watch over her.*

Wren wondered if the words had come from God or from her sister. Then she realized that either way the words had come through the power of the Holy Ghost, and therefore it didn't matter. The message was the same. And she felt the truth of that message fill her entire being with warmth. The miracle of these experiences blossomed inside her, and she wept with joy and gratitude. She got out of bed and finished her letter to Ian with the explanation of what she had just learned and her happiness in being able to tell him that he had no need to worry about Gillian, and neither did she. Everything was going to be all right. Even though Wren didn't fully understand everything that had happened and why, she trusted that *God* knew and understood it, and He would make certain that Gillian was well. Wren needed to trust the miraculous answer she'd been given and replace her fears of the unknown with faith that God would fulfill His promise that He would watch over Gillian.

The following day when the children were occupied playing and would not overhear the conversation, Wren shared with Patricia all that she had learned the previous evening, and the miracle of having her prayer answered. She was surprised to hear Patricia say that her own mother had experienced some very strange things in regard to evil spirits—dark moods and feelings without any logical explanation, and strange happenings among the family. Wren knew that every member of Patricia's family had died as a result of the persecution of the Saints, either directly or indirectly. Prior to marrying Ward, Patricia had been deeply traumatized by the events in her life. But Ward's love, combined with the healing power of the Savior, had healed Patricia in ways that were impossible to fully grasp. Wren had seen the transformation in this woman, and she was also well aware of Patricia's keen wisdom and insight on spiritual matters. She had personally witnessed the best and worst of what could occur when good people embraced a righteous cause. The windows of heaven had been opened among the Saints. Many miracles and wonders had occurred, many mysteries of God had been revealed, both through the Prophet and to righteous individuals. But Patricia pointed out something that Wren already knew, but had never before considered in the way that was being implied. "'There must needs be opposition in all things,'" she said, quoting the prophet Lehi from the Book of

Mormon. "As I see it, nothing good is going to happen in this world without Satan unleashing something equivalently evil. Of course, that's all part of the plan. We came to this world to be tried and tested, and that couldn't happen without those opposing forces. What we need to remember is that one-third of the host of heaven followed after Satan, and those spirits are keen on distracting us and keeping us from our purpose."

"What are ye saying?" Wren asked, trying to piece this together with what she'd said about her mother and the present situation with little Gillian.

"The Book of Mormon makes it very clear that angels minister unto the children of men . . . through the power of the Holy Ghost . . . under the direction of the Savior."

"Which makes perfect sense with Gillian seeing her mother . . . and what I read in the Book of Mormon last night. It said that some people have the gift t' behold angels and ministering spirits . . . and I felt the truth of it; that's the reason Gillian is able t' see her mother."

"I agree," Patricia said, and Wren was pleased. It wasn't that she doubted what she'd felt, but Patricia was wise and had more practical experience with gospel principles. If Patricia had told her this was nonsense, it might have been difficult to sort out what was going on. "The scriptures also tell us that some people have the gift of the discerning of spirits. It's in the Bible as well as in our modern-day scripture. What need would there be to discern spirits if they were all good? There are obviously evil spirits about us as much as there are good ones. Just because we can't see or hear or feel them doesn't mean they aren't there. But my mother, she had such a gift; not quite as keen as your little Gillian, but she had a gift, nevertheless. She could sense them about her. She knew things that she could not have known without such a gift; things that kept us safe and gave us strength. But she admitted that she could not be aware of the angels around her without also being aware of the evil spirits as well. At first my father was concerned that Mama was being deceived, that no such thing could be possible. Brother Joseph assured my parents that the scriptures make it very clear how to discern good from evil, and that as long as Mama was using the guidance of the scriptures in understanding what was happening, she could know for herself that it was a gift from God to be used for good. Brother Parley also had much to say on the subject."

"Brother Parley?"

"Parley P. Pratt. What an inspired man! He's helped a great many people understand the strange happenings that can only be attributed to angels and spirits, and how to discern the good from the evil."

They talked for a while longer, and Wren felt deeply intrigued. Patricia guided her to many references in the scriptures that supported what she was saying, which helped immensely in understanding what was happening to Gillian. It became clear to Wren that while Gillian's gift should be carefully guided, it was not something to be afraid of.

That night, Wren reread many of the passages she and Patricia had discussed, and she prayed fervently to feel peace over the matter if indeed Gillian had a special gift. Wren *did* feel peace, the same kind of peace she'd felt many, many times in answers to prayers. She'd come to know and recognize that feeling well, and she knew for herself that it was not a feeling that could be counterfeited by an evil source. The next morning she woke up feeling like she needed to try to speak to Gillian again, even though she wasn't certain what needed to be said. Trusting that the Spirit would guide the conversation, Wren waited for a time when they were alone while the younger children were napping. Most disconcerted by the idea that her daughter might have been lured out of the house and into danger by some kind of evil being, Wren said carefully, "Ye told me yer angel mama told ye that the man ye saw was bad and dark. Have ye ever seen any other people that are bad and dark?"

"Yes," Gillian said as if it were nothing. "No one can see them but me."

Wren felt a sudden enlightenment as she realized how much Gillian was prone to speaking to *imaginary friends*. At first it had been attributed to a vivid imagination, and then Wren had wondered, but had tried not to think about the possibility that it meant she had her mother's illness. Now Wren wondered how much her daughter could see spirits around her—both good and evil—and whether her conversations were actually with them.

Wren cleared her throat gently and went on. "Ye said yer mama told ye that ye could see the difference between the light and the dark."

"There are light people and dark people."

"Have ye seen dark people around here?" Wren asked, feeling chilled.

"Not since Mama told me how t' make them go away."

"And how do ye do that?" Wren asked.

"I just tell them to go away," Gillian said with a sudden firmness. "I tell them that Jesus doesn't want them here!" She sighed and smiled. "And they go away. They're afraid of Jesus. They know He is stronger than they are. Jesus isn't mad at them. He just doesn't want them to bother us."

Wren took all of that in, marveling at how Gillian's understanding of these things correlated exactly with the doctrine she'd read in the scriptures, and with the teachings of Apostles and prophets that Patricia had shared with her.

"That's right, my sweetheart," Wren said, feeling calm and deeply comforted. "Jesus is stronger and more good and more light than anything or anyone. He will always take care of us."

Chapter Nine
Angels

That night when Wren tucked Gillian into bed, the child said, "There's no need to keep the bell on my door anymore, Mama. My angel mama told me that now that ye know about the miracles, I won't walk in my sleep anymore." She rolled over to go to sleep as if to add an exclamation point to what she'd said. Wren kissed the top of her head and extinguished the lamp. On her way out of the room, she looked at the bell on the door handle and felt tempted to leave it there . . . just in case. Then, in her mind, it became a test of faith . . . a test of believing whether or not the things that Gillian had said and experienced were true. Wren removed the bell and put it away, knowing that her sister was watching out for Gillian from the other side of the veil, just as surely as Wren was watching out for her here.

* * * * *

As autumn began to settle into London, Ian realized he and Ward had been there for more than a year, and he found himself unexpectedly and terrifically homesick. He kept working and he kept praying—just as he always did. But the work wasn't going very well; the people they were trying to help only wanted free handouts and had no interest in anything to do with God. And the praying often seemed to be halted somewhere between his efforts and reaching God's ears. He and Ward talked it through—practically every day. It turned out they were *both* feeling much the same way. In spite of fasting, and prayer, and continued efforts, the discouragement and homesickness only seemed to worsen. They discussed the possibility that perhaps it was time to move on, but they both felt strongly that they needed to remain in London for the time being.

"Apparently God is still there," Ian said when they'd both agreed on the answer. "At least He's showing Himself enough to give us *that* answer, even if it feels like nothing else is working."

"Of course He's still there," Ward said. "You know well enough Joseph's stories of being in Liberty Jail. If our dear Brother Joseph, and those who were with him in such deplorable circumstances, could go so many, many weeks wondering if God was still listening, then surely we are not above the same kind of feelings in our own trials."

"It amazes me how you can do that," Ian said.

"Do what?"

"Always put things into perspective in a way that manages to make me feel better."

"Do you?" Ward asked. "Feel better?"

"More humble, at least," Ian admitted.

"There's also Job, you know," Ward said.

"What about him?"

"Job lost everything, then he spent forty chapters trying to understand the reasons. Of course it's clear that he never lost his testimony or his faith, but he still struggled to understand his trials. At the end of the book of Job, he was given back double of everything he lost, and he realized that God had been there all along. At least that's how I see it."

"There you go again," Ian said.

"What?"

"Giving me perspective."

Ian was grateful for the perspective, but he continued to fight discouragement hour by hour. And he knew that Ward was struggling too. He awoke one morning to see thick rain outside his window and skies so heavy and gray that they resembled his mood far too much. The thought of even going out into such weather in an attempt to get someone—anyone—to listen to a message that most people were not presently interested in, made Ian pull the covers up over his head— literally. He began to pray in that very position, but he didn't feel like his prayers were very articulate. He could only manage to come up with brief phrases of pleading for help in order to keep going.

In the midst of Ian's prayer, a distinctly clear memory of his father appeared in his head, seemingly out of nowhere. It was as if, in his mind, he were back at Brierley, sitting next to his father, with his father's arm around his shoulders, saying with firm kindness, "Everything will be all right, Ian." The words came as clearly to his mind as the image of his father's face. Something close to a jolt hit Ian in the center of his chest, as if to alert his heart to the fact that what had just happened in his mind was not his imagination. He gasped just before an unexplainable warmth radiated out from where that jolt had struck him.

"Thank you, Father," he said aloud, thinking as he said it that his words had double meaning, and that God—and the angel of his earthly father—would both understand that meaning; they would know his gratitude was to both of them.

Ian got out of bed with some enthusiasm and found the passages in the Book of Mormon about the ministering of angels—some of his favorites—in Moroni, chapter 7. As he read he knew once again, with an added personal witness, that his father had been granted permission to make himself known through the veil in order to buoy Ian up at this time. He was struck with the impression that his father was there beside him still, and that he likely had been a great deal, and that he would continue to be with him—even if Ian couldn't feel it. He wept with joy and gratitude and went to his knees to offer his thanks and praise to God for giving him such a miracle.

As soon as Ward was awake, Ian shared his experience. Ward was encouraged by Ian's words, and they ventured out into the rain with the hope of finding at least one lost sheep that would have an interest in joining the fold. It was nearly dark before they found a young man who was clearly in need of a good meal and a warm place to sleep. The boy was willing to help out at Edith's inn, and he *did* show an interest in the things that Ian and Ward wanted to teach him. It turned out that he couldn't read, so Ian and Ward taught him how. It wasn't the first time they'd done so, and the Book of Mormon was a great book to use in teaching a person to read. In spite of Ward's blindness, he had learned to read before he'd lost his eyesight, and he was very good at helping a person learn the sounds that each letter made once Ian had taught the letters of the alphabet.

Ian received a letter from Wren that contained the account of a remarkable experience regarding their little Gillian. He felt the truth of the miracles burn inside him as he read what Wren had written, and it added to his confidence that his father was with him in this journey.

The following day they went for their usual visit with Mrs. Montgomery. Once again she provided them with a lovely meal and they engaged in pleasant conversation with her. She declared that she was still working on reading that book, and she knew enough about the stories in it that they knew she was telling the truth. But she didn't have much interest in religious conversation.

Later that night, Ian and Ward discussed whether they should continue their visits to Mrs. Montgomery. They made it a matter of prayer and agreed a couple of days later that they should keep visiting her.

The young man they were teaching learned to read rather quickly. He read the Book of Mormon for himself, usually in a corner of Edith's back room in between doing whatever she asked him to do to earn his keep: three meals a day and a place to sleep on the storage room floor with a couple of blankets and a tolerable pillow. It took him the entire winter to read the book, but long before he'd finished it he knew it was true and wanted to be baptized. When spring came, they put him on a ship to America, and he promised to see Ian and Ward again someday in Nauvoo. Ian was thrilled to be sending yet one more convert on his way to the promised land. But each time he said good-bye to one of these people, he longed to be going along. In seeing this young man off, he was also bidding farewell to their final copy of the Book of Mormon. The portmanteau was empty—and worn and tattered enough to be thrown in the trash. But Ian had accomplished his quest in that regard.

Ian was surprised one morning to wake up with the distinct impression that it was time to leave London, and that they should go directly to Brierley.

"Leave?" he said into the empty silence of his room. He felt surprisingly mixed emotions over the prospect. Moving on meant getting closer to the day they could return home. Going to Brierley meant a familiar place and the opportunity to see his family. But Ian felt an unsettling concern for the impoverished people in this area who had so many needs. He knew he couldn't solve all their problems, but he would have liked to solve some of them. Edith was enjoying her opportunity to help care for those in need, but Ian and Ward had spent nearly everything they had in covering the expenses for the charity project. Faced with the prospect of needing to travel, Ian got out of bed to look where the money was kept. He managed the money for both himself and Ward, although they regularly sat together and mutually discussed their accounts and how their money was being spent. Ian was not entirely surprised, but he was certainly disheartened to realize how little they had left.

While sharing breakfast with Ward, he felt hesitant to bring up the money situation as much as he felt hesitant to bring up his feeling that they should be moving on. Therefore, he was surprised, though he shouldn't have been, to hear Ward say, "I feel like it's time to go to Brierley, but I'm not sure we can afford to get there."

Ian chuckled and said, "I feel the same way, and you're absolutely right."

"Are you saying what I think you're saying?" Ward asked.

"We're almost completely broke, my friend. We have enough to settle our accounts with Edith and perhaps stay here for a few more days."

Ian expected Ward to reprimand him for not keeping better track of their funds, or for not being more careful in his financial planning. But a second didn't pass before Ward said, "Then we might have to find some work to do in order to earn more funds before moving on. I'm certain our needs will be met . . . one way or another."

"Yes, I'm sure they will be," Ian said, but he didn't feel convinced.

After a day of working as usual, Ian lay awake far into the night, praying and pondering the situation. When his attempts to sleep became nothing but aggravating, he got up and lit a lamp, opening the Bible to read from it. He missed being able to read from the Book of Mormon, but he felt peace in knowing *why* he didn't have a copy. It still warmed something in him to think that Brother Givan and Brother Tyler had been willing to let Ian have one of their own copies of the book so that he could have it in his hands when he needed it. Ian liked to think that his own personal copy had perhaps made a comparable difference in someone's life.

Ian barely had the Bible opened before he felt an impression to read his wife's letters instead. He'd read and reread them so many times that he'd almost worn them out. But he heeded the prompting and took them out again, untying the ribbon that held them together in a bundle. He read for more than an hour before her words leapt off the page and into his heart as the obvious answer to his prayers. Everything changed in an instant. He didn't feel fear or regret or trepidation. He felt completely comforted and determined to press forward, knowing that all would be well. How could he feel any other way when he read, in his wife's delicate hand: *Always remember, my darling, what it says in Mark, chapter 6. "And he called unto him the twelve, and began to send them forth by two and two . . . And commanded them that they should take nothing for their journey . . . no scrip, no bread, no money in their purse. . . . And he said unto them, In what place soever ye enter into an house, there abide till ye depart from that place."*

And also remember, she wrote, *the wonderful words of the Savior in Matthew, chapter 6. "Therefore I say unto you, Take no thought for your life, what ye shall eat, or what ye shall drink; nor yet for your body, what ye shall put on. Is not the life more than meat, and the body than raiment? Behold the fowls of the air: for they sow not, neither do they reap, nor gather into barns; yet your heavenly Father feedeth them. Are ye not much better than they? . . . Consider the lilies of the field, how they grow; they toil not, neither do they spin: And yet I say unto you, That even Solomon in all his glory was not arrayed like one of these. Wherefore, if God so clothe the grass of the field, which to day is, and to morrow is cast into the oven, shall he not much more clothe you, O ye of little faith? Therefore take no thought, saying, What shall we eat? or, What shall we drink? or, Wherewithal shall we be clothed? . . . for your heavenly Father knoweth that ye have need of all these things. But seek ye first the kingdom of God, and his righteousness; and all these things shall be added unto you. Take therefore no thought for the morrow: for the morrow shall take thought for the things of itself."*

The following morning Ian shared the passages with Ward, and they both felt encouraged. They informed Edith that they were almost out of money and would be moving on as soon as they could afford to do so. They were reassured by her insistence that whether they had money or not, she would see them housed and fed until they could earn funds to move on. Ian and Ward both felt inexpressibly grateful, and they told her so. But it only made her cry, and they realized that she would miss them terribly when they left—as they would miss her—and that she would probably provide room and board indefinitely just to have their company and be a part of the projects they had involved her in.

On a typically foggy London day, Ian and Ward determined that they had been living on Edith's charity for more than a week; they had been unable to find any work that either of them had the knowledge— or ability—to do. They reluctantly got freshened up after a day of job hunting to go to their scheduled dinner appointment with Mrs. Montgomery. They found her in good spirits, but she reported that she'd had the doctor in twice that week to see to some ailments that were worsening with age. They politely inquired over her ailments and heard a detailed account. The subject of the Book of Mormon didn't come up at all. But they did tell her they were planning to leave London as soon as they earned the funds to do so. And she asked about Edith, since they had told Mrs. Montgomery about this warm and unique woman and the projects they had been working on together on behalf of the poor and destitute. Mrs. Montgomery was apparently entertained by their reports of Edith's antics with her customers and with Ward and Ian.

After they'd finished eating their supper, Mrs. Montgomery stood up from the table and said, "Come with me. There's something I want to show you."

"Very well," Ian said and guided Ward's hand to his shoulder so they could follow Mrs. Montgomery into a very dusty library. Ian watched the old woman take a key from a desk drawer, which she then turned in a lock on a small cupboard situated among the bookshelves. From out of the cupboard she withdrew an ornate gold and white box covered with carvings of cherubs and floral patterns.

Mrs. Montgomery put the box into Ian's hands. She said, "I want you boys to have this. I don't want you to open it until you get back to your rooms. Promise me."

"I promise," Ian and Ward both said at the same time, even though Ward couldn't see what she had given them.

"It's a lovely box," Ian told him and put Ward's hand on it so he could feel it.

"Oh, it is lovely," Ward said.

"Are you going to tell us what's in it?" Ian asked.

"No," she said. "And I don't expect to see either of you again. I've enjoyed your visits." She actually sounded a trifle emotional. "You're both fine young men, and I wish you all the best. I'm glad to have that book you've given me. I want you to know that it's become very precious to me, and I thank you for it."

"I'm so glad to know that," Ian said. "We too have enjoyed our visits, and we thank you for your kindness to us."

"I would hope," Ward said, "that the book will continue to bring you some happiness in your life."

"I'm certain it will," she said, "although I don't expect to be living much longer."

Ian wondered if there was more to her *ailments* than she had said, or if she was simply being pessimistic.

"The two of you should go," she said. "It's getting late and I'm getting tired. Besides, I hate long good-byes. Come along."

She led the way to the entry hall and opened the front door herself. "Take good care of yourselves, then," she said.

"And the same to you," Ian said, impulsively kissing her on the cheek.

She smiled in a way he'd never seen before, then turned to Ward. Ian guided Ward's hand into Mrs. Montgomery's. They were both surprised when she put it to her face, but it allowed Ward to know *where* her face was so that he too could kiss her on the cheek.

"God bless you both," Mrs. Montgomery said.

"And you," Ward said as she shooed them out the door.

Ward and Ian had little to say to each other on the way home. Ian let Ward hold the box on his lap in the carriage, and he studied its intricacies with his fingers.

"What do you think is in it?" Ward asked.

"I'm not sure, but I've got a fair idea."

"Yes, I think we both know what's in it."

Ian didn't comment. If it was indeed what they both suspected, then the evidence of miracles in their life felt too great to hold, and he wasn't certain he could speak of it without starting to cry like a baby.

Once they were back at the inn and alone in their little parlor, Ward said, "You must open it. I can't bear the suspense."

Ian set the box on the little table and took a deep breath before he turned the little latch and lifted the ornate lid. "Merciful heaven!" he muttered.

"Is it . . ." Ward could only get out the two words.

"Yes, it's money, but it's . . ." he laughed softly, "it's a great deal of money, Ward." He laughed again and Ward laughed with him. "God truly *does* work in mysterious ways!"

"He truly does," Ward agreed.

The two men shared a brotherly embrace, then got on their knees to thank God for this miracle. They counted the money and were stunned by Mrs. Montgomery's generosity. They prayed together about what exactly to do with it, and they prayed again the following morning. A mutual decision came strongly and firmly, and they knew the answer was clear. They wrote a simple note to Mrs. Montgomery, expressing their gratitude and informing her of how they planned to use the money. They wished her all the best and told her that they were certain God would bless her for this contribution to helping those in need.

With the note delivered, Ward and Ian settled their account with Edith, then they paid for passage by carriage to Scotland and purchased some things they would need for the journey. They set aside a small amount of money to take with them—just as they'd been directed to do—just enough to get them comfortably to Brierley. It was as if the Lord was making it clear to them that He would provide other means for them when the time came, but for now, they only needed to get to Brierley. It was an act of faith to be willing to turn over the entire balance of the money to Edith for her to use as she saw fit in caring for the poor.

Their final matter of business before departing was to put the beautiful box into Edith's hands. She nearly fainted when she opened it. They briefly told her the story, hugged her as if she were their mother, then hurried away with Mrs. Montgomery's sentiment uppermost in their minds: they hated long good-byes.

* * * * *

Ian felt the excitement of a child and the dread of a prodigal son as the scenery passing by the carriage windows became startlingly familiar. He reminded himself that although he'd once left home as a prodigal, he'd returned home, mended bridges, and made amends. His leaving to go to America had not been a result of any immaturity or selfishness, and he'd exchanged proper good-byes with his loved ones. But he knew they'd not wanted him to go, and the thought of facing them came with mixed feelings at best.

Ian pressed a hand absently over his chest in a way that had become an unconscious habit. Through the fabric of his shirt and waistcoat he could feel the key that was hanging over his heart. Many times through each day, and especially while going to sleep at night, he'd fingered the key, recalling clearly Wren's words when she'd given it to him. He'd imagined the hope of that moment when he would be able to use it to open the front door of his home and once again hold Wren in his arms.

When he knew he was getting closer to the valley of his upbringing, Ian's excitement at returning home began to smother any negative emotion or fear he might have felt. He loved describing the details of everything he saw to Ward. The view was so deeply familiar, but it took on an ethereal, almost timeless quality as he realized how nothing had changed. *He* had changed. Just as when he'd left home before, he was certainly not returning as the same person. But the agelessness of the Highlands was magnificent simply for the fact that it was completely unchanged. The trees might have grown just a little bigger. Other than that, it was all the same. And describing to Ward what he saw allowed Ian to take all of it into himself in a way that was more deeply profound. He felt certain that his memories of his homeland would become even more clear in the future, simply for having described them aloud. He determined then that he would write those details in his journal or his letters to Wren—or both— so that they would be preserved, and so that he might help her remember their homeland in a way that *she* might have forgotten, as well.

As the hired carriage came closer to Brierley, Ian became afflicted with an unexpected tingling of nerves that rushed from his throat to his belly and back again. But his only negative thought was knowing that he was returning home broke. He reminded himself that he and Ward had discussed the matter extensively and they were both in firm agreement that they would say nothing to his family about their financial situation. Instead, they would simply press forward with faith, taking to heart the promises made in the scriptures that their needs would be met. He and Ward also both felt strongly that Brierley was their last stop on this journey. They didn't know how long they would stay, but they did know that once they mutually felt compelled to leave, they would head directly to Liverpool in order to get on a ship and return home. Of course, they needed money in order to do that, and therefore they needed to be patient and allow the means to do so to present itself. In the meantime, Ian felt relaxed and comfortable with the prospect of spending some time with his family. And just maybe a miracle might take place and one or more of his loved ones would be willing to hear and accept the things that had irrevocably changed Ian's life.

The only other thought that bothered Ian about this situation was the fact that they didn't have a single Book of Mormon left in their possession. He'd many times in the past considered mailing one or more copies to his family, but it had never felt right. Then when he'd realized he would be coming home, he had imagined being able to give copies to his mother and brother, and anyone else who might be interested. Given the enormity of a household like Brierley, there was a tiny society of household servants in and of itself, and Ian had once been on familiar terms with most of them. He was looking forward to seeing a great many people again, and had the hope of sharing the gospel message. But without a single Book of Mormon in hand, he wasn't quite sure how to go about it. This too he had discussed with Ward, and as always, he'd been humbled by Ward's faith and positive attitude. Just as they were exercising their faith that they would find the means to meet their financial needs, they also needed to have faith that they would be able to share the message they had come to share, with or without the Book of Mormon in hand.

"We can always mail copies after we get back," Ward had said. Ian knew that was true, but it just wasn't the same as personally putting it into someone's hands. Perhaps his own experience of having the book put into his hands, and knowing how it had affected him, made this approach feel more important—and more powerful. But there was nothing to be done about it, and he knew without a doubt that every Book of Mormon had been placed into hands that needed to have it. He couldn't regret not having a copy now when he looked at it that way.

When the carriage rolled onto MacBrier land, Ian's nervous excitement increased. He wished that Ward could see the beauty of the tenant farms, which he found difficult to describe. But he did his best to do so anyway, and Ward eagerly expressed his interest in every word picture Ian painted. When the castlelike home called Brierley came into view, Ian caught his breath. He found it difficult to believe that it could actually be bigger, more beautiful, more magnificent than he had remembered. He attempted to describe it to Ward, not holding back his enthusiasm and exuberance. Ward himself had come from a very well-to-do family and had been blessed with a very large inheritance, which offered sufficient financial support for himself and his family for the rest of his life, provided it was used wisely. Ian could say the same for himself. But it seemed that Ward was truly realizing for the first time, given Ian's description of the house where he'd grown up and its surrounding properties, that Ian's upbringing had been much more extravagant than Ward's had been. Ward had known that Ian was the son of the Earl of Brierley—a position that Ian's brother had inherited—but it seemed that the true meaning of that had only sunk in now.

"I suppose while we're here," Ward said, "you'll be reverting to your old surname."

"It would be proper, I believe," Ian said. "Trying to use the new one would only cause a great deal of confusion, I fear."

"Provided you can remember and not slip up."

"Yes, that would be somewhat awkward."

Ian thought of his reasons for changing his surname from the traditional Scottish MacBrier to the more American-friendly Brierley, in honor of the home where he'd been raised. He and Wren had made the decision together, and his family was aware of the change and had not seemed offended—at least as far as they could tell through the exchange of letters. But while he was actually *at* Brierley, associating with people who had only known him as Ian MacBrier, it made sense to simply keep to his original name and not try to offer any explanations that were not pertinent to the present situation.

The carriage halted near the side of Brierley, since Ian preferred to go in a side door near the kitchen as opposed to entering at the front, which might require him being formally announced and treated as company. Ian settled with the driver, gathered their very minimal luggage, and guided Ward through a door that he'd once gone in and out of multiple times a day. He was met in the hall by a maid he didn't recognize who had apparently noticed the appearance of a strange carriage and was doing her duty in protecting her assigned territory.

"May I help ye, sir?" she asked.

"Yes, you may," he said. "I'm Ian MacBrier, and I've come to see my family, but I would prefer to surprise them."

"I'll need to consult with the housekeeper," the maid said as if she feared that Ian was actually some kind of criminal with ill intent and she would need to clear this strange request.

Ian motioned toward the nearby kitchen, from where he could hear familiar sounds and familiar voices—among them the very housekeeper being discussed. "Why don't we just speak to Mrs. Boyle here and now and clear this up, then, shall we?"

Ian entered the kitchen without waiting for a response from the maid. Ward followed with his hand on Ian's shoulder. The maid followed the men into the room, seeming a bit flustered and concerned.

Ian was struck by the pleasant familiarity of the scene before him. He recognized not only Mrs. Boyle, but the head cook, her usual helpers, and a couple of stable hands who were eating their lunch while visiting with some maids who were also eating. Ian recognized every face in the room, except for the maid he'd encountered in the hall. It was just his luck to be greeted by the only employee that had been newly hired in his absence.

"If I didn't know better," Ian said loudly enough to draw attention to his presence, "I'd think you'd all been sitting here gossiping every minute for all the years I've been gone."

All faces turned toward him, and there was a long moment of stunned silence before Mrs. Boyle exclaimed, "Bless my soul! It's our Ian come back to us!" She crossed the room and hugged him as if he were her own son, but Ian had expected it. He'd always made himself comfortable among the servants, and had grown to care very much for some of them—and the other way around. From the corner of his eye he noticed the new maid relaxing now that she knew Ian met with Mrs. Boyle's approval.

"We didn't know that we'd ever see you again," Mrs. Boyle said.

"I wasn't sure myself," Ian said. "But here I am." As others were gathering around for proper greetings, he hurried to introduce his traveling companion. "Hello, everyone. This is my dear friend, Ward. Just so you don't have to wonder, he is unable to see. But he's fairly tolerable company once you get used to him." This provoked a round of chuckles from the servants and a playful slug to Ian's shoulder from Ward.

"How do you get such a perfect aim when you can't even see me?" Ian asked.

"I can *hear* you," Ward said with a smile.

Ian received hugs and handshakes from many people he'd once encountered on a daily basis, and everyone was kind to Ward and greeted him with friendly words and warm acceptance. A couple of maids guided him to the table and asked if he would like something to eat.

"He's got a beautiful wife back in America," Ian said to the maids. "So, don't be *too* nice to him."

"I do indeed," Ward said, "but I confess that whatever you're eating smells terribly good."

"Oh, let me get you a plate," the cook said eagerly, then turned to Ian. "And what about you, my boy?"

"Thank you, but if it's all right with you, I think I'll leave my friend here in your care for a while, and I'll go and surprise my mother and my brother."

"Very good plan," Mrs. Boyle said, winking at Ian. "Lunch will be served for them in just a short while. I'll see that a place is set for you so you can eat with them."

Ian said to Ward, putting a hand on his shoulder, "Would you prefer to come with me now and join the family for—"

"I think I'm in very good hands," Ward said.

"Indeed he is!" the cook said in the same moment that a maid said, "We'll take very good care of him!"

"Why don't you enjoy a little time with your family," Ward said, "and I'll see you later."

"Very well," Ian said. "These people will know where to find me if you need something." He then said specifically to Mrs. Boyle, "Is my room still—"

"Just as you left it," she said. "I'll have it aired out, and the guest room next to it for your friend."

"Thank you," Ian said. "That's exactly as I'd hoped. Perhaps if Ward here would like to rest before I come back, you could guide him to that room and just let him know where the important things are located. He can manage fine otherwise."

"I can indeed," Ward said and inhaled dramatically when a plate of food was put in front of him. "Now, if someone will just put a fork in my hand, I'll have everything I need."

"He's easy to please," Ian said, then he thanked everyone for their kindness and expressed again how good it was to see them all.

Chapter Ten
Brierley Revisited

Ian had a pretty good idea of where to find his mother during the time just preceding lunch. He hurried up the back stairs, down one hall and up another, until he came to the door of his mother's sitting room. Since the door was closed, he felt confident she was in there; otherwise it would have been left open. He lifted his hand to knock, reminded of a similar moment when he'd returned home after his years of aimless wandering. He felt less nervous about facing his mother now—only excitement in surprising her. But he also felt heartache in thinking that he couldn't surprise his father, wouldn't be *seeing* his father. Gavin MacBrier had passed away since Ian had left Scotland to go to America, but that was the very reason he'd been blessed with being able to feel his father's companionship during certain difficult moments of his journey.

Focusing on seeing his mother, he knocked at the door and immediately heard her call, "Come in."

Ian turned the knob and pushed open the door. Years fled unnoticed as he watched Anya MacBrier sitting near the window, focused on something she was stitching in a way that was so comfortably normal. Her simply styled blonde hair and pleasant countenance didn't appear to have changed at all.

"Hello, Mother," he said before she had a chance to finish another stitch. She paused abruptly, then looked up, as if she feared that her ears were deceiving her.

"Oh, Ian!" she gasped more than spoke and rushed toward him, her sewing falling to the floor unheeded when she stood up. She wrapped her arms around him and he did the same in return, briefly lifting her feet off the floor as he laughed with perfect delight. When he set her down she took his face into her hands, saying with tears in her eyes, "I thought I'd never see you again."

"I thought the same," he admitted, feeling a little emotional himself. "But here I am. God works in mysterious ways."

"He does indeed!" she said and took both his hands into hers, looking him up and down. "You don't look nearly so bedraggled as the last time you came home. In fact, you look quite well."

"I *am* well, Mother."

"Oh!" she said. "I just can't believe it! You're really here! And your family? Are they—"

"I'm afraid I came without them," he said. "I have a friend with me . . . for reasons we'll discuss at another time."

"Oh, I see," she said, clearly disappointed that she wouldn't see Wren and the children. But he'd expected her to feel this way. He was disappointed too. As impossible as it would have been for Wren to make this journey, with a new baby and two other children, he missed her every hour of every day.

Trying not to think about that, Ian said brightly, "You can meet my friend later on. He's being well cared for in the kitchen."

Anya's face showed some enlightenment. "Wren has written to tell me that you were traveling—doing missionary work, she said."

"That's right."

"I confess I've worried, not having received a letter from you personally for . . . well over a year now."

"Going on two," he said. "Wren assured me that she was keeping you informed."

"Vaguely," Anya said, sounding only mildly put out. "When she said *traveling,* I assumed she meant in America."

"I apologize for not letting you know sooner, Mother, but I've been in England for more than a year." He knew it was actually more than a year and a half, but he preferred making it sound a little more in his favor. "I knew that I would be coming here before going back home, but I wanted to surprise you. I didn't know for certain when it would be, and time for writing letters has been minimal, and . . . well, I'm here now."

"Yes, you are!" she said as if all had been forgiven instantly. But she was like that.

Ian guided her back to the little sofa where she'd been sitting and sat close beside her.

"I do hope you'll be staying long enough to make your visit worthwhile," she said, taking his hand.

"A few weeks, at least," he said, wondering how on earth he would ever acquire funds sufficient for him and Ward to leave at all. Recalling his commitment to faith on that account, he added, "I'm not certain when we'll leave exactly. Right now, I want to just sit with you and hear about everything that's happened while I've been away."

The first thing that came to Ian's mind was the death of his father, and he knew immediately that it was the first thing that had come to his mother's mind as well. When Ian had left here, Gavin MacBrier had been struggling with illness for quite some time, and there had been no way of knowing if he would hold on for years or go unexpectedly at any time. While Ian had been in New York, word had come of his father's death. It had been a few years now, and he and his mother had exchanged many letters, but it was naturally the greatest change that had taken place, and the one that had caused the most heartache.

Ian resisted his temptation to ignore what they were both thinking and begin a different topic. He took his mother's hand and said gently, "It must be very difficult for you . . . without Father."

He saw tears in her eyes just before she lowered them. "Yes, of course. He was the truest light in my life. He was an integral part of me."

"I'm certain he still is," Ian said.

"He'll always hold a very big place in my heart," she said. Ian agreed, but that's not what he meant.

Certain this was not the right time to bring up his spiritual beliefs—especially in regard to his father—he said, "You were always the truest light in *his* life." As an afterthought he added something he'd thought many times but had never made the effort to tell her. "I believe the example I saw in the love between my parents has surely helped me to be a better husband, and to appreciate what a very good wife Wren is to me."

"That's a very sweet thing to say," Anya said, putting a hand to his face.

"It's true."

"Wren is a *very* sweet girl."

"Yes, she is." Ian looked down; now he was the one fighting his emotions.

"You miss her."

"I miss her very much," Ian said and cleared his throat before he looked back at his mother.

"Then why this long separation from her?" Anya asked. "I'm thrilled to see you, Ian, but I'm not sure I understand the reasons that you've traveled all this way without your family."

"I would love to explain it to you," he said with a smile, "but not right now. I know that lunch will be on any minute, and I'm anxious to see Donnan and his family."

"Oh, of course," she said, glancing at the clock. She immediately rose to her feet, and Ian did the same, following her toward the door.

Anya hesitated and put a hand on Ian's arm. "Before we go down to lunch, there's something you should know."

Ian felt a chill at the same time a distinct memory rushed into his mind. When he'd returned home years ago following his hapless wandering, he'd come to this very room to see his mother. And before they'd left the room to go and speak to his father, she had wanted to tell him something, to give him some kind of warning. That was the moment she'd told him that his father had developed a health condition during Ian's absence—the same problem that had eventually taken his father's life after Ian had gone to America.

Ian tried now to remain in the present and hear what his mother needed to tell him, even though he couldn't shake the associated memory that cast a certain eeriness over the moment.

"What is it, Mother?" he asked gently, steeling himself for a blow, wondering what dreadful thing might have happened within the family that had not been communicated to him through letters.

"It's difficult to explain," she said. "Perhaps as you spend some time with your brother you'll be able to discern the problem. Perhaps you might be able to help *me* understand it better."

"I don't understand," Ian said, turning fully toward her, determined to get something less vague before he faced his brother again after all these years.

"It's nothing physical," she said. "Nothing medically viable. Donnan simply has not . . ."

"Has not what, Mother?" Ian pressed when she didn't finish.

"He has not dealt well with your father's death, Ian. He is hardly himself. He claims that everything is fine, but it's evident to both Lilias and myself that everything is *not* fine."

Ian felt another chill as he wondered if this opportunity to come home might have some meaning or purpose in it beyond what he'd imagined. Although, if his brother's wife and mother had not been able to help him, what made them think that Ian could possibly have any influence? He told himself he should have more faith in himself, or rather more faith in God's ability to use Ian as an instrument in His hands to do good. If Donnan needed help, then perhaps Ian could be the one to help facilitate it. Only time—and much prayer—would tell for certain.

For the moment, all Ian could think to say was, "I'll certainly be mindful of the situation."

"I hope you might be able to get through to him," Anya said as if she were placing every hope in him to completely change the situation.

"We'll just have to see, Mother," Ian said and took hold of her arm. "Now, come along. Donnan is probably wondering by now why there's an extra place set at the table, but no one would dare ruin the surprise."

On their way down the stairs, Anya smiled up at Ian and said, "How lovely to have you come home like this! What a wonderful surprise!"

"It's wonderful to be here," he said and smiled. "Most especially to see *you*!"

They entered the dining room to see Donnan sitting at the opposite end of the long table, looking toward the window. He was as blond as Ian was dark. They were close in height and build, but differing in features enough that they didn't necessarily look like brothers. He hadn't changed at all, except for a subtle darkness in his countenance that was indicative of what his mother had told him. Donnan's wife, Lilias, was sitting to her husband's right. She was as lovely as Ian remembered, with reddish-blonde hair and kind eyes. Ian knew the children were likely having lunch in the nursery with the nanny. Donnan and Lilias had a son just a little older than Gillian who had been born not too long before Ian and Wren had left for America. They also had a daughter that Ian knew was approximately two years old. And being raised along with Donnan and Lilias's children was little James.

James was the son of Ian's brother James, who had been killed in a senseless duel. James's death had been the tragic result of his own promiscuity. He'd been a good man in many respects, but he'd seemed to have a sick addiction to becoming inappropriately involved with women. The family had begged and pleaded with James over and over to put a stop to his immoral ways; they had all agreed it would be the undoing of him. In the end, it had undone him far worse than any of them could have ever imagined. He had become involved with the wife of an abusive and very powerful earl. When the earl had discovered his wife's affair, he had challenged James to a duel. Donnan and Ian had been with their brother when he'd been shot and left to bleed to death. It was one of the worst experiences of Ian's life. Then, some months later, a maid who had insisted on remaining anonymous had delivered an infant to the MacBrier family, along with a letter that explained how the child was a result of the affair, and the mother had died soon after she'd given birth. The earl wanted nothing to do with the child, but James's family had been thrilled to take little James in and give him all the love that the child's father was no longer alive to give.

Little James would be about five by now, and Ian felt anxious to see him again. He'd remained abreast of the milestones in the child's life through letters, and he knew that he had brought a great deal of joy into the house. Of course, as soon as James had been old enough to understand, he'd been taught that his parents were dead and that he was a cousin to Donnan's children. And perhaps some day, he would be told of the tragic events that had preceded his birth—but not until he had enough maturity to comprehend such things, and to be able to favorably balance the fact that he was loved, accepted, and cared for against past situations that he'd had no control over. Ian knew through letters that the community was aware of James's illegitimacy, but Gavin MacBrier had made it clear—by actually standing up to announce it in church, according to the story Ian had been told—that if he ever got wind of anyone gossiping about his grandson, or treating him unkindly, they would have to deal with him. Ian's father had never been anything but a kind and dignified man. But he'd also been a powerful and intimidating man, and he had a great deal of influence in the community. Anya had told Ian that Gavin's declaration had apparently worked, because people—for the most part—seemed to have completely forgotten that James's existence had a scandalous beginning.

Ian hoped to spend some time with the children before the day was over, but for now he was glad to be seeing his brother again for the first time in years.

"Look who showed up out of nowhere!" Anya announced as they entered the room.

Donnan and Lilias both turned to look in the same moment, but Ian was focused on his brother. Donnan's eyes widened, and his expression went from disinterested to astonished so abruptly that he seemed to lose his breath. He let out a strained chuckle that seemed more an effort to *catch* his breath, then he came to his feet and hurried around the table to receive Ian with a firm, brotherly embrace. The two held to each other for a long moment while Ian's mind went once again to the *last* time he'd come home. Donnan's initial greeting had been positive, but then he'd belted Ian in the jaw and expressed his anger over the way Ian had left home and the amount of time he'd been gone, leaving his family to worry and wonder. The circumstances were much different now, but Ian still knew that Donnan had not necessarily been pleased by Ian's departure, or the reasons for it. Donnan broke the embrace and took hold of Ian's shoulders and smiled, but even his obvious pleasure at seeing Ian didn't conceal the cloudiness in his eyes that once again revealed the truth of what his mother had said.

"It's really you!" Donnan said. "I can't believe it! Is your family here with—"

"They're still in America," Ian said and saw Donnan's disappointment, but he quickly returned to enjoying the pleasure of this reunion.

"What brings you home, then?" Donnan asked. "Wren has written that you were traveling, but I didn't realize you'd traveled so far."

"We'll have plenty of time to catch up on everything," Ian said, aware that a maid had entered the room to serve the meal and was hovering patiently close by. "Right now, let's eat. I'm famished!"

Ian nodded toward the maid as a signal for her to go ahead and serve even though they weren't seated yet. She nodded in return and proceeded. Ian then turned from his brother to greet his sister-in-law, Lilias.

"Look at you," he said embracing her. "As lovely as ever!"

"Always so charming," Lilias said and met his eyes. "It's truly so good to have you back."

"It's good to *be* back," Ian said and they were all seated. Donnan helped Lilias with her chair, and Ian helped his mother.

"My sons together again," Anya said, beaming as she took in the two of them seated near each other. "What a grand sight!"

"It is indeed!" Lilias said, then a brief, mildly awkward silence descended—as it always did at the mention of the brothers being together. They would always miss their third and eldest brother, James. While time certainly healed wounds, Ian doubted that a time would ever come when James's absence wouldn't be noticed and remembered with some degree of sadness. Of course, the same was true of his father's absence. The household just didn't feel complete without him here. In the same thought, Ian had to consider and accept that the same was true of himself. They'd always been a close family, and the absence of *any* member would be keenly felt. Ian had known upon his decision to move to America that it would be difficult for his family, and it had certainly been difficult for *him* to leave *them*. But that didn't change his absolute knowledge that he'd done the right thing for the right reasons. It also didn't change the fact that it was a difficult situation for more people than him. Being home felt good for many reasons, but it didn't really feel like home anymore, and being here was bound to bring up some sensitive emotions and issues. Taking in the fact that he was actually *with* his family, he had to acknowledge that his time here at Brierley could very likely bring out a mixture of emotions for all of them. Eventually he would be saying good-bye again, and just like the last time he'd left, none of them would have any reason to believe that they would ever see each other again.

Ian's sister, Gillian, had married many years earlier and lived quite some distance away. Going back and forth for visits was cumbersome, and it happened rarely. But visits were still possible and they occurred on a regular, although infrequent, basis. For Ian, making his home in America was an entirely different matter.

While Ian's thoughts quickly went from the absence of his brother and father, to comparing his own situation with his sister's, the family had begun to eat, and Ian felt the reality deepen that he was no longer a comfortable participant in meals at this table. Much had changed while he'd been away—most obviously, the absence of his father and the invisible dark cloud hovering around his brother. Even if Anya hadn't mentioned the problem, Ian would have picked up on it quickly. They chatted casually about trivial matters, avoiding certain specifics of Ian's purpose for leaving home, which he preferred to discuss at a more appropriate time. He told them he'd been in London, and explained again his reasons for not warning them of his visit or letting them know why he'd been on the same continent for more than a year and not notified them. He told them about Ward, his dear friend and traveling companion, and expressed how he was looking forward to having them all get to know each other. He explained Ward's blindness, and how they had met in Liverpool before going to America. He'd explained it all in letters a long time ago, but they all seemed to want to hear it again in person, especially with the prospect of meeting Ward and having him in their home.

Ian told his family a little bit about Nauvoo, and how Wren and the children were doing according to Wren's most recent letter. He continued to avoid specific information about his religious beliefs or his reasons for leaving his family to serve a mission. He wanted to share *everything* with them, but he wanted the moment to be right, and he felt more inclined to working himself back into the comfort of being back home before he broached the more sensitive topics. He had no idea how they would respond to the full enormity of the gospel and what it meant to Ian. They knew it had meant enough to him to get him to go to America. He had certainly shared his feelings with them through letters, but he'd always felt hesitant to be too specific or delve too deeply into his feelings, instinctively believing that the time wasn't right—or perhaps simply fearing that what meant so much to him would mean nothing to these people he loved. Perhaps he just feared the rejection of his beliefs, and he wasn't certain how he might handle that. For now, he preferred to enjoy the moment and wait for another time to cross those borders.

Once lunch was over, Anya insisted on meeting Ward. Anya, Donnan, and Lilias all went to the parlor for coffee, and Ian went to the kitchen and found Ward still there, having a delightful time visiting with servants who were glad to avoid their work by visiting with this newcomer. Ward was witty and charming as always, and his blindness seemed to have an intriguing effect that evoked curiosity and interest. Ian comically ordered everyone back to work, teased Ward about upsetting the household routine, then he made certain he was doing all right and had everything he needed before they went together to the parlor to meet Ian's family.

Walking up the long hall, Ward asked, "Should I be nervous?"

"Not at all," Ian said. "They're wonderful people. My mother will be treating you like a son within minutes. I'd bet on it."

"I'm not opposed to that—her treating me like a son, that is. I *am* opposed to gambling."

"Oh, you're a funny man," Ian said in a tone that implied he didn't think so at all.

Ward chuckled. "All these months with you have dulled my sense of humor."

"*What* sense of humor?" Ian asked, and they *both* chuckled.

Ian entered the parlor with Ward's hand on his shoulder. He stopped and took Ward's arm to guide it toward his mother as she stood. "Mother this is my dear friend, Ward Mickel. Ward this is my mother, Anya MacBrier."

Anya took Ward's hand and he brought it to his lips with a respectful kiss. "It is such a pleasure to finally meet you, my lady," he said. "Ian has told me what a queen you are."

"How very sweet of you," Anya said. "It is certainly a pleasure to meet you."

Anya then held Ward's hand toward Donnan, who had stepped forward and took hold of it. As soon as Ward felt the grip of a man's handshake, Ian said, "This is my brother, Donnan."

"A pleasure, Donnan," Ward said. "I've heard so very much about you as well."

"All good, of course," Donnan said with a false lightness, as if he were trying to be appropriately jovial for company while in reality he didn't really feel that way.

"Of course," Ward said. "And since Ian has children with your names—Donnan and Anya—I've heard much about the wonderful people they were named after."

"My wife, Lilias," Donnan said, graciously guiding Ward's hand to where Lilias took hold of it, and Ward kissed it as he had Anya's.

"So very good to meet you," Lilias said and also put a kiss to Ward's cheek. "Any friend of Ian's is a friend of ours. I hope you'll be comfortable in our home for as long as you choose to stay."

"Thank you, Lady MacBrier," Ward said.

He knew well enough that Ian's brother was the Earl of Brierley, and how he should address him and his wife, but Lilias quickly said, "We prefer to avoid such formality among family and close friends. Please just call me Lilias." She put his hand over her arm and guided him to the sofa. "Let's sit down and chat, shall we? Tell us all about yourself, Ward."

They were all seated, and Anya added, "Oh, yes. Tell us everything. I understand you met Ian in Liverpool before you sailed to America. He's told us a great deal in letters, but it's much more delightful to hear it firsthand. I think you should start at the beginning."

"I agree," Lilias said, "and we'll have a much less boring afternoon than usual. Tell us everything."

Ian and Ward began to reminisce about their meeting, and their journey, each filling in bits of the story, interspersed with some friendly bantering. At moments, there was much laughter, and at others, there was some sadness in regard to the deaths of Bethia, Ian and Wren's baby, and Ward's mother.

"I do so wish I could have met your mother," Anya said. "She sounds delightful. I dare say the two of us would have had much to talk about . . . and much fun together."

"I do believe you're right," Ward said.

Donnan hardly contributed to the conversation at all, until he asked somewhat audaciously, "So, how did you lose your eyesight, Ward? Were you born that way, or—"

"If I didn't know that Ward is the kind of man to not be offended by such a question," Ian said, "I'd have to give you a bloody nose for being so obnoxious."

"You're welcome to try," Donnan said with a smirk toward his brother, but Ian saw something in his eyes that contradicted the lightness of his invitation. Ian wondered if some of his brother's brewing depression had anything to do with Ian's absence. Perhaps he would find out before he left Brierley. Or perhaps he needed to make a point of staying long enough to find out.

"I'm *not* offended by the question," Ward said. "I much prefer having it addressed directly."

Donnan nodded triumphantly toward Ian, but his gesture would have been lost on Ward.

"I was not born blind, therefore I'm very blessed to have some clear memories of what the world looks like. I understand what people mean when they describe colors and details to me."

"It must be very difficult for you," Lilias said kindly.

"It is, yes," Ward said. "But then, I've become quite accustomed to it, so I don't really think about it that much. As long as I have someone nearby to help me out here and there, I manage rather well."

"It's easier for him at home," Ian said, "where he knows the placement of the furniture, and where his things are kept in a certain order. When we're in strange places, he needs a little more help finding his way, but he actually *does* manage rather well."

"My mother, of course, had been my closest companion when the blindness set in, when I was very young. Until I met Ian, no one else had ever helped me. Following her death, I don't know what I would have done without Ian. He's the greatest friend a man could ask for."

"And vice versa," Ian said.

"And you share a home in Illinois, do you not?" Anya said. Ian knew that she knew they did, but she was likely trying to make conversation, and perhaps clarify the situation when letters didn't necessarily cover every detail.

"That's right," Ian said. "We both contributed financially to the planning and building of the house. Ward lives with his wife, Patricia, and their daughter, June, in one section of the house. I live with my family in the other section, although we most often share meals and other activities in the main living area of the house."

"It works out rather nicely," Ward said. "Our wives are very good friends as well. We're glad to know they have each other while we're away."

Ian feared that such a comment would lead to someone asking exactly *why* these men would leave their families for so long, but Ian was able to steer the conversation back toward happenings in the area and to people he knew who lived in the community.

They all visited through much of the afternoon. A maid came to the parlor to announce that the children were awake following their naps and to see if it was all right for them to be brought down to the parlor.

"Oh, of course," Lilias said. "Have them brought here straightaway. We'll watch out for them until suppertime, and Bonnie can have some time to do whatever she likes."

"Very good, my lady," the maid said and left.

Not a minute later the children came bounding into the room. Donnan and Lilias's son, Ross, ran to his father's arms, and their daughter, Nessa, ran to her mother. Little James went to his grandmother. After they shared hugs with the familiar adults in the room, Anya and Lilias took turns explaining to the children who these men were. Nessa couldn't understand and had no interest in the strangers, but the boys were both curious. Ian told James and Ross how he remembered them very well as babies, and how glad he was to see that they were growing into such fine young men.

"I'm thinking," Ian said, "that perhaps tomorrow I would like to get my brother to go out riding with me." He pointed at Donnan and clarified to the boys, "That's your father," he said pointing at Ross, "and your uncle," he said pointing to James. "And he's *my* brother. Now, my brother and I used to go riding *all* the time. Perhaps when he and I go out for a ride, we could take the two of you along . . . but only if it's all right with your mother and grandmother."

"Do I have no say in this?" Donnan asked lightly, but with that severity still present as an undertone.

"None," Ian said.

"I think it's an excellent idea!" Lilias said.

"A *very* excellent idea!" Anya added, and the boys jumped up and down with excitement.

"But not until tomorrow," Lilias added. "After breakfast, and when you've done your lessons with Miss Bonnie."

"We'll do them extra quickly," James said with enthusiasm.

"Then we'll have a marvelous time!" Ian said.

"Provided it doesn't rain," Donnan grumbled.

"Always such an optimist," Lilias said with fond sarcasm.

"And we ladies shall delight in keeping Ward entertained," Anya said. "I can't wait to tell him all about your childhood, Ian. I'll keep him laughing."

"He'll never want to be your friend again," Donnan said with more severity, as if he truly meant it, and Ian wanted to repeat what Donnan's wife had said to him a moment ago. But he just smiled at his brother and said nothing.

Ian talked a little more to his nephews, and he introduced them to Ward, explaining to them that Ward couldn't see. The boys were curious and asked questions, and they allowed Ward to touch their faces in order to see what they looked like.

"Very handsome young men!" Ward declared, then made them giggle by telling them a funny story about his mother when she was alive.

Ian finally excused himself and Ward with the declaration that they needed to get settled in and properly cleaned up before supper. Ian guided Ward up the stairs and to the room that had once been his. A guest room right next to it had also been aired out and was ready to be occupied. Ward found it ironic that it was the same room Bethia had once used, when he had once been very close to Bethia.

Ian set out Ward's things and guided him around his room enough for him to get his bearings and be able to care for himself as much as possible. Since the rooms were large, Ian said he would leave the door open between their two rooms so that he could hear Ward call if he needed any help.

"No one else is even living in this part of the house," Ian told Ward, "so you don't need to worry about disturbing anyone. You can yell as loudly as you like."

"I might do that," Ward said, "just for fun."

Chapter Eleven
Hiding

Ian found that sharing supper with his family and having Ward present was an especially pleasant experience. Of course, he missed Wren—as he always did—and he couldn't help wondering how it might be if she were there. Since she had shared many meals with the family at this table, it was harder *not* to miss her here than it had been when they'd stayed in places where he had no memories to associate with her.

Ward fit in well with his family, as Ian had believed he would. During supper and afterward as they visited in the parlor, Ian found his brother's damp mood less noticeable. He hoped that whatever might be at the root of it, he would be able to help him get past it during the time that he was here at Brierley.

Ian and Ward both had what they agreed was one of the best night's sleep they'd had since leaving Nauvoo. The beds were large and comfortable and the surroundings peaceful. It all felt wildly luxuriant in contrast to the way Ian and Ward had been living, even though it was the lifestyle they had both grown up with.

Following a good breakfast, Ian left Ward in the care of Lilias and his mother, certain that Ward could communicate any unexpected needs he might have and that they would be more than eager to help him or call one of the servants to do so. Ian and Donnan went to the stables with the boys. James had taken quickly to Ian and loved holding his hand as they walked. Ian allowed James to help him saddle the horse, while Donnan did the same with Ross. They soon set out with James sitting in front of Ian in the saddle and Donnan holding his son the same way. They had a delightful time talking and laughing and riding to the old familiar places. But since the boys were with them, Ian couldn't bring up any of the questions he wanted to ask his brother—specifically how he was doing in regard to the death of their father and in having to take over the management of the estate. But Ian knew there would be plenty of time for such conversations and he was happy to just enjoy the moment. They impulsively decided to ride into town, where they had lunch at an inn. Then they wandered around a bit, which gave Ian the opportunity to see some familiar faces and talk with some fine people that he'd come to know during his growing-up years. Everyone who knew him was thrilled to see him, and he promised to come back into town at least a few more times while he was staying at home. He told people that he had a friend with him and warned them that he was blind. He knew with the way this town gossiped that every single person would know about that long before Ian brought Ward into town for an excursion.

Upon returning to Brierley, they were gently scolded for not coming home for lunch and for the boys to take their naps. But Anya confessed that she had not really expected them for lunch, and the boys usually only *pretended* to sleep at nap time anyway. When pressed, Lilias agreed with her mother-in-law, with only a lighthearted reticence.

Within a couple of days, Ian had eased effortlessly back into the routine of Brierley. He missed his father and he missed his wife and children. But if he kept his focus on finding joy and purpose in the present moment, he certainly *did* find it. Ward fit in even more comfortably than Ian had predicted, and it only took him a day or two to be able to find his way comfortably around his room. The typical daily routine that Ian and Ward shared easily merged into the dynamics of the household. The servants who interacted with the family came to quickly enjoy Ward's charm and humor and kindness.

Since they were being favored with beautiful weather, Ian took Ward outside at least once a day for a walk around the grounds and through the gardens. He described their surroundings in detail to Ward, who could smell the differences of the flowers in the garden, and could tell when they were near water, or when birds or other animals were close by.

Ian took Ward into town to spend a day, and they had a grand time visiting with people and walking the streets. But they both agreed that it felt strange in contrast to their time in London. Ian had come to Scotland with the feeling that these people in his hometown were generally stubborn and set in their ways, and he'd prayerfully determined that it was best to keep his beliefs quiet. He felt good about that decision, and he and Ward had agreed that if a favorable opportunity presented itself for them to speak in a way that would not cause problems for Ian's family, then the Spirit would surely guide them to do so.

On Sunday Ian and Ward attended church with the family, but no comment on religion was made before, during, or after the service. Ward had asked Ian privately what he was waiting for, and Ian had simply told him, "The right moment." Ward respected that and was trusting Ian to know when that moment might be. They had already mutually decided that they would not predetermine the length of time they would spend at Brierley. They'd had enough experience in being guided by the Spirit to know that when it was time to leave, they would both know it. And once they were in agreement on any matter, they knew it was the right course.

Just a little more than a week after Ian and Ward had arrived at Brierley, Anya told her son over lunch, "Oh, a package arrived for you today."

"A package?" Ian asked, knowing that one of the servants would have brought the mail in from town earlier in the day.

"That's right," Anya said.

"For me?"

Anya laughed softly. "Yes, dear. For you. It's obviously from your wife. I'm certain she knew you were coming here."

"Yes, but with the slowness of our letters going back and forth, she couldn't have possibly known when. I'm not certain she's received word that I've left London yet."

"She must have been inspired," Ward said with the same enthusiasm that Ian was feeling. He wanted to jump out of his chair that very moment and get his hands on the package. But he remained politely seated for the duration of lunch. Having been informed that the package had been taken to his room, he slipped away with Ward at the first possible moment. He wanted Ward to be with him when he opened it, certain Wren wouldn't send something for him without Patricia including something for her husband as well.

"I can't believe it!" Ian said to Ward as they entered the room. Ian guided Ward to sit on the edge of the bed, near where the package had been left.

"You should have more faith," Ward said lightly, and Ian chuckled.

"I'm certain that's true, but . . . how could she have known?"

"As I said, I'm certain she was inspired. *God* knew when we would be arriving here. Surely you know Wren well enough to know that if anyone could hear a prompting from the Spirit, it would be her."

"That's very true," Ian said. "Yes, I should have more faith." Then he added, "It's bigger than I expected." He put the square box on Ward's lap and let him feel it.

"Heavy, too," Ward said. "What does it say on the box?"

"It's addressed to Mr. Ian MacBrier in care of Brierley."

"She must have known that if she used the new version of your name, no one here would know who you were."

"That's true," Ian said. "And she's even put that the package is from *Mrs.* Ian MacBrier, Nauvoo, Illinois."

"Ah, home," Ward said, and Ian moved his friend's hand to the place where the name of their city was written. Even though Ward couldn't feel the words, Ian knew that an awareness of them beneath his fingertips would warm him. And it did; the smile on Ward's face made that evident.

"Open it!" Ward said with excitement. He knew as well as Ian did that there were surely letters inside.

Ian had to find a letter opener before he could cut into the package. When he opened the box, his breath caught in his chest. There on the top—not at all surprising—were two letters. On one it simply said Ian, and on the other it said Ward. But beneath the letters were multiple copies of the Book of Mormon. "I don't believe it!" Ian said breathlessly.

"And again I say you should have more faith," Ward said lightly. "What don't you believe?"

Ian just took one of the books out of the box and put it into Ward's hands. He felt it for a few seconds and quickly recognized its size and weight and perhaps something special about it that couldn't be seen. Ian actually saw tears gather in Ward's eyes. They had both missed having a copy of the book to read from, and also having copies that they could share with others during their journey. Ward was well aware of Ian's regret in not having copies to share with his family, now that he was here. And now they had multiple copies in their hands again.

"I don't believe it," Ward said, completely serious.

Ian chuckled while blinking back the sting of tears in his own eyes. "Oh, ye of little faith!" Ian said with gentle humor, and they both laughed. Their quiet laughter merged into something more delightful as the reality of the miracle settled in.

"How many copies?" Ward asked.

Ian dumped out the box on the bed to count them. "Eight. Eight copies."

"All with a purpose, I'm certain," Ward said.

"I'm certain as well," Ian said.

"And letters?"

"Yes, of course."

"Oh, read mine first. It's my turn to hear my letter first."

"I'll not argue with that," Ian said, and they both got comfortable.

Ward indulged in his typical ritual of holding the letter close to his face to inhale it as if he could take in the fragrance of his wife. He touched both sides of it fondly, then put it dramatically into Ian's hands so that he could read it to him.

The men both enjoyed lengthy letters from their wives, then they enjoyed talking about all they'd read and speculating over the changes in their children during the time they'd been away. Then, as if they were experiencing a rare delicacy, Ian opened a brand new copy of the Book of Mormon and began to read one of their favorite passages. While it didn't fit word for word, in principle it very much described their feelings and experiences in having left their homes to do the work they had been doing.

Blessed be the name of our God; let us sing to his praise, yea, let us give thanks to his holy name, for he doth work righteousness forever. For if we had not come up out of the land of Zarahemla, these our dearly beloved brethren, who have so dearly beloved us, would still have been racked with hatred against us, yea, and they would also have been strangers to God. And it came to pass that when Ammon had said these words, his brother Aaron rebuked him, saying: Ammon, I fear that thy joy doth carry thee away unto boasting. But Ammon said unto him: I do not boast in my own strength, nor in my own wisdom; but behold, my joy is full, yea, my heart is brim with joy, and I will rejoice in my God. Yea, I know that I am nothing; as to my strength I am weak; therefore I will not boast of myself, but I will boast of my God, for in his strength I can do all things; yea, behold, many mighty miracles we have wrought in this land, for which we will praise his name forever. Behold, how many . . . of our brethren has he loosed from the pains of hell; and they are brought to sing redeeming love, and this because of the power of his word which is in us, therefore have we not great reason to rejoice? Yea, we have reason to praise him forever, for he is the Most High God, and has loosed our brethren from the chains of hell. Yea, they were encircled about with everlasting darkness and destruction; but behold, he has brought them into his everlasting light, yea, into everlasting salvation; and they are encircled about with the matchless bounty of his love; yea, and we have been instruments in his hands of doing this great and marvelous work. Therefore, let us glory, yea, we will glory in the Lord; yea, we will rejoice, for our joy is full; yea, we will praise our God forever. Behold, who can glory too much in the Lord? Yea, who can say too much of his great power, and of his mercy, and of his long-suffering towards the children of men? Behold, I say unto you, I cannot say the smallest part which I feel.

Ian finished reading the passage, then they both remained silent for several minutes. Ian didn't know where Ward's thoughts might be, but his were vacillating between the joyful and fulfilling experiences he had been blessed with during this journey, and the longing for home that hovered constantly with him. The two connected in today's miracle of receiving this package from Wren. In her letter she had told him she'd simply had the idea come to her that he might need more copies of the book, and he would eventually get to Brierley. *If the package arrives first, I hope it doesn't confuse the family too badly, and I hope it doesn't spoil the surprise.*

Ian took up a pen to write Wren a letter that very moment, to thank her for her inspired decision to send the books, and to let her know that they had arrived safely at Brierley. He told her in detail of the happenings there, and as always he expressed his wish that she and the children could be with him, even though they all knew it would have been impossible.

After finishing a lengthy letter, Ian helped Ward write a letter to Patricia, which was a different slant on all the same news. By the time their letters were ready to be posted the following day, it was nearly time for supper and they both freshened up before going down to the dining room.

As they were seated and the meal was served, it became startlingly evident to Ian that his brother was missing. "Where is Donnan?" he asked Lilias.

"He's not feeling well," she said in a tone that implied some mild sarcasm. But he read something in her eyes that bordered on a plea for help. She added, "He doesn't feel well a great deal these days." Both the tone and the look in her eyes intensified with the second statement.

"Has he seen a doctor?" Ian asked, already suspecting what the answer would be.

"It's nothing that any medical doctor can fix," Lilias said.

Ian caught a subtle glare from his mother toward Lilias, as if she didn't want her to speak of the problem to Ian. This seemed somewhat of a contradiction to him, since his mother had already told him there was some kind of problem. Lilias said with kind boldness to her mother-in-law, "You know we can't keep this a secret from Ian, and if we both could get past our embarrassment over this problem with my husband and your son, we might actually be able to solve it."

"He'll come around," Anya said to Ian as if she didn't believe it.

"Would you like me to talk to him?" Ian asked.

"That's not necessary," Anya said at the same time that Lilias said, "Yes!"

"Perhaps tomorrow," Ian said, trying to be respectful to both women.

Donnan didn't show up for breakfast, but little was said about his absence, as if it had become very common. Ian knocked on the door of Donnan's sitting room, where Lilias had told him Donnan spent his time when he wasn't "feeling well."

"Go away," Donnan called.

"It's your brother," Ian called back.

"I don't care *who* it is," Donnan called. "Go away!"

"Fine. I'm leaving," Ian said.

Later he spoke to Lilias and had to ask, "Is he drinking?"

"No, I haven't allowed any liquor anywhere near him since he's gone into this state of continually feeling sorry for himself. But he locks himself in that room for days at a time. He barely takes his meals, doesn't bathe, won't open the drapes."

"He sleeps in there?" Ian asked.

"Either all the time or not at all, as far as I know. He's certainly not sleeping where he's supposed to be sleeping . . . which is in the same bed with his wife."

"I'll try to talk to him," Ian said on the wave of a weighted sigh.

"Best of luck to you," Lilias said with sarcasm and walked away.

Ian watched her go, wondering what he'd come home to, and what he was going to do about it. It was a good thing he knew that he had God on his side, or he'd feel utterly helpless.

* * * * *

While Donnan continued to remain hidden, Ian found Lilias and Anya mostly unwilling to talk about the situation, and Donnan unwilling to talk to him at all. Each day Ian took advantage of the opportunity to play with his niece and nephews. They took well to his attention, especially since they weren't getting *any* attention from Donnan. The children also enjoyed Ward's company and they all had a great time together. But it didn't take away Ian's concern for his brother.

Feeling increasingly helpless, Ian was glad for a distraction when Ward suggested that while they were at Brierley, he should perhaps copy down some family information that might be important to his children and grandchildren someday. He told Ian that in his own family, the records for his father's side had been kept in a family Bible that would always remain with the family in his father's native country of Italy. At one time his mother had copied down names and dates of significant events that had been kept in that family Bible, believing such information might have value to Ward and the family he'd hoped to have. Ward suggested that Ian now do the same while they had extra hours on hand here at the home that had housed generations of Ian's ancestors. Ian had no trouble locating the MacBrier family Bible. He'd been shown the beautiful book in the library many times throughout his life. So he and Ward quickly made a habit of going to the library after lunch, and Ward kept Ian company while he meticulously copied down the names of his ancestors and the dates of births, deaths, and marriages. Ian enjoyed reminiscing about what he knew of the circumstances surrounding these events in the lives of his parents and siblings. And he also enjoyed speculating over what life might have been like here at Brierley in generations past, long before his parents or grandparents were here.

On the fourth afternoon of this activity, Ian was surprised to hear a knock at the door.

"Come in," he called, and was surprised to see Mrs. Boyle, the head housekeeper, peer timidly into the room once the door had come open a few inches. "Hello," he said to her. "Can I help you with something?"

"Forgive me for disturbing you, sir, but I wonder if I might have a word."

"Of course," Ian said. "Come in." He noticed how she peered back into the hall, as if to be certain that no one had seen her enter the room. She closed the door quietly and stood before him. She glanced at Ward, and Ian said, "It's all right. He will keep my every confidence. Whatever you need to say, speak freely."

"Thank you, sir," Mrs. Boyle said, and Ian started to feel an uneasiness about this encounter. Why would the head housekeeper seek him out—apparently in secret? And why would she seem so nervous? He couldn't recall *ever* seeing her nervous. She was a steady and unfaltering woman who took her work very seriously. If there was some problem with the household, why wouldn't she be addressing that problem with one of the members of the family who actually lived here?

"What is it, Mrs. Boyle?" Ian encouraged when she said nothing for a long moment.

"I hope you won't think I'm out of line," she said. "And I hope that if you feel the need to discuss what I'm about to tell you with anyone else that they won't think I'm out of line either."

"No one needs to know the source of any information you feel the need to share with me, if that's what you're concerned about."

"Thank you, sir," she said. "The thing is . . . the servants talk . . . and the servants, many of them, are friends with those that work the tenant farms here at Brierley."

"Yes," Ian drawled, wondering where this was headed.

"The thing is," she said again, "I've been hearing of a number of problems . . . among the tenant farmers."

"Such as?" Ian asked, trying not to jump to conclusions over what the source of these problems might be when he hadn't even yet heard what they were exactly.

"It might be best if I don't use names, but there was one farmer who got very ill and was falling behind on the rent because of it and apparently the overseer was coming down hard on him, but Lady MacBrier knew nothing about it."

"My mother or—"

"I was referring to the earl's wife, but your mother knew nothing of it, either."

Ian wondered why she'd not said that *the earl* had not known anything about it. What was going on that Donnan's duties were being deflected to the women in the household? Rather than posing such a question to the housekeeper, he simply said, "There were other problems?"

"Yes, sir. Fences broken and not getting fixed. Roofs leaking. Things like that. Of course, the overseer should be seeing that such things are taken care of, and he should be reporting them to the earl, but . . ." She stopped and didn't finish. Instead she cleared her throat in a way that seemed to say she *wouldn't* finish but hoped that he would be able to fill in the rest for himself.

Ian took a fair guess and said, "But the earl is not keeping abreast of the overseer's behavior—or anything else, apparently."

Mrs. Boyle cleared her throat. "That would be my assumption, sir. But it's not my place to—"

"It's your place to know what's going on in this house, Mrs. Boyle, and I appreciate your bringing the matter to me."

"I was so glad to see you come, sir," she said with a crack in her voice. "I believe it was the answer to many prayers."

Ward turned toward Ian as if he could actually cast him some kind of glance. But Ian knew what he meant by the gesture. Their entire journey had been in God's hands. Why would he think that coming to Brierley *wouldn't* be?

"Thank you, Mrs. Boyle. Is there anything else I should know?"

"Not that I can tell you, sir," Mrs. Boyle said. "And this conversation will stay between us?"

"Of course," Ian said, then added more lightly. "Servants gossip, you know. Who knows *where* I might have heard such a thing."

"Indeed, sir," Mrs. Boyle said with appreciation. "Thank you for your time, sir."

"And thank you for your candor, Mrs. Boyle," Ian said.

She nodded and turned to leave, then turned back. "The death of the earl has been hard on your mother *and* your brother. No one can blame them for having a hard time adjusting, but . . . life must go on, if you don't mind my saying so."

"I don't mind your saying so at all," Ian said. "Thank you again." A moment later he added, "Mrs. Boyle? Has my brother come out of his room yet?"

"Not for days now," she said. "It's becoming more and more common, and it's a real worry to all of us. He only unlocks the door long enough to take his meals, but he doesn't eat much of them. He's not asked for any clean water to wash since he holed up there."

"I'll see if I can talk to him," Ian said, and in his head he heard Lilias saying with sarcasm, *Best of luck to you.*

Mrs. Boyle gave him an appreciative nod before she opened the door carefully and peered out to be certain no one was in the hallway, then she slipped out and closed the door quietly behind her.

"So, what do you make of that?" Ian asked Ward.

"I think it's a good thing you're here."

"And where, o dear and mighty friend, would you suggest I begin to solve this problem? Should I begin by lecturing my brother?"

"I'd do that after you have more information," Ward said as if he'd already deeply considered it, whereas Ian had been mostly facetious in asking the question.

"Should I have it out with the overseer?"

"Eventually."

"Should I start with my mother, then?" Ian said, more obviously facetious.

Ward said with complete seriousness, "No one knows the problems of a man better than the man's wife."

Ian was surprised at how the comment resounded in his spirit. If anyone knew the heart of the problem with Donnan—and all else going on in regard to the matter—it would be Lilias.

"I suppose I should go and talk with my sister-in-law."

"I suppose you should," Ward said, lying back on the couch where he was sitting. "I believe she said she would be spending the afternoon in the gardens. Apparently she likes doing that sort of thing. I'll just stay here and take a nap. But don't leave me here *too* long. I might starve to death."

"Don't worry," Ian said. "I won't let you starve to death."

"Good luck," Ward said, and Ian left the room, shaking his head even while he prayed silently to know how to handle whatever might be going on.

He found Lilias in the garden as Ward had predicted.

"Good afternoon, Mrs. MacBrier," Ian said, and she turned toward him.

"Hello, Ian. What brings you out here?" She clipped a couple of spring flowers and put them in her basket, then she turned more toward him, removing her gloves.

"To talk to you, of course," Ian said. "I'll just come straight to the point. I've heard there have been some problems with the overseer."

Lilias's countenance immediately changed. She set down her things and walked toward a nearby bench, but she didn't sit down. Ian followed.

"Where did you hear that?" she asked.

"Servants gossip," he said. "What I need to know is how much truth there is to what I've heard."

"Tell me what you've heard," Lilias said, and Ian repeated the gist of it.

"Yes, as far as I know, that's all true. I've had some problems with Mr. Abbot, and I'm not sure what to do about it."

"*You* have had problems with Mr. Abbot?" he asked. She glared at him but looked away. Trying to focus on one problem at a time, he added, "And I'm assuming Mr. Abbot receives a fair and honest wage for his position."

"Oh, more than fair!" Lilias declared. "You should know better than anyone, Ian, that the MacBrier family is reputed for being kind and fair in all their dealings."

"I know that's the way it was before I left here. And I know that you have not always been a member of the family."

"I have been for enough years to know how things are and how they ought to be."

Ian took in what she was saying and responded more gently. "You've been trying very hard to cover for Donnan." She turned her gaze downward and he added, "And you've been doing it for quite some time now."

Lilias sank onto the bench, as if having her secret found out had just knocked the breath from her lungs. She hung her head, and he heard her sniffling. He stepped toward her and handed her a clean handkerchief from his pocket. "Tell me," he urged in a soft voice and sat down to face her.

Lilias sniffled again and pressed the handkerchief to her eyes. "You know, of course, that he was reluctant to become the earl."

"We spoke of it before I left. He tried to convince me to take the position. I told him that I knew my place was not here, and he told me—after he'd given the matter some thought—that he needed to rise to the position and do what was required of him."

"He was doing well working with your father after you left. They were getting along famously and all was well. Then your father left us with so little warning. Of course, we'd all known for some time of his health problems, but he'd been doing better. We'd all come to believe he would live for a good, long time. It was such a shock for all of us, but Donnan took it very hard. I did my best to offer support for his grief and allow him the time alone that he insisted on. But now I think that I shouldn't have. I think I left him alone far too much. I think if I had insisted that he show himself more and own up to his duties right from the start, he wouldn't have fallen into this terrible state. I think that I've done him harm by stepping in and taking his place so easily. Now he has no reason to believe that I won't take care of anything and everything. I'm happy to support my husband in his work, Ian. I've grown to care very much for the people who rent land from us. But I am *not* the earl. It's not my place to take care of Donnan's responsibilities. Although now that I've assumed that role, I'm not sure how to reverse the situation."

Ian wasn't certain how to address *that* problem, so he reverted to a more pressing one. "Whether or not Donnan is doing *his* job, the overseer should be doing *his*. And apparently he is not."

"I learned just a few weeks ago that some complaints had been issued to the overseer, which were supposed to then be passed on to the earl."

"Or to you in the earl's stead," Ian clarified, and she nodded.

"Not one of us had heard anything about these problems, while the people were assuming that we were just neglecting the fact that repairs were urgently needed to some fence lines; that a poor, dear man was ill and his family was struggling to pay the rent; and that more than one roof was leaking. The problems went unresolved and the tenants were angry with *us.*"

"Has Donnan spoken to the overseer?"

"Donnan does very little except lock himself away. I spoke to the overseer myself, but I admit that I'm not well versed in handling such situations, and I don't think he took my request for a change very seriously. I made arrangements for the problems that I'd become aware of to be resolved. But . . ." Her words faded and she dabbed at her eyes again.

"It shouldn't be left to you to solve such problems." Ian rose to his feet.

"Where are you going?" she demanded, doing the same.

"First I'm going to speak with Mr. Abbot, and then I'm going to have a good, long talk with my brother."

"What will you stay to him?" she asked.

Ian paused. "Whatever is necessary," he said, then added gently, "You mustn't worry, Lilias. Everything will be all right."

"I wish I could share your confidence."

"I'll not leave," he said, "until I make certain that everything is all right." He wondered as soon as he said the words if he would come to regret them. But Lilias smiled faintly, and he saw some hope in her eyes—or at least some comfort.

Ian went into the house and asked one of the servants to send word for Mr. Abbot to come and see him right away, then he found his mother, feeling the need to understand the situation from her perspective.

"I've spoken to Lilias," he said. "The situation is apparently worse than I've been led to believe."

"You were very far away. There was nothing you could have done."

"I mean that it's worse than I've been led to believe since I came back. This is much more than Donnan just having a difficult time with losing his father."

"Is it?" Anya asked and reached into the cuff of her blouse to pull out a lacy handkerchief. He was glad she had one, since he'd given his to Lilias. "I don't know what it is, Ian. I don't understand it at all. I used to feel so strong . . . so in control of my life. I knew my place here and filled it to the best of my ability."

"You always filled it marvelously."

"But when your father died, it was no longer my place to be the lady of Brierley. Lilias is a remarkable woman. I'm not certain Donnan deserves her, but I thank God every day that she married him. I shudder to think where we would be if she'd not stepped in."

"I'm certain you would have managed well enough, Mother. You're a lot stronger than you think you are. But the problem here is that Donnan *is* the Earl of Brierley, and he is not owning up to his responsibilities."

"Perhaps it's just not in him to do so," Anya said.

Ian took the words in, telling himself not to assume that she meant anything more than what she'd said. Then he realized that he *knew* she had absolutely meant to imply what she was implying.

"He is perfectly capable of being what he was born to be, Mother. *I* am going back to America—where I belong. This is *Donnan's* birthright, not mine."

"It was not meant to be his, either. It fell to his shoulders when James was killed."

"Regardless of that, Donnan is older than I am, and this is *his* responsibility. He tried to give it all to me before I ever *went* to America, and—"

"He did?" Her astonishment reminded him that he and Donnan had agreed not to discuss the matter with their parents.

"Yes. I told him I would consider the matter carefully and even pray about it. I knew more than ever that it was not my place to be the earl. At the time, Donnan agreed that he needed to step up and fill the position. He told me he was going to start working more with Father, and I had every reason to believe that he would take it more seriously."

"He did. He was doing marvelously . . . until your father died."

"If you want my honest opinion, I think he's using his grief over Father's death as an excuse to avoid doing what he didn't necessarily want to do in the first place. He needs to act like a man and do what Father would want him to do."

"And what if he won't?" Anya asked.

"What *if* he won't?" Ian countered.

While the question hovered uneasily in the air, a maid knocked at the door to inform Ian that Mr. Abbot was waiting downstairs to speak with him.

"Thank you," Ian said. "I'll be right there." After the maid left, Ian added, "I'll speak with Donnan. I'll do everything I can to help him get back on his feet, but I am not staying, Mother. This is not my home anymore."

He rushed out of the room before the full heartache of that statement could affect his judgment or spur him to irrational emotion. Before going down the stairs to meet with Mr. Abbot, he took a minute to breathe deeply and calm himself, and he uttered a silent prayer for guidance and strength in dealing appropriately with this situation so that he could go back to Nauvoo with the confidence of knowing that the affairs of his family and his beloved Brierley were in order.

Chapter Twelve
The Reluctant Earl

Ian's interview with Mr. Abbot quickly fueled his anger rather than calming it. The man was all but lying about the incidents that Lilias had told him about, and he was mildly indignant and rude. He had clearly neglected his duties, yet Ian couldn't bring himself to relieve the man of his employment. He believed it was right and fair to give him another chance. The thought occurred to him that Donnan—in the state of mind he was in—might not have been as clear as he should have been about this man's duties in regard to his employment. Still, Ian felt so angry he wanted to belt this man in the jaw. He pushed his hands behind his back and clasped them there, as if that might help keep them from doing any damage he would later regret. He took a bold step toward Mr. Abbot and spoke with a firm resolve that didn't begin to express the full depth of his disdain. "You listen to me, and listen well, Mr. Abbot. Your employment as overseer makes you the official representative of Brierley and the MacBrier family. As of this moment, your position in that regard is hanging by a thread. I'm going to assume that perhaps you were not fully clear on your responsibilities, and I'm going to assume that your present attitude is not one that you will ever show itself again to me or anyone else you associate with in regard to your employment. I'm going to assume that you need this job and you're willing to make the changes necessary in order to keep it. If that is the case, you should take this opportunity to make that clear. If I am assuming incorrectly, please inform me at once."

Mr. Abbot said nothing, and Ian spoke only a notch below a shout. "Mr. Abbot! Is there something you need to say?"

"Yes, sir," Mr. Abbot said, clearly unnerved.

"Then say it!"

"I would be most grateful t' remain employed for the house of Brierley, sir."

"Very good," Ian said. "Then this is the way it's going to be. If you become aware of anything—*anything*—amiss in any way among the people living and working on MacBrier land, you will report it at once to the earl. If the earl is ill or unavailable, you will report it to his wife or his mother. You will issue your reports with complete honesty and in a timely manner, and you will do everything in your power to rectify these problems according to the agreement of your employment. If one more incident comes up—one more, mind you—where it becomes evident that this is not the case, you will be dismissed. Do you understand me?"

"I understand ye, sir."

"Good then. My brother and I will be personally visiting the tenant farms in a week's time. I expect everything to be in good repair, and everyone to be pleased and content with the situation."

"But a week is—"

"If everything had been in order as it should have been, a week should be more than ample to solve any little remaining problems."

"Very well, sir," Mr. Abbot said with abject humility.

The overseer left and Ian took in a deep breath to calm his nerves and try to think clearly. This was *not* how he'd imagined spending his time at Brierley.

"Spoken like a true earl," Ward said, and Ian turned, startled to see him standing in the doorway to the adjacent study.

"How on earth did you get in here?" Ian demanded, sounding more upset than he'd intended.

"I brought him," Lilias said, appearing at Ward's side. "I wanted to hear what Mr. Abbot would say to you . . . and I bribed Ward. I knew you might forgive him for eavesdropping more likely than you would forgive me."

"I don't care whether or not *either* of you eavesdrops," Ian said. "I have nothing to hide. However," he pointed a finger at Ward—as if Ward could actually see him, "I am *not* the earl, nor will I ever be."

"You know how to behave like one when you need to," Ward said.

"Let's just hope I can teach my brother to behave like an earl before the whole place is in shambles," Ian said.

"Amen," Lilias said under her breath, then more loudly, "I'm very grateful for your help, Ian."

"I'm glad to do what I can, Lilias," Ian said. "But I'm not sure I can solve this. My mother wants me to stay . . . to take the position."

"She said that?" Lilias asked, astonished.

"Not in so many words," Ian said. "But I want you to know what my mother and Donnan are both already aware of. I know in my heart that my place is in America. That's my home now. This is Donnan's position to fill, and I would be doing him a great disservice to rescue him from having to fill it. Do you understand?"

"I do," Lilias said with appreciation and admiration in her eyes. He wished that his mother felt the same way.

"You and I are going to work together to help Donnan come to himself over this, and then I'm going back to America. Whether or not Donnan comes around, I'm still going back to America."

"Of course," Lilias said.

"Which means that the situation could be increasingly difficult for you."

"Perhaps I can learn a thing or two from you before you leave," Lilias said, "that might make it easier."

Ian sighed and gave her a compassionate gaze. "I'll do everything I can to help you, Lilias."

"I know you will," she said and surprised him with a quick hug. "I'm going to check on my husband . . . if he'll let me in the room."

"If he won't," Ian said, "let me know." He'd had about enough of his brother hiding away and causing so much grief for so many people. If he didn't show his face soon, Ian was going to take drastic measures.

* * * * *

That evening before going to bed, Ian talked the entire situation through with Ward. Not only did talking about it out loud help clear his thoughts, but Ward had a way of making complicated problems seem more simple. He was gifted at giving sound advice, but in this case he had to admit that he was stumped. No one could force Donnan to come out of his room and act like an earl. But Ward still had sound advice, "We can pray for him . . . for everyone involved."

"Of course," Ian said. "I have been."

"As have I," Ward said. "But we can increase our efforts."

Ian and Ward knelt together, and Ward offered a lengthy, beautiful prayer on behalf of Ian's family and the household and estate of Brierley. He also prayed, as usual, on behalf of their home and families so far away, and he expressed gratitude to God for all they had been blessed with.

After Ian made certain that Ward had all he needed for the night, he knelt by his bed and prayed again, then he crawled between the covers and prayed again. He fell asleep baffled and deeply concerned.

He woke up the next morning feeling the same way, then an idea occurred to him that took his breath away. Words had come clearly into his mind at the same moment a distinct memory had appeared there. The memory was of something that had occurred in this very house, some of it in this very room. He'd been struggling to find the answers to some problems he'd been having in his life at the time, and seemingly out of nowhere, he had remembered that he'd left the Book of Mormon discarded in a traveling bag in the bottom of a closet in his room. He'd hardly glanced at the book since he'd impulsively purchased it from missionaries in London prior to his coming home. Ian recalled how he'd rushed up the stairs that day, as if the book had taken on a life of its own and was calling to him from its abandoned place. Ian had dug out the book and had been so moved by the experience that he'd begun reading it right away. Within its pages he'd not only found the answers to his problems, but the path of his life. His gratitude for having that book come into his hands was inexpressible. It had changed his life—for the better—in more ways than he could ever count. And now, while new problems and challenges were weighing on him, the memory of that moment had come clearly into his mind. And along with the memory he had just as clearly heard the words, *You're looking to the wrong source to solve the problems, Ian.*

"The wrong source?" Ian asked aloud to the empty room. Himself! He was looking to himself to solve the problems. But he alone was certainly not capable of solving this mess. Of course, he'd been praying for help and guidance. He'd not really been trying to—or believing he could—solve it on his own. But his prayers had been answered. The solution to the problems was in the pages of that book. And Wren had been inspired enough to send him multiple copies.

Ian jumped out of bed to hurry and get dressed, feeling an extra zeal in the prospect of the day. The time had finally come to open up and share his deepest beliefs with his family. And he felt as excited as a child at Christmas. He didn't know how his message might be received, but in that moment he didn't care. He only wanted to share with these people he loved what meant most to him. Now he could fully expound on and explain his reasons for going to America, and his reasons for coming back to his homeland. Now he could explain why he'd been willing to uproot his family and change his entire life. And with any luck, what he had to say would be met with enough openness that more problems might be solved. They needed miracles, and if anything in this house could be the source of miracles, it was that book.

* * * * *

Ian knew that he would most likely find his mother in her sitting room this time of the morning, then it occurred to him that the conversation he wanted to have with her would take longer than the time they had left before breakfast. Resigned to exercising some patience, he read for a while, listening for signs that Ward was awake. Once he *was* awake, Ian helped him through his usual routine, and told him of the experience he'd had that morning and of his plan to speak individually with his mother, Lilias, and Donnan.

"I predict that the first two conversations will go very well," Ward said. "As for your brother . . . well, you're going to have to figure out how to actually be in the same room with him before you're going to be able to talk to him about spiritual matters."

"Oh, very funny," Ian said with the kind of sarcasm that was normal between them. "Have I ever told you what a funny man you are?"

"Every day," Ward said tonelessly. "And to continue my thought, I would suspect your brother is likely not in the mood to talk about spiritual matters."

"He might be more willing to talk about spiritual matters than he would be to talk about the neglect of the estate."

"That's true," Ward said. "You might be able to get to him by avoiding that which he most wants to avoid."

"Perhaps. Truthfully, he wasn't at all receptive to even my subtle hints about prayer and religion before I left here years ago. I don't know that much would have changed in that regard."

"His feelings and circumstances have certainly changed," Ward said. "Sometimes that can make an enormous difference."

"That's true," Ian said. "Either way, I know that I'm supposed to share these things with him, and to give him a copy of the book. I can only do my part and then step back and let God do His."

"Amazing how that works."

"It *is* amazing, isn't it," Ian said with enthusiasm.

At breakfast, Donnan still hadn't shown himself, and neither Anya nor Lilias had seen or heard anything from him beyond a word or two shouted through the door when they had checked on him. Near the end of the meal, Ian asked his mother if he could have some time to visit with her.

"Do you have any plans for the rest of the morning?" he asked.

"None of any consequence," Anya said.

"Good," Ian said. "Then I'll meet you in your sitting room once I get Ward settled."

"Or," Lilias said, "I could take Ward on a walk through the gardens and tell him all about my roses; they're just starting to bloom. And then *I* will get him settled . . . but only if I'm boring him terribly and you're still visiting with your mother."

"What a lovely plan," Ward said. "I would love to smell the roses."

"The pink ones do smell different from the red or the yellow, you know," Lilias said.

"Yes, I know," Ward added, and she smiled.

Ian took note of her smile and realized it was something he hadn't seen her do since Donnan had locked himself away. Apparently Ian's arrival had occurred on one of Donnan's better days. Or perhaps Ian's arrival had spurred Donnan into one of his bad spells—although, according to Lilias, they had become more frequent and longer lasting even *before* Ian's arrival. Ian felt deeply concerned, but focused again on what he had felt this morning. He had hope in knowing that God's hand was in this, and that God was mindful of the situation. Surely things would work out, and a day would come when Ian could return to his family in America with the peace of knowing that all was well here at Brierley.

After breakfast, Ward left with Lilias and Ian went to his room only long enough to retrieve a copy of the Book of Mormon. When he met his mother in her sitting room, he saw her glance curiously at the book, but he set it aside and said, "We can talk about that later."

"So, what would you like to talk about?" she asked. "If it's your concern for Donnan, I have to say that I wonder sometimes if he will ever be able to live up to his responsibilities. I fear the estate will crumble into ruin if he doesn't come to his senses."

"I admit that I'm concerned for Donnan," Ian said, *"and* the estate, but that's not what I wanted to talk to you about."

"Oh?" Anya said, sounding pleasantly surprised. He suspected that concern for Donnan and the estate had likely dominated the household for quite some time. "Tell me, then," she said.

"While I'm here at Brierley, I wanted to take the opportunity to tell you more about my reasons for making the decisions I've made. At first I told you very little, and I know that I explained some of my reasons in letters, but it's just not the same as a good conversation, is it?"

"No, it's certainly not," she said and took his hand.

Ian took in her gentle countenance and was reminded of what a thoroughly good woman his mother was. Beyond their disagreement over her wanting him to stay at Brierley, and his convictions about living in America, they'd never had cause to quarrel. She had always loved him unconditionally, always supported him in everything he did—except for his occasional rebellious and self-destructive behavior, of which she'd made no qualms about telling him her exact thoughts. Her intentions had always been the best, and even now she was likely just confused and concerned, not knowing how to solve this problem. She was also likely still grieving over the loss of her husband. With them being as close as they'd been, Ian felt sure that adjusting to life without him had not been easy for Anya, by any means.

"So, now that I'm here," Ian said, "I would like to tell you the whole story . . . if that's all right with you."

"Oh, I would love to hear the whole story, Ian," she said with such enthusiasm that the feelings Ian had awakened with that morning deepened in him.

"I know I've told you bits and pieces, so some of what I tell you might be repetitive, but if I just start at the beginning, I won't leave anything out."

"How delightful!" she said.

Ian went all the way back to his reasons for leaving Scotland years ago when he'd simply been hiding from his problems and drinking too much and had gone away with no explanation, leaving his family and loved ones to worry and wonder. He told her the story of how he'd awakened with a hangover in an alley in London, and he'd wandered to a street where missionaries had been preaching. He told her how he'd purchased a book from them, and then how he had immediately felt compelled to come home.

Ian told his mother how the book had called to him that day after he and Wren were married, and how it had answered questions and solved problems in his life. Then he told her in fine detail of the spiritual experiences he'd had that had let him know, beyond any doubt, that the book was true, and that it was his destiny to follow where the book led him—specifically to the religious group that believed in the teachings of the book.

"Is that the book?" Anya asked, pointing to where it sat inconspicuously beside Ian's leg.

"Yes, this is a copy of the book. This is what was in the package that Wren sent here. I came to England with a suitcase full of them, but I've given them all away—even my own copy. She was truly inspired to send more copies, because she didn't know the situation. I had wanted very much to give you a copy of the book—for a very long time. Many times I considered mailing one to you, but I never felt quite right about it, always believing that perhaps the time just wasn't right. I didn't know that I would actually be coming back here and have the opportunity to give one to you personally."

He set it in her hands and she took it reverently, as if what she'd heard Ian tell her so far had—at the very least—given her some respect for its contents. She thumbed through it a little, then set it on her lap and put her hands over it, turning her attention again to Ian.

"So, this is the reason you came to England? To be a missionary? Like the missionaries who helped you that day?"

"Exactly," Ian said. "I didn't want to leave my home and family, but I knew beyond any doubt that God wanted me to make this journey, just as surely as I knew He wanted me to go to America initially. How could I *not* do it when the men who had placed this precious volume into *my* hands had left *their* families behind and made the sacrifice in order to share the truths of the gospel with those in need; people like me, lost and wandering?"

"I admire your convictions, Ian," she said. "You're a good man, and I'm proud of you."

"Thank you, Mother. That means a great deal to me."

"For what it's worth, your father felt the same way."

"It's worth a great deal to me to know that," he said and looked down. "I wish I could have been here when he died, but . . ."

"You were where you needed to be," Anya said. "I know. I wish you could have been here as well. I admit that I have a certain selfishness in wishing that you would have stayed. I wish it still. But I'm glad to know why you feel the way you do." Ian nodded, and she said, "You have more to tell me?"

"If you're interested," he said.

"Oh, I am very much interested!" she said, and Ian went on to tell her about the experiences that had led to Ward's own conviction that the book was true, and all they had gone through in order to just find the location of the Mormons, and then to get to Nauvoo. Ian told her about meeting the Prophet Joseph Smith and his lovely wife Emma, and of Joseph's miraculous vision and his role in restoring the true and full gospel once again to the earth. He told her how Joseph had been inspired to call him and Ward to serve as missionaries, and he also told her about the persecution the Saints had endured, and how they had been driven from one place to another.

"That's dreadful!" Anya said. "Is your family in danger?"

"Nauvoo is a peaceful place," Ian said. "We have every hope that we will be allowed to live there in peace, and worship according to our desires without any interference from others who would oppose us." He explained to her the nature of opposition, and how everything good in the world was counterbalanced by something evil. But the presence of opposition had only strengthened the conviction of the Saints in knowing that the course they were on was right and good and sanctioned by God.

When Ian had told her all that he wanted to, he put his hand over hers where they were still resting on the book. "I would like to ask you, with all the sincerity of my heart, to read this book. I don't know that it will have the impact on your life that it has had on mine, but I do believe it will bring *something* good into your life." He wanted to add that he would never expect her to leave Brierley and join the Saints, no matter how the book affected her. In his heart he knew she never would, but he felt it was a sentiment better left unacknowledged. And it was all right. Even if, across the distance, he could know that she understood his convictions more deeply, and that to some degree she had gained a stronger relationship with the Savior through the principles of this book, he would be more than pleased.

"Would you do that for me?" he asked. "Would you read the book?"

"I would *love* to read the book," she said, "and I'm so glad that you've shared these things with me." She put her arms around his neck and embraced him tightly. "You're a good man," she said again. She drew back and put a hand to his face. "I love you dearly, my precious Ian. I always will."

"I know, and I'm grateful. I love you too, Mother. A man could not ask for a better mother."

"And a mother could not ask for a better son," she said.

The conversation became more casual, while Ian told her trivial details of life in Nauvoo. He explained more about their home, the yard, the neighborhood, the city, the vastness of the Mississippi River, and the good people they were surrounded by. Anya took in every detail with pleasure and seemed to be thoroughly enjoying every word.

Ian felt the conversation winding to a close when an impression came to his mind so strongly that it made him gasp.

"Is something wrong, dear?" Anya asked, putting her hand over his.

"No," he said quickly, then he remained silently distracted while he tried to discern whether what he felt was real, and if what he'd felt impressed to say truly came from God. It only took him a few seconds to know that both his feelings and their source were valid. He'd many times felt Satan's efforts to imitate the voice of the Lord, and he'd learned to distinguish the difference. And Ian clearly knew the voice speaking to him now, and he understood the principle through which it was possible, because he'd studied it repeatedly, and he'd had multiple witnesses of its truth.

The words came again to his mind. *Tell her I'm here.* Ian felt no need to argue with the request, but he did wonder exactly how to go about telling his mother something like that without sounding crazy. Then he reached for the book and turned quickly to the correct passage. He knew exactly where to find it, even in a copy that wasn't marked. Moroni, chapter 7.

"I would like to read this part with you, and explain to you some wonderful experiences that have happened to me."

"Very well," she said, seeming eager to have him share more, but perhaps confused over his distracted behavior.

Ian read through the entire passage that taught the principle of ministering angels, explaining to his mother that angels (meaning either spirits who had passed on, or spirits of those who were not yet born) were allowed to minister unto the children of men (meaning people in this world) under the direction of the Savior, by the power of the Holy Ghost, to fulfill the covenants—or promises—that the Father had made with His children. Ian emphasized some of his favorite phrases.

"'Wherefore, my beloved brethren, have miracles ceased because Christ hath ascended into heaven, and hath sat down on the right hand of God, to claim of the Father his rights of mercy which he hath upon the children of men? . . . And because he hath done this, my beloved brethren, have miracles ceased? Behold I say unto you, Nay; neither have angels ceased to minister unto the children of men.'*

Ian then explained plainly to his mother the principle that through the power of the Holy Ghost, any person had the opportunity to know the truth of all things. He repeated briefly how the Holy Ghost had witnessed to him of the truth of many things in his life. Then he took a deep breath and said, "What I'm trying to tell you, Mother, is that I know beyond any doubt that there is one angel in particular who has ministered to me a great deal through the course of my journey. He has given me strength and love and support. Most of the time I cannot feel his presence, but I have frequent impressions that he is there, nevertheless. There have been a few moments, however, when I have been allowed to feel his presence, and I've even had impressions of words in my mind that he has communicated to me . . . through the power of the Holy Ghost." He paused and looked at her more intently. "Do you understand the principle of what I'm telling you?"

"I think so," she said. He heard her breath sharpen, saw her put a hand to her heart while her eyes appeared both intrigued and mildly skeptical. "Are you saying what I think you're saying?"

"It could sound crazy, Mother, if you don't understand the spiritual principles that make it possible. It's not something to be spoken of freely, because it's personal and it's sacred. But I can tell you that I know, Mother; I absolutely know . . . that my father has been very close to me." Anya gasped, and a sparkle of moisture gathered in her eyes. "And I know that he's here now with us, and he wants you to know that's the case."

Anya let out a sharp whimper then pressed a hand over her mouth. Ian feared she would express doubt or allude to Ian's possible insanity. It crossed his mind that she might accuse him of tormenting her with such an idea. But she threw her arms around his neck and wept against his shoulder, murmuring softly close to his ear, "Such a precious miracle!"

Ian held his mother and let her weep, wondering if her emotion was at least partly due to her feeling the truth of what he'd said, or perhaps even feeling some kind of closeness to her husband. It truly was a miracle!

When she had quieted down and composed herself, Anya verified that she *did* believe that what he'd told her was true, and that she would find great peace in believing that Gavin MacBrier was still mindful of his family and watching over them. "It gives me comfort," she said, "to imagine him close by when I miss him, or to think of him with his children and grandchildren when they need him. Perhaps he can have some influence on Donnan . . . even if Donnan doesn't recognize it."

"I'm sure you're right," Ian said, amazed to realize that she had taken the principle into her heart with great faith, and even with great accuracy.

They talked for a while longer, and the morning progressed with neither of them giving any thought to the passing of time. They only broke away from their conversation reluctantly to go downstairs for lunch. Before leaving the room, Anya promised that she would start reading the book that very night. Ian couldn't help but be pleased, and he hoped she would read quickly so that they might have the opportunity to talk about it some before it was time for him to return to America—whenever that time might be.

At lunch it became evident that Ward and Lilias had spent the morning together exploring the gardens and then in the nursery playing with the children. Lilias had told him all about her own childhood and how she'd come to meet Donnan and fall in love with him, and Ward had shared his experiences of meeting and falling in love with Bethia—whom Lilias had known prior to Ian leaving Scotland with his family. He told Lilias more details than she'd known about Bethia's death, and he shared with her how he'd met Patricia and had fallen quickly and deeply in love with her. After Ward and Lilias had reviewed all they had talked about through the course of the morning, Lilias said, "So what did the two of *you* talk about?"

"Oh, so many things!" Anya said with a thrill in her voice.

"I told her the long version of why I went to America, and why I've come back," Ian said, "and if you think you're up to it, I'd be happy to tell you the same story."

"I would like that very much!" Lilias said with enough enthusiasm that Ian felt hopeful that she too might be open and receptive to what he wanted to share.

"Tomorrow, perhaps?" Ian said.

"What's wrong with this afternoon?" Lilias asked.

"I can certainly take care of myself," Ward said.

"Or I can talk you into keeping *me* company," Anya said.

"It's settled, then," Lilias said. "I think that a tour of the rose garden would do *you* some good as well, dear brother."

"I'm sure it would," Ian said, and he would have winked at Ward if Ward could have seen it.

* * * * *

Ian couldn't help being pleased when Lilias proved to be every bit as receptive as he'd hoped she'd be. While she didn't exhibit the same level of enthusiasm for his experiences that his mother had shown, she was interested and positive and agreed to read the book.

"Perhaps you can get your brother to read the book," she said. "He could bear to have some good Christian principles in his life."

"I'll certainly try," Ian said.

"It's not that he's necessarily unkind," Lilias said, "but I do believe he's become rather selfish. And I know enough about Christ to know that He is the only way that we can truly heal from our sorrows."

"I agree completely," Ian said, and his hope on behalf of both Lilias and his brother increased.

Following his conversation with Lilias, Ian returned to his room and got on his knees to offer a lengthy prayer before he made an attempt to approach his brother. He made certain Ward had what he needed before he went to the door that Donnan kept locked between himself and the world. He knocked and heard his brother predictably call, "Go away!"

"I'm not going away," Ian called back. "I want to talk to you. I promise not to talk about the estate or anything related to it. I just want to talk."

"I'm not in the mood," Donnan shouted.

"I don't care whether or not you're in the mood," Ian said. "I'm not staying in Scotland so very long, Brother. You should be polite and at least have some genteel conversation with me while I'm around."

"Genteel?" Donnan echoed with a growl. "Since when have *we* ever been genteel?"

"Exactly!" Ian said. "And to show you just how *un*-genteel I can be, if you don't open this door, I'm going to break it down and *force* you to talk to me, whether you like it or not. So open the door or you'll be hiring a locksmith to come and fix it before you'll ever be able to lock the door again."

Ian waited about half a minute before the door came open. He stepped in to find the room dark except for a vague trickle of daylight pressing reluctantly through the draperies. Once his eyes adjusted to the lack of light, he looked at his brother and said, "You look terrible. Have you been drinking?"

"I have *not* been drinking."

"You probably would be if your wife didn't quarantine you from the liquor."

"Probably," Donnan said and closed the door. Ian pulled back the drapes and Donnan snarled, "Don't *do* that!"

"Some sunlight would do you good," Ian said and turned to get a better look at Donnan. "You *really* look terrible!"

"Did you come to discuss my personal hygiene?"

"No, but someone should," Ian said in a tone of light banter that had, at one time, been very common between them.

Ian sat down, ignoring the foul aroma surrounding his brother and the staleness of the room that indicated a human being had been holed up in here for days.

Donnan sighed as he realized that Ian would not be easily gotten rid of. He sat down as well, folded his arms, and said, "So talk."

"I'd love to," Ian said, setting aside the book he'd brought with him. He could tell Donnan was surprised when Ian started the conversation by expressing his desire to share more details about his reasons for going to America and of his life there. Donnan's countenance began to soften while Ian talked, as he apparently realized this conversation truly did have nothing to do with Donnan or the problems in his life. Ian told Donnan all the same things he'd told his mother and Lilias, except that the conversation was suited to a brother. And he didn't say anything about the miracle he'd experienced with his mother; that was meant to remain private between them. He finished with a heartfelt plea for Donnan to read the book, then he handed it to him. He said with sincerity, "I know you haven't been feeling well, and I don't know what you've been doing to occupy your time, but some reading couldn't hurt. What have you got to lose?" Donnan didn't answer, and Ian pressed him for a commitment. "Will you read it? Will you read it for me? Preferably soon, because I'd like to be able to talk to you about it before I go back to America."

Donnan thought about it for a long moment, then said, "Yes, I'll read it. Thank you. And thank you for sharing these things with me. I don't know that I could ever feel the way you do, but I'm glad to know what my brother's been up to, and why."

Ian nodded and smiled, then asked, "Is there anything I can get for you?" He said it as if he truly believed that Donnan had been ill.

"No, thank you," Donnan said, and Ian left the room as if nothing were out of the ordinary.

Chapter Thirteen
Confrontation

Donnan came to supper that night, bathed and looking normal. He mentioned to Ian that he'd started reading the book, and Lilias and Anya both declared that they had as well. Donnan teased Ian about leading some kind of conspiracy in the household, then the conversation turned to trivial matters. For the next couple of days, Donnan behaved more normally, although he still managed to avoid estate business, and Ian was aware that Lilias was dealing with the overseer. He tried to help her some but not become too involved, knowing that he wouldn't be staying long enough to follow through on any serious involvement.

Ian spent a great deal of time with his niece and nephews, enjoying their company while he tried not to miss his own children and wonder what they were doing and what they looked like now. He prayed for his children and tried to focus on the present, knowing that the time would soon come when he could return home to his family.

Ian wanted to believe that as soon as his loved ones started to read the Book of Mormon, everything would start to get better. In truth, just the opposite happened. He was grumbling about it to Ward when his friend interrupted and put it neatly into perspective. "For a man who claims to understand the nature of opposition, you sound awfully surprised that it would happen within your own family. Did you really think that Satan would just allow these people to merrily go along reading and have some great magical transformation happen without any fuss whatsoever?"

Ian had to admit, "Maybe I did."

As he pondered what Ward had pointed out, he assumed a new attitude and started praying harder that opposition would not keep his loved ones from grasping the messages in the Book of Mormon that might touch their lives for good. He also took the opportunity to explain the principle of opposition to each member of his family who was reading the book, hoping to help them understand *why* they might feel that every little thing was going wrong around them, distracting them from their reading and discouraging them about life in general. They all seemed to understand what he was saying, and agreed that they would keep reading and try to be open to what they were learning. However, Donnan seemed to find it necessary to completely lock himself away in order to read the book, ignoring his appointments with Mr. Abbot and leaving Lilias to deal with the overseer. Ian stepped in to try to help, not wanting all of it to fall on Lilias's shoulders, but he knew that by doing so, he was only creating a bigger problem. It was evident that Donnan *preferred* to have Ian solve the problems. Lilias agreed with Ian that they needed to do everything they could to make Donnan face up to his responsibilities, but Anya became so frustrated with the situation that she made it clear she preferred Donnan's solution to the problem.

"I just don't believe that Donnan is cut out for this position," Anya said to Ian.

He'd come to her sitting room, hoping to discuss her reading with her. He'd imagined talking about the stories she was reading, and the powerful Christian principles integrated into them. But she jumped right into listing all the reasons that Donnan was proving himself incapable of being the Earl of Brierley. Prior to now, Anya had only implied that Ian should take his brother's position, but this time she came right out and said, "We need you to stay, Ian. The family needs you here. The people of this household and those living on the estate need you here. This is where you're supposed to be."

Ian swallowed carefully while he reminded himself of the principle of opposition. He also reminded himself that his mother was a good woman with good intentions, and in spite of her having been told his reasons for moving to America and settling his family there, she obviously didn't fully understand them. And perhaps she never would. It occurred to him that it would be better to not become immediately defensive about his determination to stand his ground. At this point, he believed that avoiding contention was the best plan, but he already knew that he could never do what she was asking of him. He cleared his throat and steadied himself, maintaining a calm demeanor. Before he could comment, she went on.

"I'm not just asking, Ian; I'm begging you. Please . . . come back to us. We need you here. We need your family here."

In Ian's mind, a thousand protests threatened to burst out of his mouth. While he was attempting to sort them into reasonable categories, he chose to address an obvious point. "Even *if* I made the decision to do so, I could never have Wren make the journey alone with three children. It would take me more than two months to get back to Nauvoo, time to settle matters there, and the same amount of time again for me to return here. By then, things could be much better here."

"Or much worse!" Anya said.

"At any rate, I cannot make a decision of that kind based on such unpredictability. And certainly not without consulting my wife."

"You went to America *entirely* based on unpredictability," Anya said, not unkindly but certainly with the firmness of a mother who was on the edge of putting her son in his place.

"Because I knew in my heart it was the right thing to do," Ian protested, equally kind but certainly firm. "I knew it beyond any doubt. I know it still. And Wren knew it too. The decision was one of mutual consent and full agreement. Nauvoo is my home now, Mother. We have a house and friends there—people who need us."

"*We* need you," she countered.

"We live among people who share our religious beliefs," Ian said. "That is the greatest source of our happiness, Mother. We sacrificed *so* much to be among these people, and yet our sacrifices are nothing compared to some. We are supposed to be there, and I know it!"

"Ian," Anya took hold of his upper arms and looked up into his eyes, "maybe what was right for you then isn't right for you now. I'm asking you to seriously consider the needs of your family here. Pray about it and see if you don't get the answer to move your family back."

Ian felt complete confidence as he said, "I'll pray about it, Mother, and I will do so with sincerity. Will you do the same?"

"What do you mean?"

"I should think the question is obvious. You're asking me to pray about this decision, and you seem to believe that I will get an answer. I'm asking you to pray to know if I am really the solution to this problem, or if the solution is that Donnan needs to make some changes in his life."

"How can I tell Donnan that he just needs to get over this strange . . . melancholy that controls him?"

"How can you tell *me* that I just need to leave behind the life I've built for myself? Why is it easier for you to ask *me* to fix the problem, than to ask Donnan to do so? This is *his* problem, to begin with. God didn't send us to this world in a certain order by accident, Mother. Donnan inherited this birthright. I know where my place is in this world. Donnan needs to figure out his and rise to the demands of his position. Perhaps you should be praying harder for him to change rather than praying that I will stay. Either way, we both have some praying to do. Agreed?"

Anya looked as if she wanted to protest, but she nodded and looked down. "Agreed."

Ian moved toward the door, needing some time alone. Before he left the room he said, "And it wouldn't hurt for you to keep reading that book. Whether you believe it's true or not, you really might find some answers there. It might actually surprise you."

Anya didn't comment, and Ian realized he felt on the verge of anger, but he didn't know who to be angry with. His mother felt desperate, and any mother would instinctively want her family to be close by. Perhaps in some way she was unconsciously believing this was simply a good excuse to get Ian and his family to come home because she missed them. Either way, Ian couldn't let his mother's emotions— or anyone else's, for that matter—sway what he knew to be true.

After talking the matter through with Ward, he knew that he needed to do as his mother had asked and pray about this decision. Even though he knew in his heart what the answer would be, Ward pointed out that if he took it to the Lord now, with an open heart, he would surely be blessed with a reaffirmation of his need to be with the

Saints. And he could face his mother—and his brother if necessary—with added confidence in knowing where he stood.

Ian took the matter very seriously, and over the next few days he prayed intensely to know for certain where he needed to be. He also prayed sincerely that Donnan *would* come to his senses, and that Ian could return to Nauvoo with the peace of knowing that all was well with his family here at Brierley. The answer came with a firm but gentle reassurance, and Ian knew beyond any minuscule doubt that he had been born to become an American, so that generations to come would be the same. He also knew that he needed to start preparing to leave Brierley, and the impression came strongly to him that he should only stay another two weeks before getting home as quickly as possible. He discussed his impressions with Ward and was not at all surprised to hear that Ward had gotten the same impressions. It had always been that way, but it was an added reassurance to Ian that he was getting the right answers, and he felt grateful for the way that God not only answered his prayers so undeniably, but he gave Ian the added witness of his companion's personal revelation to bolster his confidence in doing what he knew he had to do.

That evening at supper—with Donnan absent—Ian announced to Lilias and his mother that he and Ward would be leaving in two weeks. His mother opened her mouth to protest, and he put up a hand to stop her. "Please let me finish. You asked me to pray about this decision, and I have. I've prayed very hard and I have absolutely no doubt that my place is in America. I know it's difficult for you, Mother, and I'm sorry for the grief it causes you, but I must do what God asks of me, and I know that this is the answer—for me and for my family." He turned more to Lilias and said, "In the time I have left, I will do everything I can to help Donnan understand how important it is for him to do what needs to be done. I will also do what I can to help *you* make certain everything is in order so that if he continues to struggle you will be able to manage without so much of a burden on your shoulders. We'll discuss ideas, and I'll do everything I can to help you."

"Thank you, Ian," she said with sincerity. "I'm very grateful you came home when you did, and your help means more than I can tell you. It's already made a big difference for me, and I'm certain we will be able to manage."

Ian nodded and smiled toward her. "I'm glad to do what I can." He glanced toward his mother, whose expression was humble and without protest, but he could also see in her eyes what he'd seen there when he'd initially left for America. Her heart was breaking, and he could do nothing to keep it from doing so. He could not honor God and make his mother happy at the same time. He could only do what he knew was right in his heart. He knew that his mother understood that, and she respected it. But it still broke her heart. And consequently, it broke his heart as well.

Ian was glad he'd waited until the *end* of supper to make his announcement. Now that he'd said what he'd needed to say, no one seemed to have any appetite or desire to eat. Ian stood and said, "I think I'll get some fresh air. Ward, would you like to join me, or—"

"I think I'll stay and visit, if you don't mind," Ward said, and Ian hoped that Ward could soothe the taut emotions in the room. Perhaps that was his intention. He was very good at that sort of thing.

"I'll see that he gets to his room," Lilias offered.

"Thank you," Ian said and kissed his mother's cheek. "I'll see you ladies in the morning."

Ian hurried from the room and then from the house. Once alone in the gardens, he sat on a bench, hung his head, and cried. He knew what was right, but why did it have to be so painful?

* * * * *

The following morning a thought occurred to Ian, and he mentioned it to Ward while they were preparing for the day. "Now that we've announced our intention to leave in two weeks, we have to face a rather large problem."

"What's that?" Ward asked.

"We have no money," Ian said. "Or had you forgotten? We can't get home without money, and a fair amount of it."

"The Lord will provide," Ward said as if expecting Him to do so was the most natural thing in the world.

During the next few days, Ian found the opportunity to have some private conversations with a few of the servants—including

Mrs. Boyle—with whom he shared a personal relationship, and he took Ward along with him. Together Ian and Ward gave away each remaining copy of the Book of Mormon except for one. They both felt that they needed to have one with them for their journey home. Ian and Ward agreed that they had a strong sense of fulfillment, and they were satisfied that they had completed the work they'd come to this land to do, and it was now time to embark on the long journey home.

The next day Ian awoke with a thought in his head that took his breath away. He looked around the room he was sleeping in to reassure himself that it was indeed the room he had slept in all through his youth. Nothing had changed. Some of his clothes that he'd worn prior to going to America were still hanging in the closet. His handkerchiefs and some other odds and ends were in the bureau drawers. The house was huge, and his room would have never been needed as a guest room. Nothing had changed.

Ian squeezed his eyes closed and said a prayer, hoping that what he was thinking might actually be true, and that it wasn't simply an obscure memory that might give him false hope. He finally gathered the courage to get out of bed and stand before the bureau. He opened the top center drawer, then lifted it off of its runner, pulled it out, and set it aside. He reached his hand to the back board of the bureau, holding his breath. He let it out sharply when he felt an envelope tacked there. He peered inside, where barely enough light found its way in to show him where the tacks were so he could remove them. He took the yellowed envelope out and held it in his hands as if it might explode. For a long moment he thought of his reasons for hiding money. His parents had known that he was using most of the allowance they gave him to buy liquor, and his drinking had become a very big concern to them. When they'd threatened to withhold his allowance with the hope of solving the problem, he had hidden money just in case they carried through on their threat. They never had, and with ample money at his disposal, he'd never thought of it again—until now. He couldn't believe it! He had no idea how much he'd put in this envelope, and he couldn't remember if he'd taken part of it out at some time. Given the amount of drinking he'd done in his youth, there were a lot of things he couldn't remember.

Ian took another deep breath, turned the envelope over, and opened it. His heart began to pound as he realized that a significant amount of money was there in his hands. He wasn't sure it would be enough to get them all the way home, but it was a brilliant contribution to the necessary expenses of the journey. He laughed, then he felt the warm sting of tears in his eyes, then he laughed again before he went to Ward's room to tell him that he'd been right. The Lord was indeed providing.

Over the next couple of days, Ian devoted his time to helping Lilias understand some of the workings of the estate so that she could be better equipped to handle it. He was proud of her for taking her position in being Donnan's wife so seriously—and he told her so more than once. He also talked to her some about the book, pleased to know that she was reading it and that she *had* found some strength from its passages.

Ian shared some conversations with his mother that made him feel better about the situation between them. She admitted humbly that she respected his decision, and she knew that her desire to have him and his family there had tainted her perspective of the situation. She too was reading the book, more quickly than Lilias, and she was eager to talk to him about some of the things she'd read. She came right out and told him that she would never leave Brierley, and something as bold as embracing a new religion held no interest for her. But she expressed a sincere love for the book and heartfelt gratitude for Ian having shared it with her. Under the circumstances, Ian knew he could likely hope for no more than that. At least now his mother would more fully understand his beliefs, and it might give them more to talk about in their letters to each other.

With little more than a week left before Ian planned to leave Brierley, Donnan had hardly shown himself for days, and Ian felt a growing urgency to do something about this problem—even though he wasn't certain exactly what to do. When Donnan didn't show up for breakfast, and it was reported that he'd once again refused the meal that had been taken to his room, Ian said, "I am so fed up with this."

He stood from the table, only vaguely aware that he'd left the women looking stunned, and perhaps afraid. But he didn't think about that. He could only think of how he had to do whatever it took to solve this problem, once and for all, or he could never leave here in peace.

Ian went first to find Mrs. Boyle, saying directly to her, "I would like a hot bath prepared in my brother's bedroom, and once he's had some time to get cleaned up, I would like a good meal brought to the dining room."

"Very good, sir," Mrs. Boyle said with a conspiratorial smile. She might as well have come out and said, *It's about time somebody did something about this.*

With Mrs. Boyle's silent vote of confidence, and a determination inside of him that he had to believe was inspired, Ian went to the sitting room that Donnan had turned into his own personal prison. Feeling more angry than he knew he should, he went back to his own room and took some time to pray and calm himself. On his way back to Donnan's room, he saw some maids taking buckets of water into the bedroom Donnan was *supposed* to share with his wife. Ian stopped at the door of the sitting room, took a deep breath, and said another quick prayer that he could have the courage to do what needed to be done.

"Open this door," Ian called. "We need to talk!"

"Go away!"

"I'm not going away!" Ian said firmly. "Open the door!"

"I'm tired. Go away!"

"Open this door, Donnan!" Ian shouted, "or I swear to you I will break it down!"

"You wouldn't dare!" Donnan shouted back.

Ian felt so frustrated that he didn't give the matter another moment's thought before he took hold of the doorframe with both hands and lifted his foot with all the force of aggravation he felt. The lock broke beneath his boot and he threw the door open. In the shadowy room he saw his brother's stunned expression just before he took him by the collar, pulled him up out of his chair, and backed him up against the wall.

"I don't know what all of this is about, big brother," Ian said, "but I am sick to death of it, and so are the women who love you. Your parents did not raise you to behave like this, and every day that you hide away like some cowardly, sniveling fool, you dishonor them by your avoidance of living the life you were born to live. Now, you listen to me, and you listen well. You are going to do whatever it takes to be a man and do what needs to be done. Note that I didn't say you were going to *act* like a man; you are going to *be* a man. I don't care how hard it is. I don't care how much effort it takes. You have a wife and children and responsibilities that come with your name and your privilege. And every day for the rest of your life you are going to put your feet on the floor and get out of bed and face those responsibilities in a way that would make your father proud of you. No more shame. No more guilt. No more hiding. We are *finished* with this."

"Are you done trying to bully me?" Donnan snarled.

"Is that what you think I'm doing?" Ian countered.

"What would you call it?" Donnan retorted like a snotty schoolboy.

Ian took hold of Donnan's arm and practically dragged him into the next room where the bath had been prepared. "Get yourself cleaned up, and then we're going to talk about this."

"Why don't you just go back to America and leave me to my business?"

"Your *business*?" Ian snarled. "You haven't given a moment's thought to your *business* in months."

"Whatever I have or haven't done," Donnan snapped, "is of no concern to you."

Ian took him by the collar again, glad that Donnan was in a weak enough state not to protest. "*This* family and *this* estate certainly *are* my business."

"Then why don't *you* take care of them?"

"Because it's not *my* responsibility!" Ian said. "Now, get cleaned up so we can talk about this!"

"Why don't *you*—" Donnan said but was interrupted by Ian landing a fist to the side of his jaw. The force sent Donnan back into the tub full of water, fully clothed.

While Donnan was gasping and shaking his head in an attempt to get his bearings, Ian said, "I'm coming back in half an hour and I expect to find you bathed and dressed. If not, I will take a scrub brush to you myself, and I will have every manservant in this house here to help me if I need to. Don't think I won't do it!"

Ian left the room and slammed the door for emphasis. He stood there in the hall for a moment, surprised to realize that what he felt was not anger. He didn't feel at all out of control or fueled by any negative emotion. He felt as if everything he'd just said and done had been controlled and purposeful, however differently it might have appeared to his brother.

For the next half hour Ian paced the hallway, listening for evidence that Donnan was doing what he'd been told to do, and making certain that his brother didn't try to leave and sneak out of the house in order to avoid facing what needed to be faced. He chuckled softly to hear Donnan grumbling and cursing, but then he heard noises to indicate that he was getting out of his wet clothes and getting cleaned up.

When Donnan opened the door, looking better than he'd looked in weeks, Ian was leaning against the wall of the hallway, his ankles crossed and his arms folded. He looked up to see that Donnan was surprised to find him there.

"Making certain I don't escape?" Donnan asked.

"Exactly," Ian said, ignoring Donnan's disgusted expression. "Now, we're going to get you something decent to eat, and then we're going to get some fresh air while the maids clean up the disasters you've left in your rooms." He took hold of Donnan's arm. "Come along, brother."

Donnan shook off his brother's grasp. "I can walk of my own accord."

"Just don't go trying to dash off," Ian warned lightly, "or I'll be making the other side of your jaw a perfect match."

"Resorting to violence?" Donnan growled.

"You have no room to talk," Ian said, trying to keep the tone light. "When I came back from London, you handed me a fierce bloody lip."

"You deserved it," Donnan said.

"One good turn deserves another," Ian said and chuckled, but Donnan didn't seem to find it humorous.

Ian sat at the dining table with Donnan while he ate his meal. He ate voraciously, and Ian asked, "Did that belt in the jaw awaken you to the realization that you've been practically starving yourself?"

"Maybe," Donnan said and kept eating.

When Donnan was finished, the two men walked out to the gardens, ambling slowly among the meticulously trimmed shrubberies and the flowers of early summer. After walking in silence for many minutes, Donnan said, "So, why don't you just come out and say it?"

"Say what?" Ian asked.

"Whatever it is you have to say," Donnan said.

"I already said *everything* I have to say," Ian said. "I'm leaving soon and I need to know that everything is all right here with you . . . with the family . . . the estate. I need to know I can count on you to do what needs to be done."

"Would you believe me if I told you that you can? Count on me?"

"I'll believe you if you mean it," Ian said, wanting to ask Donnan if he'd heard him correctly.

"Truthfully," Donnan said, putting his hands behind his back, "I've felt like such a heel about the way I've been behaving, but I wasn't sure how to undo my bad conduct once I'd developed the habit of behaving in that way. Maybe I just needed to be slugged into a bathtub to knock me to my senses."

"Maybe," Ian said with a nonchalance in his voice that was a stark disguise for the inner joy he was feeling to hear what his brother was saying—and the sincere humility with which he was saying it.

"However," Donnan said, "getting slugged into a bathtub in and of itself might not have been enough, if I hadn't already . . ."

"Already what?" Ian pressed when Donnan hesitated, and Ian sensed that his hesitation was due to his struggling with some kind of emotion.

Donnan came to a bench and sat down. Ian sat beside him. Donnan leaned his forearms on his thighs and clasped his hands together. "I read something in that book that I must admit . . . well, it really got to me. I read it over and over." Donnan sighed and Ian had to try to not hold his breath, waiting to hear more evidence of the miracle unfolding before him. "Since you *are* my brother," Donnan said, "you know that we were raised with strong Christian principles, and we were certainly taken to church on Sundays. But such things have never felt directly applicable in my life . . . until I started reading that book. I realized that I had let the grief of losing Father take far too great a hold on me. My fear of not being able to measure up to what he'd left to me just mixed into that grief and I . . ." he shook his head, "I'm ashamed to say I just . . . fell apart." He sighed loudly and sat up straight. "I haven't read very far into the book, because I keep reading the same passages over and over. The way Ishmael's daughters were grieving too long for the death of their father. The faith that Nephi displays over and over in the face of difficulties in his life. But what struck me most deeply were the words of Nephi following the death of his own father."

Donnan closed his eyes and lifted his face slightly toward the warmth of the sun as he recited memorized words. *"Nevertheless, notwithstanding the great goodness of the Lord, in showing me his great and marvelous works, my heart exclaimeth: O wretched man that I am! Yea, my heart sorroweth because of my flesh; my soul grieveth because of mine iniquities. I am encompassed about, because of the temptations and the sins which do so easily beset me. And when I desire to rejoice, my heart groaneth because of my sins; nevertheless, I know in whom I have trusted. My God hath been my support; he hath led me through mine afflictions in the wilderness."*

Ian looked heavenward, almost expecting to hear angels singing. The miracle felt so intense to him that he wouldn't have been surprised. God had answered his every prayer, even more than he'd ever believed possible. He was still trying to take it in when Donnan turned to look at Ian and said, "I can see now that I've not allowed the Lord into my life, Ian. I can see that I need to allow Him to help me take on these burdens that feel so heavy to me. I can never thank you enough for your patience, and for sharing your beliefs with me. Believe it or not, everything's going to be all right now. I *will* make our father proud, Ian. I will!"

"Oh, I believe it!" Ian said, and the two brothers embraced tightly.

They talked for a while longer, then they went into the house to find Ward and the ladies just sitting down to lunch. Lilias rose to greet her husband with a kiss when she saw him. It was evident by the glow in her eyes that she had immediately picked up on the change in Donnan's countenance. Donnan greeted his mother with a kiss as well, then they were all seated.

"Before we eat," Donnan said, "there's something I want to say. I'll keep it simple and we can discuss the details later." He took a deep breath. "I want to apologize for my behavior of late, and I want to promise both of you—Lilias, Mother—that it will never happen again. I will never again leave burdens on your shoulders that should be mine. I promise you!"

The women both got tears in their eyes, and Ian saw Ward smile. The two of them had certainly seen evidence of a great many miracles during their journeys together.

* * * * *

The day before Ward and Ian were scheduled to leave Brierley, Ian counted his money once again, silently figuring an estimation of how much it would take them to get home. He imagined them having to find some kind of work in Liverpool before sailing, or perhaps in New York City before they could afford to get home from there. He prayed once again to know what to do, and then tried to make it a matter of faith and simply not think about it.

Later that day, Anya found Ian in the library with Ward. They all chatted comfortably for a few minutes before Anya put an envelope into Ian's hand.

"What is this?" he asked.

"Before you left," she said, "your father gave you your inheritance in full."

"That's right," Ian said, his heart pounding as he realized this was about money.

"After he died, some investments he'd made were cashed in, and I set aside your portion with the intention of sending it to you when the time felt right. It never felt right. Now I can place the money safely into your hands and not worry about it getting lost or stolen if I were to mail it. I'm certain you'll find good use for it."

"I'm certain I will," he said and kissed his mother's cheek. "You'll never know what this means to me."

"I think I might," she said and winked at him, then she abruptly changed the subject by asking Ward if he would like to join her for a walk while Ian visited with his brother about some estate business that needed to be settled before Ian's departure. Ward graciously accepted the invitation. Ian silently thanked God for blessing him so abundantly, then he went to find his brother, knowing their hours left together were quickly running out.

Chapter Fourteen
Pall of Silence

Wren loved spring in Nauvoo, and she especially enjoyed being able to spend some time outdoors when the air was pleasant. The children also loved being outside, and it was a joy to share their pleasure in observing the evidence of the world coming back to life. Wren loved pointing out to them how the leaves on the trees were sprouting, and the green stalks of future flowers were poking up out of the ground. She loved hanging the wash outside on a sunny day, instead of spreading it around in the house to dry. The sunshine and fresh air always made the clothes and linens smell better, and she was glad to finally have another winter behind them. And she hoped with all her heart that before winter came again, she might have her husband back home with her and the children. Having spent two winters without him felt like two winters too many.

She'd not grown to miss him any less, even though she had learned to manage well enough. She held a prayer in her heart continually that he would be brought home safely to her. She'd come to accept that his work out in the world was the most important thing for him to be doing, and she completely respected that. She knew that Ian would come home when the Lord let him know the work was finished. She accepted God's will in the situation, both in the fact that he was gone to begin with and in the timing of his return. Still, she prayed every day that it would not be too much longer, and she found it difficult to relinquish her own will to God's in that regard. She told God that she would accept His will even if she didn't understand it. But she would always find herself praying in the same breath that Ian would come home soon.

Spring also brought an improvement of health with the children. No one had been seriously ill through the winter, but there had been a lot of coughing and stuffy noses that had never seemed to go away. Now that the air was getting warmer, it felt as if the windows could be opened and all of the stale air could be expelled from the house. Wren and Patricia knew the same was true of other households and other children. They sometimes took turns attending Relief Society meetings, and even Sabbath meetings, when the children needed to stay in due to illness. They participated enough in such things to be aware of similar struggles in other homes and also to remain apprised of local happenings. But it seemed that when spring arrived, people were getting out more and were more prone to sharing news with one another. At first Wren felt this was a good thing, then news started coming to her ears that an air of unrest was growing in Nauvoo, and it made her terribly uneasy.

Wren had certainly been aware in the past of little incidents happening here and there in which anti-Mormon fanatics did something to frighten or cause harm to the Saints. But as far as she'd known it had been rare here in Nauvoo, and she'd never felt unsafe, surrounded as they were by many good neighbors in the heart of the city. Of course, she was also well aware of how the Mormons had been driven from other places prior to settling in Nauvoo. She had heard the horrors of those times from many sources, most especially from Patricia, who had seen and experienced unspeakable things. But Nauvoo felt safe. Nauvoo was a place of peace and prosperity, and Wren had no reason to believe that they wouldn't grow old here and see their children raised. A temple was being built, and Wren—along with everyone else in the community—longed for the day when it would be completed and the Saints could partake of great blessings within its walls. Joseph had taught the people about the great work that would take place in temples, and about the promised blessings to those who were willing to participate in that work. Wren looked forward to the day when Ian would return. She imagined him once again being among the men who donated their time to the construction of the temple. Since Ian had financial security and didn't need to work for a living, she knew he would gladly give time each and every day to the temple effort. She had written to tell him the details as the work had progressed, and he had expressed his desire to do exactly that. Wren loved imagining how it would be. He would of course be very busy and come home tired. But at least he would come home. Every day he would come home.

The knowledge that a temple was being built here in Nauvoo helped ease Wren's concerns when word came to her that some of the Saints were experiencing persecution. But with the warmth of spring, the most troubling news that came was in regard to their beloved Prophet, Joseph. For reasons Wren didn't fully understand, it seemed that Joseph's life was being sought, and he was in danger—again. He had announced his intentions to run for president of the United States. Wren considered it a noble goal, to be sure. But she wondered how he would ever manage to do such a thing and continue to do all that he did for the people of Nauvoo. There was talk on the streets and among the Saints of political controversies and conspiracies and of legal threats that had nothing to do with the law. Wren wished that Ian was here so that they could talk about such things. She felt certain that Ian would better understand all that was taking place and help her to understand it better. As it was, Wren simply felt unsettled, knowing that events were unfolding among the Mormons and it was all very complicated. But she didn't begin to understand it. She *did* understand, however, the feeling in the air that something just wasn't right, and it seemed likely to get worse before it got better. She did her best to care for her home and family, serve others whenever she could, and live her life as God would have her live it. She tried not to entertain thoughts of fear and doubt, but rather to look to the future with hope and faith.

Wren saw Emma Smith rarely, and she'd only had the chance to actually speak to her once in the space of many months. She was a very busy woman and often struggled with her health. She was also dealing with the early stages of pregnancy. But Wren had noticed a growing cloudiness in Emma's eyes, and it worried Wren. What did Emma know that the women around her *didn't* know? Or perhaps Emma was as ignorant as the rest of them. Perhaps for all that she was the Prophet's wife, the Prophet chose to not tell his wife things that might worry her. Or perhaps he was just too busy to share every detail of the goings-on. His life as a religious leader *and* a political one was likely more complicated than Wren could begin to imagine or understand. But she understood the look in Emma's eyes, and it left her uneasy. Still, Wren knew she was a simple person with a simple life, and the most or best she could do was pray for the Prophet and his wife, press forward with faith, and strive to be her best self.

Spring warmed into summer, and Wren didn't know whether to be sad or thrilled to realize her husband had been gone for two years. She was sad to think how long they'd been apart, and thrilled to know that there were two years behind them in this separation, and they were two years closer to being together again.

At that very time, the situation regarding Joseph seemed to explode. Wren's ignorance became especially frustrating. She and Patricia tried to piece together what little they knew, but it was very little. They knew that the Nauvoo Legion, which had been created to protect their city, had been put on high alert. And they knew that Joseph and his brother Hyrum were supposed to go to Carthage Jail, some miles away, to answer to some kind of trumped-up charges that the people all knew were not founded in any real truth. It was not unusual for Joseph to be facing charges of one kind or another. Satan had been using this as a method to oppose the young Prophet right from the beginning. And Joseph had spent time in prison before for the sake of the cause. But word among the Saints was that Joseph believed if he went to Carthage he would not come back alive. Apparently it was more about some kind of conspiracy to undo him than it was about anything legal.

Patricia came home from town one afternoon quite agitated with the news she'd heard. Wren had remained with the children so that Patricia could do her errands quickly. She reported that the news among their fellow Saints was that Joseph and Hyrum had fled Nauvoo, that they'd crossed the river and gone west in search of a place where the Saints could eventually follow and live in peace.

"Leave?" Wren echoed, her heart wrenching. "But . . . the temple . . . the city. Everything we have is here."

"If the Prophet feels the need to leave," Patricia said, "and he's had inspiration regarding where the Saints need to be, we cannot dispute that."

Wren couldn't argue, but she slumped into a chair, feeling sick to her stomach.

"It will not likely be anytime soon," Patricia said, "but that's what I heard."

"Then it's all worse than we've believed," Wren said.

"Apparently so. And it would seem that Joseph knows it will continue to get worse."

Wren looked hard at Patricia. "D'ye think there is *any* place the people can go and live in peace?"

"There must be!" Patricia said with conviction. "Joseph has said there is such a place. We must believe that it's true!"

Wren nodded, but she wondered what they might have to go through to find that place and settle there. Wren and Patricia were far from the only women in Nauvoo whose husbands were away on missions, but it felt especially disconcerting to hear this kind of news and not have their husbands here in the face of such uncertainty. Wren and Patricia talked the matter through and came mutually to the only possible conclusion. They could only press forward with faith and strive to do God's will, each and every day. Together they focused on the necessary household tasks, finding joy with their children, and reminding each other frequently to have faith and a positive attitude.

That evening after the children were in bed, they read together from the scriptures and shared a lengthy prayer. But when Wren was alone in her bed, surrounded by darkness and silence, the happenings of Nauvoo combined with the absence of her husband left her decidedly afraid. When the fear began to overtake her, she had to force her mind to a place of faith while she prayed aloud and with fervor for God to remove her fear and replace it with faith. Faith that her husband would come home safely, faith that Joseph and Hyrum would be protected, faith that the Saints would be able to live in peace. And faith that no matter what happened she—and those she loved—would be able to press forward with hope in Christ and the promise of great eternal blessings that would make any mortal sacrifice worth it.

Wren finally slept with the promise of those blessings wrapped around her, but the next day brought news that Joseph and Hyrum's absence was only making the situation worse for the Saints, and some people were accusing them of being cowards. Wren and Patricia both felt outraged that *anyone* could call these great men cowards. The things they had faced and endured would have undone most men. They prayed together right then and again at bedtime, specifically asking God's blessings to be upon these men who had sacrificed so much for the Saints. They prayed for the families of Joseph and Hyrum, and they prayed that the Saints would be protected, guided, and strengthened. They prayed, as always, for their husbands, and they asked God that they might be allowed to return home soon. Of course, they always finished their prayers with submission to God's will above their own. But after the amen was spoken, Patricia said to Wren, "It can't hurt to ask."

"No, it can't hurt t' ask. And I'm going t' keep asking until they come home safely."

Wren and Patricia shared a hug, then went to their separate rooms to endure another night of sleeping alone, struggling to repress their fears and nurture their faith.

The next news that Wren and Patricia heard was that Joseph and Hyrum had returned to Nauvoo, and it was their intention to go to Carthage and face the charges against them.

"No!" Wren said when Patricia repeated the information to her. "I thought that Joseph believed they would not come back alive if they went t' Carthage."

"That's what I've heard," Patricia said. "But how can we know if all of what we've heard is true? And I'm certain it's much more complicated than we can possibly imagine."

Wren groaned and began to pace while her thoughts ran in circles. Could it be true? What of Emma? How was she doing with all of this? While Wren missed Ian and worried over him every day, she couldn't even begin to imagine what Emma might be going through. And Emma was now about halfway through her pregnancy. Wren wanted so badly for Ian to be here, to talk all of this through with him, to have his arms around her and his shoulders to lean on. But at least he wasn't being forced to face illegal charges and possibly death.

Wren and Patricia continued to discuss the situation amidst the need to care for the children, although they were careful to speak cryptically of things that might upset them—especially when Gillian was around. She was smart and perceptive, and she knew very well who Brother Joseph was. They didn't want *her* to be upset and add the need to soothe her to the strain of the situation. Both women decided that they just had to believe that Joseph and Hyrum would survive this. Surely some miracle would intervene! The people needed their Prophet, and the Prophet's brother was a great sustaining force among the people of the Church—and to his brother. Surely God would not allow anything too horrible to happen. Joseph had been miraculously spared many times before; surely he would be again!

The following morning it was Wren's turn to go into town to pick up a few things while Patricia stayed at home with the children. She was starting for home when she became aware of some people gathering on the street, and some whispers among them. She quickly realized that Joseph and Hyrum were riding slowly past on horses, along with a small group of men accompanying them. They were leaving Nauvoo to go to Carthage, and it seemed a general sentiment among the whispers Wren heard that there was a chance they wouldn't come back alive. While Wren refused to believe it, her heart was struck with an unexpected tightness when she got a good look at Joseph as he rode past. He wore an expression of dignity and courage, as he always did. But there was a solemnity about his countenance that Wren had never seen before. Tears came to her eyes—hot, unyielding tears that caught her off guard and made her wonder over the depth of their source. Did a part of her believe this *was* the last time she would see Joseph and his brother alive? Or was it simply the poignancy of the situation that was affecting her so deeply? She watched the group of men ride past, and stood there in silence long after they were gone from sight. She prayed for them and for their wives and families. She said an added prayer for Emma, who had been so very kind to her and Ian when they'd first arrived in Nauvoo. She was a good woman. She'd been through so much. She needed her husband to come home to her, just as Wren needed her own husband to come home to *her*.

Wren returned home to tell Patricia what she had seen and what she had felt. They knelt together to pray that very minute, and prayed again a while later, including the children in their circle even though most of them were too young to understand what was taking place. Wren had quietly explained it to Gillian the best that she could, realizing that the situation had become too prevalent in their lives to be ignored or avoided. Gillian took it in with mature matter-of-factness, but that night, when Wren knelt with Gillian beside her bed to listen to Gillian's prayer, she was astonished with the maturity the child exhibited in asking that Joseph and Hyrum and their families would be blessed, as well as the men who were with Joseph and Hyrum. And at the very end of her prayer, Gillian simply said, "Whatever happens, let Jesus take care of everyone. In the name of Jesus Christ, amen."

Long after Gillian had been tucked into bed and Wren was lying in her own bed, gazing toward the ceiling into the darkness, her daughter's tender words kept resounding in her head. *Whatever happens, let Jesus take care of everyone.* Wren felt in awe of this child's simple and humble example of allowing God's will to override all else, and to simply believe that no matter what happened, Jesus would take care of everyone. No matter the trials and persecutions, no matter the losses and the grief, Jesus would comfort every heart and soothe every hurt. And in the end, the atoning sacrifice of Jesus Christ would restore all things to those who exercised faith in Him and did their best to endure faithfully to the end.

The following morning at the breakfast table, Gillian said to Wren, "Mama told me that when it's time for Brother Joseph to go back to heaven, everything will be all right. She said that Jesus would take care of Joseph and everyone who loves him."

Wren exchanged a quick glance with Patricia that promised further conversation at some more appropriate moment later in the day. She then looked directly at Gillian and said, "Of course everything will be all right, my sweetheart. Of course Jesus will take care of everyone who loves Brother Joseph. I'm so glad that yer mama told ye that, because it's true."

Gillian was satisfied enough with the comment to go on eating as if nothing was out of the ordinary.

The following day word came that Joseph and Hyrum had been murdered by a mob with painted faces. Wren and Patricia wept as if a member of their own family had been cruelly taken away. Gillian cried some too, as if she felt the loss as deeply as the adults. The other children seemed concerned with their mothers' tears, but were too young to understand the reasons for their sadness. Wren couldn't remember feeling any more devastated than this when she'd lost her own father, her sister, her baby. Not only had she been well acquainted with Joseph, but she knew he was a prophet of God. It was through him that this glorious gospel of Jesus Christ had been restored. She stood stoutly among the Saints who had pledged their allegiance to God and to His living prophet on the earth who spoke for Him. Now Joseph was gone. What would become of the Saints? Of Nauvoo? And what of Emma, and Hyrum's wife, Mary? What of their dear mother, Lucy? What of the children? It was all just too horrible to even feel real.

Wren found it difficult to function at all through the remainder of the day, and Patricia was equally devastated. They only did what was absolutely necessary to care for their children in between repeated efforts to talk about what had happened and to express their grief— perhaps to convince themselves and each other that it had actually taken place.

Wren cried herself to sleep that night, and she was not awake for long the next day before tears overtook her again. The grief of this horrible loss was tangled into fear on behalf of the Prophet's family, and of the Saints as a whole. The uncertainty of the future was as difficult to grasp as the horror of the present.

Word spread through town that the bodies of Joseph and Hyrum were being brought back to Nauvoo that day. Wren and Patricia were gathered at the edge of the street, along with their children, when the wagons went slowly and silently past. The bodies were covered with green branches and not to be seen until they'd been prepared for burial. But Wren didn't have to see them to know in her heart that it was them. They were truly dead, and their spirits had moved on. The entire spirit of the city felt different. Grief was etched into every face. Wren felt perfectly empathetic; she completely understood the silent communication that passed between the Saints when they met on the streets. The loss was mutual and deep, and the fear intertwined into the loss was undeniable. If a prophet of God could be murdered in cold blood—and his brother at his side—then what might evil men be capable of doing to a body of people only wanting to live their religion in peace? The history of the Mormon people to this point had already proven that it could get so bad that the extermination of

Mormons could become legalized. Would it reach such proportions again? Would they be driven out of Nauvoo as the people had been driven out of Ohio and Missouri? Where would they go? How would they survive? And if such an exodus was to occur, what would Wren and Patricia do if their husbands did not return home first?

Through the following days a pall continued to hover over the city. Wren and Patricia waited in a very long line for the formal viewing of the Prophet and his brother. While it was difficult to view the evidence for herself, Wren knew that doing so made it easier to believe. She looked for Emma but didn't see her anywhere. She was dealing with her grief privately, no doubt.

Wren and Patricia also attended the public funeral, which was difficult as well, but it also carried a message of hope. The very gospel that Joseph had been an instrument in restoring to the earth was the source of hope for all people who were mourning his loss.

Within weeks it became evident that life would go on, and the Church would continue to thrive. The death of the Prophet had ended a great era in regard to the restoration of the gospel, but the keys and authority needed to keep that gospel alive and functioning had been left behind in Joseph's stead, and God would continue to lead His people. While the possibility of leaving Nauvoo remained a topic of discussion, the work on the temple continued, and life went on as before.

Wren often wondered about Emma, and wished that there was something she could do to help her in this time of grief. She wished that she and Emma were more than just acquaintances, so that she could be in a position to make more of a difference to her at this time. After prayerfully considering what she might do within the parameters of their established relationship, she wrote Emma a lengthy letter that expressed all of her love and concern and prayers. She had it delivered to Emma's home, sending it with a prayer that it might be received with just a tiny bit of the love and comfort that Wren had felt when writing it. Each day she continued to keep Emma and each member of the Smith family in her prayers, and each day she prayed that Ian would return home to her—soon! She needed him. Oh, how she needed him!

* * * * *

When it came time to leave Brierley, the final good-byes were every bit as difficult for Ian as they had been the last time. When all had been said and final embraces shared, Ian felt mixed emotions as he and Ward stepped into the carriage. Ian turned back to gaze at Brierley for as long as it was visible through the carriage window, then he looked ahead, knowing that he was finally going home. Home to America. Home to his sweet Wren and his precious children. Home at last!

As soon as Ian and Ward arrived in Liverpool, they went straightaway to purchase their passage on the next ship bound for New York City. It would be leaving in three days. Ian and Ward agreed that they were glad it was three days and not five, or six, or ten. But they both felt so anxious to get home that every day felt like a week. Unlike when they'd left New York, they both felt completely good about making this journey in the steerage. It would conserve their funds and ensure that they didn't run out of money after they got to America and needed to still travel a long distance. It also seemed right—according to Ward's reasoning on the previous journey—that it might give them more opportunity to interact with the other passengers and perhaps share their message of peace and hope. They both felt mildly concerned about being in such close quarters when there was always the possibility of illness breaking out. But they had prayed about the decision and had both felt peaceful with it. They simply had to put their trust in the Lord that all would be well, and that they would be able to return to their families safe and healthy and strong.

They found adequate accommodations in Liverpool—barely adequate, but adequate nevertheless. During the few days, they went twice to the tea shop where they had first met prior to their initial passage to America. They reminisced over the situation that had led them to sit at the same table in the crowded shop. Ian had been with Wren, Bethia, and Bethia's traveling companion, Shona. Ward had been with his mother. They talked about how Ward and Bethia had immediately felt drawn to each other, and it hadn't taken long for them to fall in love. They'd become very close in a very short time, and Bethia's death had been extremely hard on him. But Ward admitted now that losing her had been very humbling for him, and it had perhaps softened his heart prior to Ian putting the Book of

Mormon into his hands. Ward's mother had read the entire book to him while they'd been living in New York, and Ward had gained an undeniable testimony of its truthfulness. Now that he was married to Patricia and had a beautiful daughter, the heartache over losing Bethia had been softened, but her death would always be a tender place in his heart.

Ian and Ward sometimes laughed as they recounted certain memories about their journey from Liverpool to Illinois, and sometimes they were overcome by a pall of silence as they wandered together into memories that were still difficult to talk about. They'd both made peace with the deaths of Ward's mother and Ian's daughter, but they hadn't stopped missing them, and some memories would always be difficult and were likely best avoided. They chose instead to talk of the peace and joy in their lives that the gospel had given them, and of all they'd been blessed with—including dear wives and precious children.

Longing to get home quickly to their wives and children, they were glad to finally set sail, and they began counting days at sea. Ian put a mark for each day on a page in his journal so that he could keep track. The six weeks—give or take depending on the weather—that it took to cross the Atlantic seemed eternal, but they were determined to make the most of it.

They hit a long spell of rain, which thankfully did not bring much wind with it. The ship sailed along mostly undisturbed, but going out on deck for fresh air and diversion was impossible without getting drenched and therefore very cold. Ian and Ward and the passengers with them had all agreed that staying warm and dry would more likely keep them all healthy. They were mostly a pleasant group of people, friendly and conversational. Among the passengers were children who got easily bored and often cranky, but everyone—for the most part—was patient and willing to help keep the children occupied.

When the tedium and boredom began to get especially cumbersome, Ian asked the group if they would mind if he read to them from his favorite book. He told them it was a book of ancient scripture that was not very well known. He told them it had many wonderful Christian principles in it, and also some truly great stories. No one protested, and a few sounded eager to hear anything that would ease their boredom. So Ian began reading aloud from the Book of Mormon each day for an hour or more after breakfast and lunch, and for a while each evening before bed. Once the habit was established, Ward suggested that they all pray together as a group before going to sleep. Some politely went along; others were pleased. But this too became a habit.

The crowd that gathered to listen to the readings and pray together became larger in number over the days, and more and more attentive. Ian regretted that he had no more copies of the Book of Mormon to give to these people, but he assured them that arrangements could be made for copies to be delivered to them if they would write to him in Nauvoo. Many people lingered after the reading sessions to engage in conversations that not only included the topics encountered in the Book of Mormon, but also included discussions regarding Joseph Smith and his experiences in bringing it forth. Ian and Ward both found opportunity—just as they had many times in London—to share their testimony in regard to Joseph being a prophet. Privately, Ian and Ward discussed how privileged they were to know Brother Joseph personally, and they looked forward to being able to see him again. Before they reached New York City, there were several people who had told Ian and Ward they were planning to travel to Nauvoo as soon as circumstances allowed. Ian made certain that all of these people knew where to find him so that he could help them when they arrived. Deep bonds of friendship were forged with a few of these people, and the weeks of the journey went much more quickly for Ian than he had anticipated. He felt richly blessed for the opportunity of this particular phase of the journey, and was grateful for how it had enriched his own life by giving him a chance to share with so many people what was very dear to him. They read the entire Book of Mormon and some favorite passages over again. And not one of the passengers in the steerage became ill through the entire voyage. Many declared that it was the power of prayer and of the book they'd been reading that had helped keep them all healthy and safe.

The ship docked with the morning tide, and once breakfast was over, passengers began to disembark. The minute Ian and Ward stepped off the ship, they immediately went to arrange transportation west. It would take a series of hired carriages traveling for long stretches to finally get them to their destination, and home still felt so far away. But now that they were actually back in America—back on the same continent as their families—they could think of nothing but getting home and being reunited. They didn't even bother trying to find a room in New York City. They were on a carriage before supper time, with some bread and cheese they'd purchased tucked into their bags so they could travel through the night and not stop for a meal.

"It's funny," Ian said to Ward once they were headed west, "I feel now more than ever that our work is done, that there is nothing more to do except get home safely. I felt that way when we left Brierley, but since we got off that ship, the feeling has settled in more deeply."

"I couldn't have said it better myself," Ward said emphatically. "I'm missing Patricia more right now than I've allowed myself to do for many months now."

"I couldn't have said *that* better myself," Ian said, then clarified in a comical tone. "I mean . . . missing Wren . . . the way you miss Patricia."

"I know what you meant," Ward said and nudged him gently with an elbow. The middle-aged couple sitting across from them couldn't help overhearing what they were saying. The man ignored them; the woman smiled as if she enjoyed the way they were speaking of their wives.

"How long have you been away from home?" the woman asked.

"More than two years," Ward said.

"For what purpose?" the woman asked, astonished.

"We're missionaries," Ian said. "We've devoted this time to sharing the gospel of Jesus Christ with many people that we've encountered."

"How fascinating!" the woman said. Her husband glared at her, then at Ian and Ward, silently stating that he wasn't interested and he wasn't pleased with his wife's interest. But the woman ignored her husband and said, "Tell me your message. It would be a lovely way to pass the time."

Ian and Ward took turns sharing their beliefs, their experiences, and their hope that others could find the peace and joy they had found in their own lives. In the end, before the couple arrived at their destination and left the carriage, the woman admitted that she was quite content with her own religious sect, and the husband seemed relieved to hear it. But she thanked them for sharing their message with her, and she wished them well. She also said, "Do you boys have what you need to get home?"

Ian said, "I'm certain we'll manage, thank you." He didn't want to admit that with the carriage fares being what they were, he wasn't sure they could afford to have enough to eat through the remainder of the journey. And he and Ward had decided that while stopping at an inn along the way a couple of times to get a decent night's sleep would be preferable, it likely wasn't possible with the amount of money they had left.

"Oh, I'm certain you will," the woman said, but as she stepped out of the carriage with Ian's assistance, she discreetly placed some money in his hand. She winked and nodded, silently declaring that she wouldn't take it back, and that she didn't want him to draw her husband's attention to the fact that she had given it to him. Ian nodded in return, silently thanking God for His blessings that came from many different sources. "Thank you for your kindness," he said and winked back at her, adding, "It's been a pleasure visiting with you."

"And you," she said and walked away toward her waiting husband. Ian stepped back into the carriage and it rolled on.

After seemingly endless hours in different carriages, Ian and Ward were glad to stop at an inn where they could get a nice, hot meal and a good night's sleep in tolerably comfortable beds. They were on their way again the following morning, watching miles pass by the carriage windows and counting the possible days until home appeared on the horizon.

They talked about stopping in the town where Ward's mother was buried in order to visit the grave and leave some flowers there. But when Ward realized how much time it would take away from their traveling, he insisted that they just keep going. He declared firmly, "I'm certain my mother understands our need to get home to our families, and I'm certain her spirit is nowhere near that cemetery."

"Yes, I'm certain she'll understand," Ian agreed.

The final days of the journey dragged incessantly. They had to endure the breaking of a carriage axle that created more than half a day's delay. But Ian and Ward both agreed that at least the problem had occurred in a way that had not put anyone in danger. Since Ward's mother had been killed in a carriage accident, it was a sensitive topic for both of them. Trying to count blessings instead of wasted hours, Ian did his best to help fix the problem, while Ward comically pretended to supervise. Since he couldn't see and had no idea what was going on, the driver and his traveling assistant found Ward's advice humorous, which helped keep the situation from becoming overly stressful. When it became evident that the axle *couldn't* be fixed, one of the men took a horse from the team and rode to the next town to get a different carriage to bring back and secure the passengers and to deliver the necessary items to fix *this* carriage.

Ian and Ward were soon on their way again, and the counting of days narrowed down to the counting of hours until the shores of the Mississippi River would appear before them, and they would be home.

Chapter Fifteen
Home at Last

When the two men finally arrived in Nauvoo, it was well past dark, and they feared that their wives would have already gone to bed.

"I can smell the river," Ward said when they stepped out of the carriage. "We're really home!"

"We really are!" Ian said.

With Ward's hand planted firmly on his shoulder, they walked as quickly as they could safely manage down familiar streets to the home they loved so dearly. A clear night and a partial moon made the walk easier, and Ian stood for a long moment just outside the gate, looking up at the house with awe and gratitude.

"It looks just the same," he said to Ward. "Such a beautiful house!"

"Indeed!" Ward said as if his imagination made the image every bit as clear to him as it was to Ian. "Are the windows dark?" he asked.

"No," Ian said eagerly. "I see some light in a couple of windows, so we're in luck. We won't have to wake them, which might scare them to pieces." Ward chuckled and Ian added, "But with any luck the door will be locked."

"Why would that be lucky?"

"Because," Ian reached beneath his shirt to take out the key he'd worn on a chain around his neck since the day Wren had given it to him, "I need to use the key my wife gave me to get in the door."

"How quaint," Ward said with light sarcasm. "However we get in the door, could we just . . . get in the door?"

"Sorry," Ian said, realizing how long they'd been standing at the gate when they were so close to being inside and with their sweet wives again. Ian suddenly realized that holding Wren in his arms was only moments away. The thousands of times he'd imagined how it might be made his heart pound and his stomach flutter.

Ian opened and closed the gate quietly, and the two men walked up to the porch where Ian put the key into the door and turned it, laughing softly to feel the lock give way and the door open. How could he not think in that moment of Wren's words when she'd given him the key. They were etched clearly into his memory, and were almost as tangible to him as the key itself.

This already belongs t' ye. It's yer key t' the front door of our home. Its literal purpose is to open that door when ye come back, but I want ye t' wear it and not take it off until ye're able to use it again. When ye see it, when ye feel it next t' yer heart, I want ye t' think of home, but I also want ye t' remember that this is also the key t' my heart. Ye've had my heart for many years, Ian Brierley, and ye'll have it forever.

* * * * *

Wren sat on the edge of the bed with her hairbrush in hand, engaging in a ritual that she had literally done hundreds of times while she wondered where Ian was now, how he was doing, and when she might see him again. She ached for him so deeply she had to conclude that the ache had only deepened and accumulated through each day of his absence. To simply try to comprehend the full depth of the love she felt for him seemed impossible. There was nothing in her life to compare with it. The light of the gospel meant more to her than she could express, but it was intertwined somehow with the love she shared with Ian. Because their love was true and pure, it only enhanced all she felt in regard to the gospel plan. And having the gospel in their lives only enhanced the love that she and Ian felt for each other. It all seemed a part of the same circle in ways she didn't understand but knew nevertheless that it was true. And their children were a part of that eternal circle. The love that she and Ian felt for each other—even across the miles—made her love her children more in ways that she knew she could never put to words. Pondering the enormity of her feelings, the absence of Ian in her life felt increasingly difficult. In a strange way she had become accustomed to his absence. Or rather, she had developed an acceptance of being able to manage—both physically and emotionally—without him. What choice did she have? During this season of their lives, it had been his place to be elsewhere, and it had been her place to be here. They'd each had their own purpose, their own calling, their own mission to accomplish. But the months had dragged on, and she missed him deeply, utterly, and sometimes painfully. God had been merciful with her. He had given her comfort and strength. He had protected and provided for her and her family. And unless something had happened since Ian had written his last letter, she had no reason to believe that the same was not true for him. But, oh, how she missed her dear, sweet Ian! Oh, how she longed to be in his arms, to feel his embrace, to accept his kiss and return it with all the fervor of love that she felt for him!

An unusual sound somewhere downstairs made her heart jump. Her first thoughts went to the possibility of danger, then her mind fully received what her ears had heard, and her heart pounded for an entirely different reason. Only the sound of a key turning in the lock of the front door, just at the bottom of the stairs, would make such a noise. She unmistakably heard the knob turning and the door coming open, as if the sounds had been magnified tenfold and she could hear every detail, even from this distance.

Wren tossed her hairbrush to the dresser and rushed down the stairs in the dark, holding tightly to the stair rail to help guide her and keep her steady. About halfway down, she checked herself and stopped for a long moment, wondering if her ears had deceived her, or if there was some other explanation for the sounds she'd heard. Then she heard the door open from the other side of the house, and Patricia's voice saying, "Oh, it's true!"

"So it is," Wren heard Ward say. It *was* true. They had really come home! Home at last!

Wren hurried down the remainder of the stairs just in time to see her husband replace the glass chimney on the lamp he'd just lit that always sat on the table just inside the door. Ward and Patricia were holding tightly to each other. The bags the men had brought with them had been discarded near the door. Wren clung tightly to the bottom of the stair rail, waiting for Ian to turn and face her. The pounding of her heart was accompanied by a fluttering stomach, sweating palms, and trembling fingers. The combination of her symptoms felt as if they might make her faint, while a couple of seconds felt like as many minutes.

"Ian!" she breathed as their eyes met and the years of his absence fled away as if nothing had changed and no time at all had passed.

"Wren!" she heard him say just before she flew from the bottom of the stairs and landed firmly in his embrace.

"Oh, Wren!" she heard him mutter close to her ear while they held each other so tightly it was a wonder that either of them could breathe.

They both relaxed their embrace at exactly the same moment, as if they both had an identical need to actually see each other's faces. Their eyes met, and Wren laughed softly at the same moment she realized she was crying. Seeing tears on Ian's face as well, she pressed her fingers across his face at the same time he wiped at *her* tears. He too laughed softly and murmured, "You're real."

"Ye're here," she responded.

"I'm home," he said.

"It's over," she muttered.

Their embrace was resumed, even more tightly, as if they might be able to hold each other close enough to reunite the oneness of their soul that had been separated for so long. Again they drew back to look at each other, touching every feature on the other's face, each pressing fingers through the other's hair while they laughed and cried intermittently. And then he kissed her. At first their lips came together tentatively, as if he'd never kissed her before. Then their lips seemed to remember that they were husband and wife and had shared more kisses—both meek and passionate—than either of them could ever count.

Ian seemed to remember that they were not alone and glanced over his shoulder, chuckling to see that Ward and Patricia were also kissing each other, oblivious to Ian and Wren. The two couples barely said good night to each other before they locked the front door and went their separate ways. Ian carried the lamp and held Wren's hand as they walked together up the stairs, hardly able to take their eyes off of each other, lost in the silence of knowing that it would be difficult to find words to express feelings that didn't really need to be expressed.

"The children are sleeping," Ian said at the top of the stairs. Although he was stating an obvious fact, his disappointment was evident.

"Yes, but ye must have a peek at them. They've changed so much, I wonder if ye'll even recognize them."

"We'll become reacquainted in no time," Ian whispered as they went quietly into little Donnan's room first. "Oh, my boy!" Ian whispered with a tremor in his voice as he bent over the child's bed and carefully pressed fingers over his soft hair. "He *has* grown!"

"He has indeed," Wren whispered. "Come along and see the girls. In the morning ye'll be able t' laugh and play with them t' yer heart's content."

"I certainly will!" he said with pleasure as they went quietly into Gillian's room. Again Ian commented on how much she'd grown. He told Wren how beautiful their daughter was, and how he'd missed her. "As I've missed you all," he added, pausing in his admiration of Gillian to kiss Wren again. He forced his attention away from his wife to go with her into the third child's bedroom. Little Anya had changed the most. She'd only been about a week old when Ian had left. Now she was more than two, with a head of thick, blonde hair and a dear, angelic face that looked all the more angelic while she slept.

"Oh, she's precious!" Ian whispered. "I haven't even been able to imagine what she might look like."

"I've tried t' tell her about ye," Wren said, "but it might take some time for her t' become acquainted with ye."

"What a delightful thought," Ian said, and again he became distracted with kissing his wife. When the distraction became especially pleasant, he guided Wren across the hall to the bedroom they had shared before he'd left more than two years earlier. He kept kissing her as he closed the door and set down the lamp. He kissed her the way he'd dreamed of kissing her at least a thousand times while he'd been gone, and he held her while he kissed her as if something in his soul had feared he might never have this moment again. Now that this moment was upon him, the reality of her presence, her closeness, her sweet beauty that had hovered so vividly in his memory, all combined to consume him with a remembrance of the full depth of his love for her. He breathed her into his every sense as if he were a dry sponge and she was the water he needed to sustain himself.

After more than two years of sleeping alone, Ian had wondered if it might be a challenge for the two of them to become accustomed to sleeping close together once again, the way they had for so long before his departure. But they snuggled up to each other and drifted contentedly to sleep almost simultaneously, as if neither of them had been able to fully relax while they'd been apart. Now they were together again, and life could begin once more for both of them.

* * * * *

Ian came awake to an unusual sound. It took him a moment to realize that it was a baby crying, but his confusion lasted only a moment. As he became oriented to the fact that he was sleeping in his own bed, back in this beloved city of Nauvoo, a trace of tears warmed his eyes. A minute later Wren climbed back into bed with little Anya in her arms. He couldn't get a good look at his youngest daughter in the dark, and he knew that lighting a lamp would likely prevent her from falling back to sleep. He simply remained quiet and examined Wren's face with his fingers while she nursed the baby.

"She's still nursing," Ian whispered, thinking of all he'd missed in Anya's life, at the same time admiring the beauty of his wife and daughter, even though he could only see shadows in the darkness.

"Only a little bit at night," Wren said. "She's very grown up during the day, but at night she seems t' want t' be a baby still."

"I'm glad she's still a little bit of a baby," Ian said.

Wren took the sleeping Anya back to her bed, then returned and eased effortlessly into Ian's arms. She found his lips with hers and he held her closer, wondering how he had ever survived all these long months without her. He hoped to never be without her again, and when the time came for one of them to leave this world, he hoped the time of separation between their deaths would be very brief. He couldn't imagine how he could ever live without her—on either side of the veil.

Ian eventually fell back to sleep with Wren in his arms. He awoke to find the room filled with daylight. He rolled over and found Wren watching him. He sighed and smiled and made himself as comfortable as she was. They just looked at each other's faces for many minutes before she said, "It really is the same Ian Brierley I know and love."

"I am not an imposter," he said with a chuckle.

"No." She smiled and touched his face. "Ye're not. But ye've changed . . . a little bit, at least."

"How have I changed?" he asked.

"I'm not certain. I'm trying t' figure it out."

"When you figure it out, you let me know." He touched *her* face. "You haven't changed a bit. You're only more beautiful than my memory was capable of recalling."

"That's a lovely thing t' say, Mr. Brierley."

"It's true; simply a fact."

Wren thought of the terrible thing that had happened in his absence. She had no reason to believe that he knew. If he knew, he surely would have mentioned it by now. And while the thought had crossed her mind more than once in the hours since he'd returned, she'd not wanted to mar their reunion with talk of something so very sad and grievous.

While she was searching for the right words to tell him, he asked, panic edging his tone, "What's wrong?"

"What do ye mean?" she asked, a little startled by the intensity of his question.

"I can see by your expression that something's wrong. Something's happened, hasn't it? Something you don't want to tell me."

"Have ye taken t' reading minds?" she asked, looking away.

"I just know you, Wren. And if you were me—and you could see your face right now—you would be wondering exactly what I'm wondering right now." He leaned up on his elbow to look down at her. "What's happened?"

Wren couldn't hold back tears. She looked at her husband again. "The most horrible thing, Ian," she said. "It happened near the end of June; only a couple of months ago. There was no way t' get word t' ye."

Ian's mind ran circles with the possibilities. His family was safe and fine. His home was still standing. He started thinking of their friends here in Nauvoo. What could have happened to cause such a reaction in Wren? He couldn't even imagine, but his heart was thudding as he waited for her to explain.

"It's Joseph," she said. "Joseph and Hyrum." Ian sucked in his breath while his mind tried to connect their names with her having said *the most horrible thing.* Before he could even grab hold of the idea, she sniffled and murmured, "They're dead, Ian. They were murdered."

Wren watched Ian while his expression indicated that he was trying to accept the terrible reality. She wondered if Patricia and Ward were having the same conversation. If they hadn't already, they soon would.

"No!" Ian muttered breathlessly and fell back onto his pillow. He put a hand over his chest when it became constricted and he had trouble drawing breath. "It can't be!"

"I'm afraid it is," she said.

Ian squeezed his eyes closed, and tears leaked from their corners into his hair. "Tell me what happened," he said without opening his eyes.

Wren repeated the story, or at least as much of it as she knew. She was glad for this time alone with her husband while the children were sleeping. When she'd told him all she could think to tell for the moment, he looked at her almost sharply and asked, "What now?"

"What now?" she echoed as if she'd not heard him correctly. "The work goes on, Ian. The kingdom of God will roll forth. Joseph's death is a tragedy, but those who killed him will be disappointed if they believe that doing so will somehow change the conviction and purpose of the Saints. The gospel has been restored, and it will not leave the earth again. Ye know that as well as I know it." She sighed and added more softly. "Brother Brigham now stands at the head of the Church. He is the prophet now, Ian. He will lead the Saints as God's chosen vessel."

"Are we in danger here?" Ian asked, wondering what she might have omitted from her letters during his absence.

"Everything seems t' be all right for the moment, but . . ."

"But?" he asked firmly. "Tell me what you know."

"There have been some problems; it's complicated. I've wished that ye'd been here t' help me understand. It seems that . . . we will have t' leave Nauvoo . . . eventually. No one knows when for certain. We must trust in the prophet and have faith t' press forward."

Ian took in her words—and her faith—and he sighed deeply, then sighed again. The Prophet dead, the people in danger. It was not what he'd expected to come home to. It would take time for him to adjust to such news, but Wren was right. When it came to matters of faith, she always was. What could they do but trust in the prophet and press forward with faith?

They heard noises from the other room, and Wren announced, "Little Anya's awake. I'll get her." She touched his face, kissed his lips, then smiled. Her silent implication was that they needed to find joy in the moment, in being reunited, in spending time with their children. They would have to talk more about these things later.

Ian got up and put on breeches and a shirt while Wren was in the other room, changing the baby's diaper. She returned, carrying a beautiful little girl who seemed like a complete stranger to Ian. He could see a remarkable resemblance to his own sister, but he'd not seen little Anya since she was a tiny infant.

"Oh, look how beautiful you are," Ian said, and the child timidly tucked her head down on her mother's shoulder.

"It's yer papa, come home again," Wren said to Anya, who seemed to be examining this man closely while clinging tightly to her mother. "She'll warm up t' ye in no time," Wren said to Ian. He knew she was right, but he still felt saddened to see how his own daughter didn't even know him.

A moment later, Gillian ran into the room, shouting with jubilance, "Papa! Papa!"

He couldn't help but feel better as he laughed and twirled with her. "Look how beautiful and grown up you are!" he said.

"I'm five now!" she announced.

"I know you are!" he said. "I thought about you every minute on your birthday."

"You did?" she asked, looking at him inquisitively while he continued to hold her.

"I did!" he said. "And I'm glad you remember me. You weren't very old when I left, you know. You must have a very good memory."

"Of course I remember you," she said very maturely, and Ian laughed.

"Such a young lady!" Ian said.

"Indeed she is!" Wren added.

"And Mama told me last night that you'd be home soon," Gillian said. Wren and Ian exchanged a glance that he read to mean Wren didn't know what the child meant. As if Gillian had read their minds, she said, "My angel mama. She came last night after I'd gone to bed. She told me you were coming home soon and everything was going to be all right."

"Did she now?" Ian asked, grateful for Wren's letters that had helped him understand the wonderful gift this child had.

"Do you believe me?" Gillian asked with a scowl.

"Of course I believe you!" Ian said firmly. "No matter what anyone else might say or think, I will *always* believe you!"

Gillian smiled at this, then squirmed down from his arms, saying, "We must tell Donnan you're home, Papa." She took his hand and dragged him into Donnan's room. Wren followed, still holding Anya. "Look, Donnan!" Gillian said to the little boy who was just coming awake. "Papa's come home!"

"Papa?" Donnan said with a sleepy voice, looking at Ian with mild trepidation.

"Do ye remember Papa?" Wren asked him. "We've talked about Papa."

"Papa went far away," Donnan said in childish tones that weren't easy to understand.

"That's right," Wren said. "And now he's come back."

Donnan looked at Ian again, surveying him up and down as if he were connecting all that his mother had told him with a few very vague memories. He finally smiled and said, "Papa."

"Give Papa a hug!" Gillian said as if it were an order, but she said it kindly.

Donnan jumped to his feet on top of the bed and reached up his arms. Ian laughed and picked the boy up, hugging him tightly as he twirled him around the way he had done with Gillian. Wren and Gillian laughed, then Ian said, "I think the two of you should help me make some breakfast."

Donnan and Gillian squealed with excitement, then Wren sent Gillian off to get herself dressed while she set Anya down so she could help Donnan do the same. Anya kept quietly watching Ian, as if she simply didn't know what to think. Ian started playing peek-a-boo with her from behind the door. Anya's quiet surprise eventually turned to some mild laughter, giving Ian the hope that before the day was over she might actually let him hold her. It was remarkable to see how much the children had changed, and certainly somewhat saddening. But he was home now, and he could look forward to getting to know them all again.

When peek-a-boo had lost its fascination and Donnan was dressed, Ian gave his wife a lengthy kiss—something he couldn't seem to keep himself from doing frequently. The children observed the kiss with curious expressions that made Ian and Wren laugh when they turned to see their faces.

"Let's go make breakfast, shall we?" he said, and the day officially began.

Wren watched Ian go down the stairs with Donnan hanging tightly to his neck and Gillian holding tightly to his hand. She had to take a moment to swallow a sudden rush of tears. The joy just felt too enormous to hold without some inevitable overflowing. He was back! He'd come home to her, healthy and strong and safe. It was over! Everything had changed. Everything was better. She would never take his presence in their home for granted. She would never stop being grateful for every day they shared together. He'd come home!

* * * * *

Ian quickly got busy in the kitchen, gladly accepting some help from Wren when allowing the children to "help" caused more havoc than assistance. Ward and Patricia soon joined them, bringing along little June, who had also changed immensely in their absence. A new round of greetings were exchanged before the breakfast efforts continued, and the kitchen was full of more joy and laughter than it had been in more than two years. Occasionally the work stopped while Ian embraced Wren, or Ward embraced Patricia, or Patricia and Wren shared a hug as they shared the joy of having their husbands back.

They all stayed in that day, just basking in the joy of becoming reacquainted with each other. There was no need to go out, and no incentive to do so when they had so much to talk about and Ian and Ward were enjoying every minute of getting to know their children again. Wren and Patricia enjoyed observing the playfulness and laughter that was more typical of the way men played with children. Before suppertime, Anya had finally decided to join in the fun, and she had warmed up to her father rather nicely.

Wren loved having Ian by her side to help with the children, bring in the wood, dry the dishes she was washing, and just to take her in his arms now and then. She thanked God a hundred times that day for bringing him home safely to her, and when night came again, she thanked him more formally while on her knees beside the bed. To pray with Ian beside her, his hand in hers, was such a great joy! To hold him in her arms while she was falling asleep, and to find him beside her when she awoke in the morning, were blessings she would never take for granted again.

Wren loved the look she saw in Ian's eyes each time she caught him staring at her. But then, he often caught *her* staring at *him*. It was difficult not to when she felt so very much in love with him, not to mention utterly attracted. She felt like she couldn't look at him enough when she'd been so completely deprived of even being able to see him for so long. Apparently he felt the same way according to the lengthy gazes he often indulged in. When Ian Brierley looked at her like that, Wren felt beautiful and loved and absolutely adored. She concluded that every woman should feel that way when her husband looked at her, even though she knew such was not always the case. Knowing that Ian was an especially kind and doting husband made her appreciate all the more how very blessed she was. And she enjoyed every moment that she found him looking at her like that—especially when they first awoke in the morning. It was as if coming awake to the discovery of not being alone was such a thrill that they both just had to stare at each other for several minutes in order to accept that it was real.

Through the following days, Ian and Ward worked themselves back into the routine of the household. It took no time at all to feel as if they'd never been gone. The adults spent much of their free time reading from the journals their spouses had kept during their separation—or in Ward's case, allowing his wife to read to him the details of all that had happened. They had long conversations that helped fill in the gaps as memories were enhanced by what had been written.

During that first couple of weeks home, Ian took care of some household repairs and some work in the yard that had definitely needed a man's attention. He loved being able to care for his family again, but he couldn't deny that his family had been very blessed in his absence.

He also began once again putting in some work on the construction of the temple, glad to be a part of the project, and praying in his heart that they would not have to leave this beautiful edifice behind.

Once word got out that Ward and Ian had returned, many people came to call—including a number of them who were living in Nauvoo as a direct result of the missionary work that Ian and Ward had done. They were pleased to see many faces that were familiar from their encounters in England, but they were especially pleased to see Hugh Montgomery. His visit provoked a detailed reminiscing of the day that Gillian had been lost and Brother Montgomery had been the one to find her. The ironies were not lost on any one of them, and they were all grateful—for varying reasons—for the miracles that had taken place and the outpouring of blessings they'd all received.

A couple of weeks after Ian had come home to her, Wren was distracted from hanging the clean wash on the line by the giggling coming from the other side of the yard, where Ian was playing with the children in the shade of the big trees. She left the wash and crossed the lawn to observe more closely. All three of the children were taking turns jumping on Ian's back, then he would roll over to toss them gently onto the ground and tickle them into a giggling fit until the next one would attack him. Sometimes there was no break between turns, and he would have more than one child on his back at a time.

When Ian saw Wren there, he collapsed on his back as if he were suddenly exhausted. Looking up at her he said, "Well, hello, Mrs. Brierley. Don't you look beautiful there in the sunshine!" He chuckled. "But then . . . you look beautiful anywhere."

"Mama be boo-tee-ful," Donnan said, and Ian chuckled again.

"Indeed she is!" Ian said.

Wren moved closer, into the shade, and looked down at her husband while the children all snuggled up close to him to take advantage of this apparent rest time between bouts of giggles.

"What *are* you looking at?" Ian asked when she only stared at him.

"I've figured it out," she said.

"Figured *what* out?" he asked, completely baffled.

"I want t' ask ye a question first," she said and sat on the lawn beside him, curling her legs up next to her, beneath her skirts.

Gillian saw a butterfly and jumped up to go and chase it. The other two children followed her, all laughing with perfect delight. Ian sat up and took Wren's hand. She took note of his disheveled curly hair, the way his shirt hung over his shoulders, and the fit of his boot over his calf as he set one foot on the ground and tucked the other leg beneath him. There were so many little things she loved about him that she now took notice of more keenly than she ever had before.

"This must be a very serious question," Ian said.

"What makes ye think so?" Wren asked.

"That look on your face."

Wren didn't tell him that her concentration hadn't had anything to do with the question. She simply said, "I suppose it is."

"So ask me."

"Was it worth it?"

"Was *what* worth it?" he asked.

"Leaving? Being gone from us for so long? Was it worth it?"

Ian leaned a little closer and his voice became gentle. "Was it worth it to you?" he asked.

"I asked ye first."

"But I want to know," he said.

"And I'll be glad t' tell ye after ye've told me first. If we're being honest with each other—which we always have been—then whether I think it was worth it should have no bearing on what ye might say."

"Of course not," he said and tipped his head thoughtfully. He glanced to where the children were picking leaves from a low-hanging tree branch, the butterfly apparently having fluttered away. He thought for a long moment, then turned back to look directly at Wren. "Yes, my darling, it was worth it."

"If ye went back t' the day ye left, would ye do it all again?" she asked.

"Yes," he said firmly. "I would." He tightened his hand in hers. "It was the hardest thing I've ever done, Wren—to leave you and the children, and to be apart for so long—but how can I deny the joy of seeing the lives that have been changed? How could I ever regret what my humble efforts have done for those people? I've often wondered what life might have been like for every one of those people if I'd made the decision to stay home . . . to not go. It hurts my heart to even consider the question." He smiled at her. "So, there's your answer. As difficult as it was, I would never trade it away to have the blessings I have now. I'm here with you and the children again. And I have the joy of my memories, and even many new friends here in Nauvoo to remind me regularly of the fact that it *was* worth it." He tightened his gaze on her. "Now, it's your turn, Mrs. Brierley. Was it worth having me gone all that time? For you this was a completely different experience. You weren't out there seeing the changes take place in people's lives. You were left here to live the same life, but you had to manage without me. I wondered every day how hard that might be for you." He brushed her hair back from her face. "Was it worth it for you?"

Wren looked down and hesitated. Ian added, "I won't think less of you if you say no, Wren. I would understand."

Wren looked back up at him and saw his surprise when he noticed the tears in her eyes. He immediately misunderstood them. "Oh, my darling, I'm sorry this was so hard for you."

"Ye should let me answer the question before ye go jumping t' conclusions," she said.

Ian laughed in response to her saucy tone, then said, "Of course. Forgive me. Answer the question."

Wren pressed a hand to the side of his face. "Ye've always been a good man, Ian. Even when ye were young and confused and wandering, ye always had a good heart. Over the years I've seen yer goodness grow. Ye love me and the children so very much, and ye take such good care of us. I've seen what the gospel means t' ye, and I love and admire ye all the more for the sacrifices ye've made and the hard things ye've endured. The answer to yer question is yes." She blinked, and tears spilled down her face. "I hated every day without ye, and I missed ye so very, very much. But t' see ye now . . . t' see yer joy in the work ye've done . . . t' see how it's made everything good about ye just that much better . . . I would do it all again. I have no regrets, Ian. I love ye so very much, and being yer wife is the greatest gift that God has given my life."

"Oh, my sweet Wren," he said, taking her face into his hands. "I feel the very same about you. I can't imagine what I ever would have done . . . how life would have been without you. You are so very precious to me."

Ian leaned closer still to give her a tender kiss. She smiled at him, and he kissed her again, while the sound of the children's laughter wafted through the air.

About the Author

Anita Stansfield began writing at the age of sixteen, and her first novel was published sixteen years later. Her novels range from historical to contemporary and cover a wide gamut of social and emotional issues that explore the human experience through memorable characters and unpredictable plots. She has received many awards, including a special award for pioneering new ground in LDS fiction, and the Lifetime Achievement Award from the Whitney Academy for LDS Literature. Anita is the mother of five and has two adorable grandsons. Her husband, Vince, is her greatest hero.

To receive regular updates from Anita, go to anitastansfield.com and subscribe.